Letters *from* Alice

A tale of hardship and hope. A search for the truth.

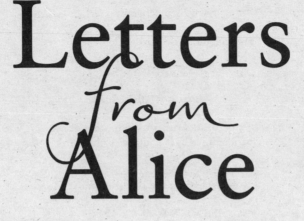

Letters from Alice

PETRINA BANFIELD

HARPER
element

HarperElement
An imprint of HarperCollins*Publishers*

1 London Bridge Street
London SE1 9GF

www.harpercollins.co.uk

First published by HarperElement 2018

1 3 5 7 9 10 8 6 4 2

© Petrina Banfield 2018

Petrina Banfield asserts the moral right to
be identified as the author of this work

A catalogue record of this book is
available from the British Library

ISBN 978-0-00-826470-3

Printed and bound in Great Britain by
CPI Group (UK) Ltd, Croydon, CR0 4YY

MIX
Paper from
responsible sources
FSC
www.fsc.org FSC˚ C007454

This book is produced from independently certified FSC paper
to ensure responsible forest management.

For more information visit: www.harpercollins.co.uk/green

Happy memories
SYLVIA ELLEN LOCKYER

NOTE TO READER

I was thirteen years old when I first discovered that my father spent his childhood in care. Until then he had never spoken to me about his past and, as children are so adept at doing, I somehow picked up that it was a subject to be tiptoed around, without ever having been told. The truth came out one Sunday afternoon after I plucked up the courage to ask for the names of my paternal grandparents, so that I could complete a genealogy project for school.

Perhaps he felt I'd reached an age of understanding because after a moment's hesitation he told me that he knew very little about his parents, who had died long before I was born. Even this snippet of information was fascinating to me and I listened eagerly as he told me about the grandmother I'd never met – a petite Irish woman who had experienced too much pain and not enough love. By the age of twenty-five she had given birth to five children.

The shadow cast by childhood trauma stretched far into the future though, and in 1941 three of her children were taken into care, including my father and his twin brother – the youngest, at six months old.

Ever since hearing my father's story I've been captivated by the idea of the corporate parent; society waiting with a safety net to cradle those most in need. For as long as I can remember, I've wanted to be part of that narrative. I finally applied to become a foster carer in 2006.

On my initial 'Skills to Foster' training course, the tutor told us that three fates awaited unwanted children of the distant past: death by exposure, prostitution or Christian adoption. We learned that homeless children and orphans in Britain were first 'boarded out' with foster carers in the latter part of the nineteenth century and that hospital almoners were the forerunners of modern social workers. But it was only in 2014, in trying to reassemble the scattered fragments of my father's childhood puzzle, that I learned more about the almoners' remarkable work.

I knew that Dad suffered with severe eczema as a child (he was separated from his twin at the age of five, his weeping wounds perhaps a physical manifestation of his sense of loss) and spent prolonged periods of time in hospital in London at some time during the Second World War, so I visited the London Metropolitan Archives (LMA) and began my search there.

Not really knowing where to start, I put in a request for old files from the Royal Free Hospital and its associated hostels in London. Within half an hour, several boxes had arrived in the reading room. Excitedly, I started going through the first one and, beneath the envelopes filled with receipts and manila files tied up with string, I found a smaller box containing almoners' reports from the 1920s.

As I worked my way through the dusty papers I read about girls 'very young, not more than sixteen or seventeen years old', who had 'fallen into trouble' as a result of living in conditions that were 'past belief ... involving very grave and unusual risks of infection'. As well as being pregnant, homeless and 'turned adrift' by their families, some of the poor girls were in agony as a result of a double infection of syphilis and gonorrhoea.

One almoner recorded that one of her patients, a girl suffering from gonorrhoea, was 'one of six siblings who all slept in one bed, in a room like a cupboard, with no outer air'. Another young girl 'lived over a stable with no access except by a ladder-like stair'.

On arrival at hospital many were 'in a state of nervous and physical exhaustion, and of resentment requiring great tact and care in dealing with them. Some [were] put to bed, till the irritable condition of their nerves [was] soothed, and many of them [slept] for days ... some descend[ing] to the depths of despair [,] bringing them to the verge of insanity'.

As I leafed through the file of fragile papers, a small bundle of handwritten letters written by one of the almoners – here, I will refer to her as Alice – fell out from between the pages. Beautifully written in a gently sloping script of fading black ink, and without a trace of the toxic condemnation that awaited the girls in society at large, they showed the almoner reaching out to her contacts in the community in search of 'well-disposed people' who might find it in their hearts to take them in.

A picture of Alice began to emerge: a fiercely intelligent woman from a sheltered background, filled with a sense of purpose and unafraid to challenge the conventions of the day. In *Letters From Alice*, Alice's character, her attitudes and motivations are drawn from the common experiences of women of her time and social station; she belongs to a generation of women emboldened by the progress of the Suffragette movement and ready to make their voices heard. Striding around some of the poorest parts of London in her ankle-length skirts, I imagined Alice immersed in a world of complex social problems, ones that resonate strongly with me as a foster carer today: homelessness and deprivation, incarceration, domestic violence, intoxication from opium and alcohol, and, inevitably, the neglect and deliberate abuse of children.

What follows is a retelling of the experiences of one of the girls (I will call her Charlotte) through the eyes of Alice, using the letters, almoners' reports and case files from the LMA as inspiration. Quotes have been lifted directly from the archive material, unless otherwise stated. Weather reports have been sourced from the Meteorological Office. Where the records are scant or incomplete, I have drawn on my research of the morals and expectations of society through the 1920s and my own imagination, to inject character into the disembodied voices in the reports and bring the stories to life on the page.

PROLOGUE

Unlike doctors and nurses [the almoner] is a newcomer in
the hospital world, but she finds all the benefits of its
traditions at her disposal. Whether the almoner is there or
not, a tapestry is being woven by the work of the hospital,
but it may be an incomplete piece of work and apt to
unravel if she does not play her part in gathering up
and connecting the broken threads.

(*The Hospital Almoner: A Brief Study of
Hospital Social Science in Great Britain*, 1910)

It was a little before seven o'clock in the evening on 17 April
1921 when twenty-eight-year-old almoner Alice Hudson sum-
moned the police constable for help.

PC Hardwicke's heavy boots tramped over the icy pavements in the east London district of Bow, Alice leading the way
a few steps ahead. The weather during early April had been
milder than usual, but over the last few days the temperature
had plummeted, a depression from Iceland bringing gales over
the eastern coasts and snow showers to the capital.

Daylight was beginning to fade as they reached their destination: a two-storey boarding house flanked by a derelict pub and a paper merchants. Alice had stopped by to see Molly Rainham half an hour earlier through concern for the young mother's welfare, she later reported to the coroner. Despite knocking for several minutes and tapping on the frosted window pane, the only response had been an unidentifiable, plaintive bleat in the distance.

Hospital almoners were accustomed to a variety of reactions to their unannounced visits, but there was something strange about the silence echoing around the hall on the other side of Molly's front door; a ghostly stillness that had sent Alice hurrying to the local police station.

From the notes in the almoner's file back at the Royal Free Hospital, Alice knew that Molly may have been suffering from post-natal psychosis. According to reports she had initially coped well with motherhood, but seemingly overnight her demeanour had changed. With her husband on a military posting in Constantinople and no other family to speak of, Alice made a point of calling in on her patient whenever her schedule allowed.

'We need to break in,' the almoner insisted, as PC Hardwicke rapped again on the front door.

He was still tapping half a minute later as Alice scrabbled at the downstairs window and wrenched it upwards. Before the PC managed to reach the almoner, his long-tailed dark blue coat flapping behind him, she had already bunched the damp hem of her long skirt up in one hand and was clutching at the window frame with the other. In one motion she crawled forwards and hauled herself over the sill, the bobby pivoting on his heels and averting his eyes behind her.

A hundred yards to the east, the bells of St Mary le Bow boomed the hour. As the policeman followed Alice through the window, a seagull cried out mournfully in the darkening sky above, a reminder to the onlookers that had begun to gather outside the small property of their proximity to the docks and the wide sea beyond.

The passageway was dark. Perhaps to soften the impact of a sudden intrusion, Alice and the PC slowed when they reached the top of the stairs, then exchanged glances. Besides an unpleasant smell, there was an undertone of something else in the air, something disturbing. With a grim expression, the bobby turned towards the master bedroom at the front of the house.

A few steps later he faltered, stopping so abruptly that Alice almost walked into the back of him. The groan that escaped him should have offered some warning of the scene awaiting her, but when Alice stepped forwards she gasped in horror. Inside the room on a bloodstained mattress, Molly was stretched out on her back, her eyes and mouth gaping. The sinews in her neck were taut, her powdered cheeks etched with the chalky deposits of dried-up tears.

It was Alice who reached the bed first. The emergency drills she had learned as a Voluntary Aid Detachment (VAD) nurse assessing casualties during the war years came back to her instantly. She ran her eyes over Molly, methodically checking for vital signs. Half a second later, she turned to the constable, gave a grim shake of her head then hurried past him into the hall.

The door to the small bedroom at the back of the house stood open. Alice hesitated in the doorway for a brief moment, then ran over to the cot by the window, where Molly's infant son lay. Bracing herself, she leaned over to feel the skin at the back of his neck. Her legs buckled then – it was warm to the touch. Had she been half an hour earlier in rousing the alarm, the deputy coroner for east London later reported to the inquest held in Stepney, the baby boy might have been saved.

The death of Molly and her son was the first in a series of shocking cases that Alice Hudson became involved in, one that marked a turning point in her career, redefining the way she viewed herself and the world around her. When Alice returned to the Royal Free Hospital on Gray's Inn Road and wrote up her report of the incident, she was unaware of the tangled threads that tied Molly to a case that rocked her above all others: the web of deception that began to unravel months later, on New Year's Eve, 1921.

CHAPTER ONE

The question of the abuse of voluntary hospitals is one of
wide knowledge. It has led to the creation of the hospital
almoner, and there is a great future in front of her ...
Students should be between the ages of twenty-five and
thirty-five, and the more knowledge of the world and of
general interests that they can bring to their training,
which lasts at least eighteen months, the better.

(*Pall Mall Gazette*, 1915)

By the middle of the afternoon on 31 December 1921, Alice
Hudson had ticked off almost all of the duties on her weekend
list.

It was three degrees Celsius, the sort of weather that pre-
scribed hot drinks and thick blankets, and the almoner might
have spent the day huddled in front of the log fire in the nurses'
home instead of trudging across the icy streets of east London,
had it not been for the pile of urgent home visits weighing
down the desk of her basement office.

Although December 1921 had been generally mild, Londoners shouldered frequent high winds and gales towards the

end of the month. Today, Saturday, there was a cloud of sulphur in the air, the sky stretching over the Thames as grey as the sediment lurking at its depths. Conditions were likely to worsen over the next few hours but, all being well, Alice would be back in her room before dark.

The signs were promising. It was 2.30 p.m. and she was already three calls down, with only one to go.

The almoner took hurried, lopsided steps along the pavement overlooking the river, a briefcase full of patient files bumping against her ankle-length cape. In the distance, the faint blue glow from the lamplighter's pole twinkled reflectively over the surface of the Thames as he worked his way, much earlier than usual, along Tower Bridge. Several children had walked unwittingly through the vapours into the frozen waters during the last terrible smog. The flickering lights glinting over the water offered at least some degree of reassurance for pedestrians.

Fifty-seven years old and possessed of an unruly beard, portly physique and a loud but undeniable charm, Frank Worthington strode ahead, smoking his ever-present pipe. A newly appointed board member of the Charity Organisation Society, or COS, Frank had shadowed Alice in the last fortnight, apparently to report back to the board on the benefits of the almoners' work.

Besides arranging financial assistance and practical support for patients in times of crisis, or improving their living conditions so that they were able to benefit from their hospital treatment, Alice was expected to identify those families with the means to make a small contribution, thereby increasing the hospital's income and justifying the cost of her own salary.

Peering beneath the veneer of the family and making judgements about their financial situation while at the same time maintaining a friendly, trusting relationship was a tricky balancing act for the almoners, however, one that could easily swing out of kilter.

Some families fiercely resented the intrusion of home visits, particularly those that were unannounced. Alice quickly learned to brace herself against the inevitable shock on the faces of her subjects, the rising unpredictability that could beset any unannounced visit, the ever-present possibility of violence.

Not that it always helped to be mentally prepared. On one surprise home visit, Alice was pelted from an upstairs window with some foul-smelling, ominously yellow soggy rags. Another time, she lost her thumbnail in a ferociously slammed door.

According to the almoner's file on the last family they planned to visit, the Redbournes persistently claimed poverty, but were known to frequent several of the newly opened jazz clubs in the West End. While the question mark over their earnings was a matter that required further investigation, however, it wasn't the almoner's biggest concern.

The Redbourne family file was marked with an asterisk; a code to indicate to the team that theirs might be a case that warranted closer inspection.

When Alice's boss, Bess Campbell, had first visited the family in their small house in Dock Street, she later documented that she had found the children home alone. Mrs Redbourne had staggered back arm-in-arm with one of her neighbours singing 'It's a Long Way to Tipperary' at the top of her voice while the Lady Almoner conducted a conversation with one of her youngest through the letterbox.

There were five children in the family, three of whom had received treatment in the outpatients department for dysentery. It was a condition feared by parents across the city: the summer diarrhoea of 1911 claimed the lives of 32,000 babies under the age of one, the plethora of flies attracted by horse manure on the streets speeding up the transmission of disease. The Red-bournes' youngest, a boy of around a year old named Henry, had fallen sick with pneumonia soon after recovering from his bout of dysentery. According to the physician who treated him, he had been lucky to survive.

As a porter on the railways, Mr George Redbourne earned a reasonable wage, one that, according to Miss Campbell, should have been sufficient to allow the family to contribute sixpence a week towards the cost of their medical treatment. A typical wage for someone like Mr Redbourne in the early 1920s was around thirty to forty shillings a week (in old money, there were twelve pennies in a shilling, and twenty shillings to a pound).

The Redbournes insisted that the rest of their income, after the eight shillings and sixpence a week they paid out in rent, was swallowed up by tram fares to and from work, payments to elderly parents and other essentials. So far, not a penny of the costs of the family's treatment had been recouped.

Trouble with nerves prevented Mrs Redbourne from working, or so she claimed, but she was a reluctant interviewee, and her word was not entirely trusted. The margin of the Redbournes' file was marked with the letters 'NF': the almoners' code for 'Not Friendly'. It was a practice taught in training, one that forewarned visiting staff to be on their guard.

Across the river, a barge billowed steam into the air. Frank stopped abruptly as a horse cantered past, its cart loaded with coal. 'Miss Hudson, you've made your point,' he said, tilting his head towards the briefcase. 'You're as capable as any man, I accept it. I just wish you'd give up your desire to become one.'

Alice stopped, resting the briefcase on the ground and shaking her hands to get the blood flowing again. Tentatively, she loosened the silk scarf she was wearing, wincing as she tucked the end inside her cape. A collection of scarves in assorted colours hung in Alice's wardrobe back in her room. She alternated them throughout the seasons to conceal the burn injury she sustained in the trench fire that had sent her home to England, the rough scars running across her left shoulder, up to the nape of her neck and over the back of her left hand.

'Don't worry, Frank,' came the curt reply. 'If ever I had such ambition, you are more than enough to contain it.' Frank chuckled and set off again through the resulting cloud of smoke, unburdened but for the folded umbrella he tapped on the ground in front of him.

Alice picked up pace, the bells of Southwark Cathedral jangling in time with her steps. As they neared Whitechapel, walking the same streets stalked by Jack the Ripper a few decades earlier, they passed several tenements, silent but for the distant yowls of a stray dog. With shoeless children using stones for marbles on the icy pavements and coatless beggars huddling against crumbling walls, it was an area well known to the almoners.

Hurrying past the destitute with nothing to offer but a concerned smile must have been demoralising for a committed social reformer like Alice, but the almoners soon learned the difficult and humbling lesson that all social workers through the ages come to accept: you can't help everyone.

Frank slowed as they neared a warren of three-storied houses with overhanging eaves. The smoke rising from chimneys all along Dock Street would likely worsen the weather conditions, but at least offered the promise of a room warmed by a log fire.

Alice reached Frank a few doors away from their destination. The trail of acrid smoke he left in his wake caught in her throat and she gave a sudden cough. Frank stopped mid-pace, draped the handle of his umbrella over the crook of one arm and held out his other hand to take possession of the briefcase. 'May I?' he asked, pipe dangling from between his teeth. With a slow roll of her eyes, Alice relinquished the suitcase. Frank immediately stood aside, gesturing for her to take the lead with a flourish of his brolly.

The Redbournes' rickety wooden gate gave a resentful moan on opening, the yard empty but for a skinny cat curled up inside an old cardboard box. Lifting its head, the creature eyed them sorrowfully and then gave a mournful yowl. Alice crouched down, stroked its cold, velvety ears and whispered a soft hello.

The rug appeared out of the door without warning, just as Frank reached the front step. With a pitiful yelp he dropped both briefcase and brolly and staggered backwards to the gate, flapping his hands madly at his hair and face. Seemingly oblivious to her visitors, the woman brandishing the rug continued with the task, shaking it violently, eyes and mouth pinched tight against the spiralling dust.

It was only when Alice rose to her feet that Mrs Redbourne noticed them.

'Oh,' she said, staring at them agog. Frank, doubled over and gasping as he clutched at the fence post for support, looked for all the world as if he'd just left the battlefield. Alice's mouth twitched as if stifling a giggle. A movement of the curtain at next door's window, and the appearance of an elderly woman with curly grey hair on the other side of the glass, was a reminder of the need for discretion.

'I am sorry to trouble you, Mrs Redbourne,' Alice said softly. The cat raised itself and coiled her ankles in a figure of eight, disappearing beneath the hem of her skirt and reappearing at intervals. A passer-by stopped outside the house. Hat in hand, the elderly gentleman stared unabashedly at their small party. Alice lowered her voice still further. 'We are from the Royal Free Hospital. Would you mind if we came in?'

Mrs Redbourne gave Alice a long look. The files back at the Royal Free stated that she was in her early forties, but her stern expression made her appear much older. Her hair had been combed into a grid–like pattern, each square grey tress curled, secured with pins and kept in place with a dark scarf. The rim of the scarf pulled tightly on the lined skin around her forehead, rendering her pink–rimmed eyes severe. She began to work her mouth as if chewing and then she said: 'We're in the middle of things just now.'

'We shan't take much of your time. We would like to check a few facts with you, and leave you with some information about our subscription scheme.'

The woman's face contorted further. 'That won't be necessary. We have all the information we need, thank you very much.' Steadfastly blocking their entrance with her wide girth, she folded the rug against the apron she wore like a shield, her lips stretched into a thin line.

Alice opened her mouth to speak. Before she managed to say a word, however, Frank, recomposed, grabbed his umbrella and nudged it against her skirt, half-pointing, half-thrusting it into the hall. 'If you'd be so kind, Madam,' he said, easing Alice aside with a fractional movement of his wrist. The expression on Mrs Redbourne's face suggested that she wasn't going anywhere, but a few moments later the woman flattened herself against the open door and let them through.

Alice met Frank's satisfied look with another curt nod. She followed him into the hall, hovering at the open door for a fraction of a second before moving aside to allow Mrs Redbourne to close it behind them.

The almoner ran her eyes around the Redbournes' hall. It was bright and clear of debris, the floor recently swept. There was a darkened rectangle where a rug must have been, the rest of the space dominated by a large coach pram.

In the front room, several logs glowed brightly in the fireplace. A pot of water bubbled away over the flames, children of varying ages playing close by. The high number of children arriving at hospital with severe burns and scalds meant that Alice frequently offered strong words of advice about the use of fireguards. It was one of the warnings that often fell on deaf ears, probably because finding the money for a guard was low down on the list of priorities for families who were worried about where their next meal might come from.

After eleven months in the post, the almoner was at least well practised in running through all of the necessary checks she needed to ensure that the financial information provided matched the family's apparent means. She had also been trained to note down any evidence of harm to the children, bruising to the skin and other tell-tale signs of neglect, as well as any other issues that might negatively impact on a patient's health. The rudimentary medical knowledge she had gained as a nurse with the VAD in a field hospital in Belgium helped her to discriminate between those injuries resulting from natural rough play and those of a more sinister origin.

The British Red Cross, recognising that the VADs had much to offer on their return to England, had offered scholarships to those willing to train as hospital almoners. Sent home after being injured from the fire resulting from the blast of a mortar bomb, and passionate about improving the living standards of the ordinary working people, Alice had jumped at the chance.

Back in 1916, when she had first arrived at the casualty clearing station in Belgium, unqualified and with no medical experience, she had only been allowed to carry out the most menial of chores, like cleaning floors and swilling out bedpans. The qualified nurses from Queen Alexandra's Imperial Military Nursing Service (QAIMNS), already battling for professional recognition, had resented the onslaught of hundreds of untrained women from middle-class homes. Inevitably, the grottiest of chores were directed towards the new arrivals.

Alice uncomplainingly cleaned up the stinking, putrid dead skin that had been scraped from the feet of soldiers suffering from trench foot. She swept up the discarded fragments of bloodstained uniform that nurses had pulled from infected wounds. She stoically hid her blushes when confronted with her first glimpse of a naked male.

Gradually the qualified staff recognised Alice's dedication. As their attitude towards her softened and their appreciation grew, she was granted closer contact with injured soldiers. Like many of her contemporaries plunged into the aftermath of battle, she discovered that she possessed a natural ability to console. It wasn't unheard of for Alice and the other VADs to lower themselves into the trenches to comfort dying soldiers, ignoring the roar of cannon fire and the smell of charred flesh. Mothers back in England found comfort in knowing that someone gentle had held their sons as they passed away.

Alice wrinkled her nose. There was a faint smell of drains, sour nicotine and something like old lard in the air – sometimes the dank smell inside the homes she visited was enough to make her retch – but the house was clean enough. The Redbourne children were whey-faced and snuffly with colds but there was no sign of fever or the dreaded influenza virus that had driven so many people to the Royal Free that winter. All of them were clothed and there was no sign of rickets among them. Neither were any of them possessed of that shrunken, unhealthy appearance that so worried the almoners whenever they came across it.

A small boy lay languidly on his tummy under a wooden clothes horse covered in linen cloth nappies and, incongruously, a white silk chemise. About a year or so old, his appearance was consistent with the description of Henry recorded in the Redbournes' hospital file. Alice's eyes lingered on his damp, flushed cheeks. With his head on his forearms, he looked close to dropping off, but healthy enough otherwise.

An older girl of around twelve years old was kneeling nearby, trying to field off blows from another young boy who was standing behind her. Around four years old, he alternated between slapping the top of her head and grabbing handfuls of her hair. He giggled when she pulled him over her shoulder and onto her lap, but then lashed out, slapping her in the eye when she tickled his midriff.

In light of what was to come, the child's behaviour might have set some alarm bells ringing. As it was, the overall impression offered was one of need, but not destitution, or something graver. And yet somehow there was enough money left at the end of the week to finance nights out in the West End, and, so it seemed, luxury lingerie.

Alice scanned the room for a second time. In the corner, an older girl was sitting on a small sofa with her face turned towards the window. A sickly-looking toddler was perched on her knee. The conversation between Mrs Redbourne and Frank became increasingly loud and animated. By distracting the homeowner with his extravagant gestures, Frank was offering Alice the opportunity to carry out an inspection unhampered; one of the oft-used subterfuges employed by the almoners.

Even with the dust motes clinging to his beard, Frank looked fantastically conspicuous in the room. Alice and her colleagues had initially been perplexed at the idea of a man turning up whenever he felt like it to observe them at work, but his humour had put them quickly at ease. Beneath his buffoonery lurked a sharp mind and keen intuition, something he appeared keen to keep under wraps.

Quietly, Alice edged past the pair into the room. Frank shifted his weight subtly from one foot to the other to aid her passage. A ripple of interest at the arrival of yet another stranger rolled over the children. The young boy who was in the process of pinching his older sister sprang to his feet and walked over to her. 'Hello,' Alice said softly, crouching down in front of him. 'What's your name then?'

'Jack,' the boy answered and began fiddling with the sleeve of Alice's cape. 'You one of them busybodies?'

The almoner smiled then removed her hat and rested it on one knee, instantly softening her features. Some of Alice's nursing colleagues were beginning to experiment with cosmetics, something that would have been considered vulgar before the war. When readying themselves for a night out, they would cajole her into darkening her lashes with a mixture of crushed charcoal and Vaseline, the more exuberant characters outlining their eyes in a dramatic sweep. Alice generally went make-up free when on duty, taming her long brown curls in a tight chignon at the back of her head. It was a style that gave her square jaw and high forehead prominence over her softest feature: her large, thickly lashed brown eyes. The resulting rather prim look came in useful when dealing with the least cooperative of patients. 'Erm, I suppose some might say so.'

'Mummy usually sends you lot packing.'

His older sister shifted around and gave a shake of her head. Alice pressed her lips together, eyes shining. 'And who is this?' she asked, kneeling in front of the young boy who was sitting on his older sister's lap, bare knees dangling beneath a worn blanket. About two years old, the child regarded her shyly and buried his face in his sister's chest. The latter planted a brief kiss on top of his hair. When she pulled away, her eyes remained downcast. The logs crackled in the grate as Alice stilled, waiting for an answer.

The girl, though wearing a morose expression, was pretty. Her cheeks were plump and prominent despite the thinness of her wrists, her eyes a feline green. After a few moments she met Alice's gaze. 'John,' she mumbled, regarding the almoner with the sort of suspicion that anyone involved in social work quickly becomes accustomed to.

'Hello, John,' Alice said, with a brief touch to his knee. She looked up at his sister. 'And you are?'

'That's Charlotte,' Jack offered, stealing Alice's hat from her knee and planting it lopsided on his own head. 'She's trouble, Mum says. Him's Henry,' he added, pointing to the young boy almost asleep on the floor. 'And Elsa's over there.' The young girl sitting next to Henry chewed her lip and regarded Alice from beneath lowered lashes. Charlotte rolled her eyes and glared.

The tell-tale signs of a scabies infestation were visible along John's forearm. Track-like burrows ran around his wrist where a mite had tunnelled into the skin, the tiny black dots of faecal matter visible around an angry rash. It was something Alice and the other VADs had often seen in the field hospitals; soldiers driven half-mad by the intense, irrepressible itch. The entire family would need to be treated with benzyl benzoate emulsion. 'Not at school, Charlotte?' Alice asked, in a precise but friendly tone.

It was a question designed to engage, rather than a genuine enquiry. The almoner had been taught specific interviewing strategies in training that helped her to disguise carefully planned interviews as casual chats, thereby gaining valuable insight into the living conditions of her patients: their relationships, finances, thoughts and fears. By examining individuals in the context of their social setting she was able to identify issues that might be impacting negatively on their health. Practical help honed to individual needs could then be offered, improving outcomes and the chances of a good recovery.

One way to encourage an interviewee to relax was to start a conversation with questions that were most easily answered, in much the same way as the devisers of written exams open with a problem easily solved. Since patients almost universally enjoyed talking about themselves, she learned that a readiness to listen, a keen interest in people and a sincere desire to help were all that was needed to encourage loose tongues.

'I'm fifteen,' the girl said, sounding offended. 'I left ages ago.'

Alice nodded. 'So are you working outside of the home now?' The almoners knew it wasn't unusual for older children to take a job so that they could contribute towards the family purse, even skipping school to do so. The income generated was often kept under wraps by families being assessed. Alice had been taught to be thorough in her questioning to uncover a true picture of a family's finances.

'Not really,' Charlotte answered quickly. Her thin chilblained fingers worked continuously at the blanket on her brother's lap, as if she had more to say. Alice waited, but the girl's eyes flicked over to her mother and then her expression suddenly closed down. Her shoulders rounded further away so that the child on her lap wobbled and almost lost balance until she reached out and wrapped her arms around his waist.

Alice pressed her lips together, rescued her hat and rose to her feet. Over by the door, Frank's charms were working a treat, Mrs Redbourne smiling up at him coyly. She barely seemed to notice when Alice slipped past. Behind her, Charlotte sat quietly, eyes watchful.

In the hallway, Alice hesitated. She stood in solitary silence for a few seconds, head cocked as if listening. After a moment she turned sideways to squeeze past the pram and then moved towards a closed door at the end of the hall. A soft thump stopped her in her tracks. There was a creaking sound, and then the door gave way, a pair of eyes peering through the crack.

After a short pause in which no one moved, the door was opened to reveal a fleshy, puffy-eyed man with a glossy sheen across his forehead. Alice strode towards him, thrust out her hand and smiled, as if a meeting had been planned between them. 'You must be Mr Redbourne?' she said. 'Alice Hudson. Pleased to meet you.'

The man looked down at her and passed his tongue over his lips, then took her proffered hand. 'You'll be from the hospital,' he said in an uncertain voice. 'The wife could do without the added pressure,' he added, when Alice confirmed her occupation. 'We do what we can, but you can't expect us to give what we don't have.'

He followed her to the living room, but when his wife caught sight of him she shooed him away with her hand. 'I thought you were at the market, George? Get going will yer, there's things we need.' Mr Redbourne pulled a pack of cigarettes from his pocket, took one into his mouth using his teeth, then, without another word, slipped out of the house.

When the front door clicked to a close, Alice entered the room he had just vacated. The back parlour was a dark room with a single bed in the centre, the wooden base held up by a pile of bricks at each corner. There was a bite to the air, the room colder than the street outside. A dozen shirts hung from a rope stretched diagonally across it, one end caught between

24

the slightly open window and the other wedged between the top of a Welsh dresser and the wall.

Alice closed the door and peered into the nearby kitchen. Through the small window at the end of the room, a partly stone-flagged backyard was visible, a patch of bare earth beyond. An old lean-to housing the lavatory blocked what little winter light there was from entering the kitchen. There was no sign of running water; most working-class families were still filling buckets from a pump at the end of their street. The approaching twilight bathed the small area in shadows, the air fermenting with the smell of old dinners. With so many people living in the house the room was likely a place of much activity but, aside from a few black beetles scurrying across the floor and over the draining board, the overriding air was one of long abandonment.

The feeling of bleakness prevailed as the almoner made her way up the stairs. The rising wind caused a stray branch to tap rhythmically at the panes of the landing window, almost as if in warning.

It was a degree or two warmer upstairs than the kitchen had been but Alice shivered nonetheless as she ventured into the first bedroom. Bare, chipped floorboards bowed towards the middle of the room, the undulating surface and the sour tinge in the air adding to the general sense of unease.

Nothing stood out as being out of place. The bed, presumably belonging to Mr and Mrs Redbourne, stood low to the floor. Covered with a tatty, slightly stained tufted counterpane, it sagged drunkenly, as if in sympathy with the floor. Droopy curtains hung half-closed at the windows and an old leather suitcase stood up on end in front of a dressing table of dark wood, perhaps as a makeshift stool.

Back in the hall, another staircase wound itself over the first, leading to the second floor. Notes in the file showed that Mrs Redbourne had been specifically questioned about the empty rooms upstairs by the Head Almoner, Bess Campbell, who suspected that they may have been sub-let. Mrs Redbourne claimed that the space was uninhabitable due to damp walls and unstable floorboards, but the almoners had visited families who had carved living spaces into stables and coal bunkers; a loft space, however unsafe, would have been appealing enough to command at least a few shillings in rent from a desperate family.

Foreign voices and a clattering of footsteps drifted down through the floorboards, followed by a loudly slammed door. The window in the hall rattled in protest. Alice turned and stared at the cracked ceiling before moving further along the hall to a much smaller room.

Here, the entire floor was hidden by a horsehair mattress and an assortment of fraying blankets and clothes. In the twenty-six years since the first almoner was appointed in 1895, much intelligence had been gathered about the sort of secrets that could lay buried within families. As seekers of truth, the almoners knew that sometimes the sinister could be masked by a cloak of ordinariness. It was one of the reasons they were told not to hurry their home inspections, but to take their time, so that the hidden might somehow reveal itself.

Alice stood quietly in the doorway, running her eyes around the room. It was only at the sound of purposeful strides on the stairs that she finally turned around.

The face of Mrs Redbourne's eldest daughter rose over the top of the banisters. The rustle of linen as the hem of Charlotte's skirt brushed the stair beneath her feet seemed to whisper something other than her arrival. In the light of the upstairs hall, the shadows under the girl's eyes became apparent, her cheeks speckled with a deep scarlet flush.

The almoner didn't say anything; probably hoping not to attract attention from other family members. Instead, she took a step closer to the young woman and gave a reassuring smile. In that fleeting moment, the teenager's desperation became evident.

After a wild glance behind her, Charlotte bit her bottom lip and then opened her mouth to speak. When no words came, Alice frowned and whispered: 'Charlotte, are you alright?'

'F-fine,' the teenager stammered, the word at odds with her countenance. 'But I-I think you should know –' She stopped, then burst into tears. Alice's fingers curled towards her palms, as if trying to encourage her to speak. 'W-what I mean is, I should have said something sooner, but it's too late now and …', she faltered, her choked whispers stilted by the click of a door latch above.

Alice looked up. A middle-aged bespectacled gentleman wearing a long overcoat descended the stairs, a scarf knotted under his bearded chin. Charlotte whirled around and then scurried away, her long skirt fanning out behind her.

'Good day, Madam,' the man said in a heavy accented voice. Alice nodded and waited in the hall as the man traced Charlotte's footsteps downstairs. The almoner's expression was serious. As soon as she had crossed the threshold of the Redbourne's home, something had struck a false note.

By the time she left, she later recorded in her case notes, it appeared as if something truly disturbing were about to unfold.

CHAPTER TWO

The out-patient department, which annually receives
over 40,000 cases, is at present conducted in the basement,
which is ill-lighted and insufficient in accommodation ...
The hospital is situated in one of the poorest and
most crowded districts of London ...

(*The Illustrated London News*, 1906)

It was still dark when Alice woke two days later, on Monday, 2
January. Three years into the future, in 1925, the live-in staff of
the Royal Free would move to purpose-built accommodation
on Cubitt Street. The bedrooms of the Alfred Langton Home
for Nurses were clean and comfortable, according to the *Nursing Mirror*, each one having 'a fitted-in wardrobe, dressing table
and chest of drawers combined. Cold water laid on at the basin
and a can for hot water, and a pretty rug by the bed ...
everything has been done for the convenience and comfort of
the nurses'.

As things were, the nurses managed as best they could in the
small draughty rooms of the Helena Building at the rear of the
main hospital on Gray's Inn Road, where the former barracks

29

of the Light Horse Volunteers had once stood. Huddled beneath the bedclothes, they would summon up the willpower and then dash over to the sink, the flagstone floor chilling their feet.

Alice's breath fogged the air as she dressed hurriedly in a high-necked white blouse, a grey woollen skirt that skimmed her ankles and a dark cloche hat pulled down low over her brow. After checking her appearance in the mirror she left her room and made for the main hospital, where the stairs leading to her basement office were located. Outside, a brisk wind propelled young nurses along as they ventured over to begin their shifts, their dresses billowing around their calves. The skirts of their predecessors a decade earlier, overlong on the orders of Matron so that ankles were not displayed when bending over to attend to patients, swept fallen leaves along the ground as they went.

Just before the heavy oak doors leading to the hospital, Alice turned at the sound of her name being called from further along the road, where a small gathering was beginning to disperse. In among the loosening clot of damp coats and umbrellas was hospital mortician Sidney Mullins. One of the tools of his trade – a sheet of thick white cotton – lay at his feet, a twisted leg creeping out at the side.

Sidney, a fifty-year-old Yorkshire man with a florid complexion and a bald crown, save for a few long hairs flapping across his forehead, often strayed to the almoners' office for a sweet cup of tea and a reprieve from his uncommunicative companions in the mortuary. Standing outside a grand building of sandstone and arches of red brick, he beckoned Alice with a wave of his cap then stood back on the pavement, rubbing his chin and staring up at one of the towers looming above him.

Shouts of unseen children filled the air as Alice took slow steps towards her colleague. She dodged a teenager riding a bicycle at speed on the way, and a puddle thick with brown sludge. 'What is it, Sidney?' Her eyes fell to the bulky sheet between them, from which she kept a respectful distance away.

The mortician pulled a face. 'Forty-summat gent fell from t'roof first thing this morning,' he said, scratching his belly. A flock of black-gowned barristers swept past them, their destination perhaps their courtyard chambers, or one of the gentlemen's clubs nearby that were popular retreats for upper-middle-class men.

'Oh no, how terribly sad,' Alice said.

'A sorry situation, I'll give you that,' Sidney said in his broad country accent. He rubbed his pink head and frowned up at the building. 'But I just can't make head nor tail of it.'

Alice grimaced. 'Desperate times for some, Sidney. It's why we do what we do, isn't it?'

The mortician pulled his cap back on and looked at her. 'Aye, happen it is. But I still can't work it out.'

'What?'

'Well, how can a person fall from all t'way up there and still manage to land in this sheet?'

Alice gave a slow blink and shook her head at him. 'Sometimes, Sidney …'

31

He grinned. 'Oh, don't look at me like that, lass. You've gotta laugh, or else t'pavements'd be full with all of us spread-eagled over them.'

Sidney recounted the exchange inside the basement half an hour later, Frank banging his barrelled chest and chuckling into his pipe nearby. The smell of smoke, damp wool and dusty shelves smouldered together in an atmosphere that would likely asphyxiate a twenty-first-century visitor, though none of its occupants seemed to mind the fug. 'Never was a man more suited to his job than you, Sid,' Frank said, gasping. 'You were born for it, man. What do you say, Alex?'

Alexander Hargreaves, philanthropist, local magistrate and chief fundraiser for the hospital, was a tall, highly polished individual, from his Brilliantine-smoothed hair and immaculate tweed suit all the way down to his shiny shoes. A slim man in his late thirties, his well-groomed eyebrows arched over eyes of light grey. In the fashion of the day, an equally distinguished, narrow moustache framed his thin lips. There was a pause before he answered. 'I prefer "Alexander", as well you know, Frank,' he said, without looking up from the file on his desk. 'In point of fact,' he added in a tone that was liquid and smooth after years of delivering speeches after dinner parties, 'I don't happen to think there's anything remotely amusing about mocking the dead.'

The walls behind Alexander's desk were lined with letters thanking him for his fundraising efforts, as well as certificates testifying to the considerable funds he had donated to various voluntary hospitals over the years. Framed monochrome photographs of himself posing beside the equipment he had managed to procure, developed in his own personal darkroom, were displayed alongside them.

Sidney's podgy features crumpled in an expression of genuine hurt. Years in the mortuary had twisted his once gentle humour out of shape until it was dark, wry and, to some, wildly offensive, but his respect for the gate-keeping role he played between this life and the grave never wavered. 'Right,' he said a little forlornly, clapping his hands on his podgy knees. 'I reckon I'd best get back to the knacker's yard.'

Alexander's nostrils flared. Frank arched his unkempt brows. 'Come on, Alex, where's your sense of humour?'

'Lying dormant for the time being,' came Alexander's reply. 'To re-emerge whenever someone manages to display some wit.'

Stocky office typist Winnie Bertram blew her nose into a hanky and tucked it back into the handbag that rarely left her lap. 'God rest his soul,' she said, her reedy, wavering voice momentarily cutting through the office banter.

Alexander glanced up from his work. 'Are you coping, Winnie?'

Winnie adjusted the black silk shawl she was wearing around her shoulders, the one she had worn religiously since Queen Victoria had been interred next to Prince Albert in Windsor Great Park more than two decades earlier. 'Not particularly, dear, no,' she said, straightening her spectacles with a mottled hand.

Winnie could be relied upon to mourn every loss the hospital notched up, even if the first she had heard of the patient was after they'd departed. She too was in the ideal job in that regard, especially with Sidney keeping her abreast of every last gasp, choke and coronary going on above them.

'You look tired,' Alexander pressed gently. 'Perhaps you should consider spending the day at home?'

Winnie patted down her short grey hair and gave Alexander a wan smile. 'I've been tired since 1890, dear. Don't worry about me, I'll soldier on.'

Alice rolled her eyes. Witnessing the aftermath of war had left her with a sense of urgency to improve the lives of society's most unfortunate, as well as a lack of patience for those with a tendency to complain about trifling issues.

She herself recognised her good fortune, having enjoyed a largely happy childhood. Quick intuition made her the ideal student and as she grew older, she delighted in the new opportunities becoming available to women. Influenced by her parents, who were both pacifists and active peace campaigners, Alice became aware of society's ills at an early age. She and her elder brother, Frederick, sat quietly in the corner of the sofa during the meetings of the National Peace Council – a body coordinating smaller groups dedicated to furthering the cause of non-violent opposition across Britain – that took place in the living room of their Clapham home.

In later years Alice became brave enough to interject, shaping the skills of negotiation and the moral compass that were to guide her as she tended to wounded soldiers on the battlefield, the ear-splitting crack of shell-fire in the distance, plumes of gas looming high above her head.

'But I don't understand why they had to invade!' thirteen-year-old Alice had burst out passionately, in response to an argument about the Austro-Hungarian annexing of Bosnia-Herzegovina.

Her father glanced at her tenderly. 'The Austrians are flexing their muscles, love. They want to ensure their empire is taken seriously. We'll see where their flag-waving nationalism gets them soon enough, I suspect.'

'War, in the Balkans and beyond, you mark my words,' one of the men, a Quaker, answered hotly, causing a great deal of muttering and concern on the faces of those present.

A hiss of steam from the old boiler caught everyone's attention. In the lull that followed, Alice asked Frank if he was ready to join her in outpatients. She was scheduled to spend the day conducting assessments on some of those waiting, all the while keeping an eye out for cases of fraud. It was an information-gathering exercise, and the ideal opportunity for Frank to gain a sense of her work.

'I've decided to carry on with my review of the paperwork down here this morning, dear Alice,' Frank said, checking his pocket watch and slipping it back into his waistcoat. 'Besides, you females are so much better with the ailing than us men.'

'But I have juggled everything around, as you asked me to. I haven't been through the inpatients lists yet, *and* I need to organise wigs and prosthetics for several patients.'

'Don't you worry about that,' Frank said. There was a hopeful glance from Alice, before he continued. 'It will still be here when you get back.'

'That doesn't sound particularly fair,' Alexander offered from the other side of the room.

'No,' Alice said, turning to him. 'But then *some* men believe a woman's sole purpose is to bend to their every whim. In fact, I suspect that *some* would prefer it if we didn't exist at all.'

'Ha! Not true, if indeed the lady is referring to me,' Frank said. He stuck out the tip of his tongue, removed a flake of tobacco and planted it back in his pipe. 'I love the female of the species. Fascinating creatures.'

Alice grimaced, grabbed her notepad and pen, and left the office with a cold glance towards her colleague.

When the first almoner, Mary Stewart, took up her post at the Royal Free in 1895, for which she was paid a modest annual salary of £125, she was allocated a small corner of the outpatients' department to work from. Visitors to her 'office' perched themselves on the edge of a radiator in the dark, airless space, a thin screen partitioning them from the view of the throng of patients waiting to be seen.

Six years later and a few miles away to the south, the first female almoner of St George's Hospital, Edith Mudd, was to carry out her duties from a screened-off area in the recovery room next to the operating theatre. She got on with the job conscientiously, doing her best to concentrate despite the activity across the room as patients came round after anaesthesia.

Since the almoners were used to moving around between London hospitals to cover each other's shifts and gain wider experience, they quickly learned to adapt to unusual working environments; one of Edith Mudd's successors at St George's managed to run a fully functioning almoners' office from one of the hospital's bathrooms.

It was in a similarly small space known as the watching room that Alice seated herself in the outpatients department; somewhere from which she could keep an eye on the comings and goings with a degree of discretion. It was just before 9 a.m. but already there were few gaps on the wooden benches that were arranged in tight rows across the large atrium. Incessant rain pelted the small recessed windows of the double doors at the entrance to the building, the wind penetrating the gap beneath the doors with a ferocious whistle.

After arranging her notepad and pen on a small desk, Alice interviewed a woman who was convinced that her daughter's knitted woollen knickers had caused a particularly nasty outbreak of intimate sores. 'Well, what else could it be?' the woman asked Alice earnestly, her overweight daughter cringing behind a curtain of long greasy hair beside her. The almoner suggested that the woman should return home, then discreetly booked her daughter into the VD clinic.

Her next interviewee was a charlady who was more in need of something to wear on her feet than medical treatment. When Alice told the woman that she would source some charitable funds to buy her a pair of shoes, she was rewarded by a wide, gap-toothed smile. The almoner glanced up and narrowed her eyes between interviews, checking on the comings and goings beyond the screens.

One of the most enjoyable and rewarding aspects of an almoner's work was being able to witness the benefit of their interventions. When Alice presented her next visitor – an elderly watchman suffering with eczema whose sore hands had blistered after spending several cold nights in the watchman's shelter – with a pair of cotton gloves, he danced a little jig in delight, drawing applause from the patients waiting on the other side of the screen.

The day passed productively; four full financial assessments completed, several patients booked in with the relevant doctors and one fraudulent claimant given his marching orders.

At a little before 4 p.m., after securing the patient files in a tall cabinet, Alice ventured out into the main reception area.

'Hello again,' she said with a nod to the elderly couple who were sitting together and holding hands in the far corner of the outpatients department waiting area. Ted and Hetty Woods had spent almost every day of the last week huddled side by side in the same spot, their few belongings stowed in a dog-eared bag at Ted's feet.

'Hullo, Miss,' Ted said as his pale-blue eyes fixed on Alice's face. Mrs Woods, a plump woman with hair of faded copper, gave her a tired but cheerful smile. The lines on her face were deep, the upward edges of her mouth suggesting a character that was determined to remain hopeful, despite all the difficulties that were thrown her way.

'We spoke about you both perhaps spending a day or two at home, didn't we?' Alice said, crouching down in front of them and resting a gloved hand on Ted's knee. She was due to meet with Dr Peter Harland, the physician who had treated little Henry Redbourne's bad chest, at the end of his shift. Their meeting had been arranged to exchange notes on other chest clinic patients, but the list of questions pinned to the front of the file in the almoners' office reflected Alice's hope of steering the conversation towards the Redbourne family.

The young woman, Charlotte, had said little during their welfare check on the family, but working closely with families had honed Alice's intuition. Quickly, she had learned to distinguish between the troubles that blighted most families from time to time and those rising from something more sinister; it was a sort of occupational sixth sense.

'We're all at sixes and sevens at home, love. We're alright here, if it's all the same to you.' Ted doffed his cloth cap, but anxiety lay beneath the civility. The skin on his face was chapped and his lips were pale and translucent, but his thin hair had been carefully combed and his clothes were clean and well pressed. Mrs Woods was similarly well groomed and yet, despite the rose water she was dabbing on her wrists and her well-scrubbed pink skin, a peculiar smell rose from beneath her clothes.

'And you, Mrs Woods? How are you?'

'Fine, duck. Lovely, thank you.' Alice's eyes lingered on the elderly woman, her brow furrowed. She had visited the couple at home months earlier after Ted's treatment for a severe leg ulcer. With a single room in a three-storey boarding house, they were better off than some, but the mould on the walls and lack of running water meant that it was far from comfortable.

Alice sighed, glancing across the large atrium. Two doctors wearing white laboratory coats stood whispering near a set of fabric screens, nurses bustling past them into the anterooms. A few feet away, another nurse stood in front of a plump elderly woman, trying to help her onto her feet.

An unpleasant musty smell prevailed in the department, overlaid with a hint of carbolic soap; a consequence of every available space being filled with the poor. Numerous ill-clad elderly locals huddled together with threadbare blankets draped over their knees, several in the grip of severe coughing fits. It was likely that more than half of those filling the space weren't interested in seeing a doctor. If there was a chill in the air it wasn't unusual for the almoners to find the outpatients department thronging with people like Ted and Hetty, hopeful of passing the time in a place that was warmer and less dreary than their homes.

Alice reached into her handbag and pressed a coin into Ted's frail hand. She had learned in training and keenly felt that it was her duty to remember the person behind the illness. She had been taught that there was little point in administering medicine to the sick only to discharge them back to a life of near destitution. Sometimes the smallest of interventions was all that was needed to relieve hardship and change lives.

'I think perhaps –' Alice began, but broke off at the sound of a shout. Several patients started and turned their heads towards a heavily pregnant woman who was standing by one of the curtained examination cubicles and yelling at a stocky man wearing labourer's scruffs.

Angling herself sideways on so that she could reach him around her considerable bump, the woman landed a punch on the man's chest and another on the side of his head. Spots of blood glistened from the resulting scratch on his cheek, and another just above his lip. 'Will you leave off me, woman!' the man yelled breathlessly, doing his best to dodge her blows while coughing explosively.

Alice gave Ted's leg a quick pat and rose to her feet. She wove purposefully around the packed rows of wooden benches, the pregnant woman gesticulating and shouting as she made her way over. 'I swear you've done it now, Jimmy!' the woman screamed.

'Excuse me,' Alice said firmly, seizing the scruffy man's arm. 'Nurse,' she called out, angling her head towards the treatment area. Several patients stared at the smartly dressed woman who had suddenly appeared, their mouths open in hushed, awed silence.

'Sit down, please,' she ordered the man, who was still coughing and frantically gasping for air. She motioned him away with a tiny flick of her head, her expression stern. Obediently, he backed away and collapsed onto a nearby seat.

A nurse emerged from one of the cubicles. Her eyes flicked from Alice to the pregnant woman, who was still trying to attack the heavy-set man, and then she hurried over to help. 'Stay outta this, Miss,' the expectant mother shouted to Alice. 'Someone needs to sort 'im out, once and for all.'

'No one is sorting anyone out, thank you,' Alice said, her voice carrying across the hall. 'I'll deal with this.'

'He's a filthy lying hound!' the woman yelled, spittle spilling out from the edges of her mouth.

'Be that as it may, he's now *our* patient,' Alice returned, her voice low and steady. Behind her, the nurse handed the man, who was now coughing up blood, a handkerchief. 'If you want to come back and see me later today, I'm happy to talk things through with you. But for now, please, I'd like you to leave.'

'You'll pay for this, Jimmy!' the woman screamed over Alice's shoulder, as the nurse led him away. 'I hope you cough up your guts and strangle yourself with 'em,' she added, before turning on her heel and waddling to the door.

Alice pulled down the cuffs of her blouse, straightened her hat and gave several still-gawping patients a reassuring smile. The almoner often needed to draw on every ounce of diplomacy she could muster to deal with the loud confrontations that sometimes broke out in the outpatients department.

The man was still coughing when Alice joined him in the watching room. 'She's agitated 'cos I'm not earning what I-I used to on account of this cough,' he told Alice in a thick Irish accent. 'And what with the baby soon to join us –'

Alice opened a new file and jotted down some notes while Jimmy spoke. A thirty-five-year-old labourer, Jimmy had sailed for England from Ireland a year earlier looking for work. He managed to find employment on the Wembley Park site, where work was under way preparing the ground for a new restaurant to be built near the planned new sports stadium, but had not yet managed to save enough to cover the cost of a deposit on his own lodgings.

Alice managed to elicit that he had spent most nights sleeping with three other workmen in a small shed on site, while his pregnant wife camped out on her parents' sofa. Waking in the same damp clothes he had worked in the previous day, his health had worsened through the winter. ''Tis a fine place here though,' Jimmy said, when Alice confirmed that his meagre earnings and imminent dependant qualified him for entirely free treatment at the hospital. 'And you're a fine woman, so you are,' he gasped, after she told him that he'd been booked into the chest clinic. A deep hacking cough issued from his lungs. He rubbed his red-rimmed eyes, watery with the strain of coughing, and said: 'Too fine to be wasting your time helping a vagrant like me.'

As the almoner made her way back across the atrium, Hetty Woods nudged her husband with her elbow. When she neared, Ted signalled to her. 'We was wondering, Miss Alice. Do you think you might have the opportunity to visit our daughter, Tilda? She's expecting but her husband won't let us near the place. He's got some sort of hold over her, I think. We haven't seen her for months. But my Hetty thinks that if anyone can sort them out, you can.'

Alice glanced over to the double doors, where another line of people were waiting to file inside. When temperatures plummeted, as they had in London in the last twenty-four hours, it was difficult to impose some order on the chaos reigning in outpatients. The doctors found the crowded conditions near impossible to work in, but the worsening storm and poor visibility at least provided her with an excuse to grant the most destitute a temporary reprieve.

'I will see what I can do in the next few days,' Alice told the couple, after noting down their daughter's address.

'Don't go after six though, duck,' Hetty said warningly. 'That's when our son-in-law gets home.'

The almoner nodded. 'I cannot promise anything, but I will try.'

Ted and Hetty watched Alice as she headed off for her meeting with Dr Harland, their rheumy eyes watery with gratitude.

CHAPTER THREE

The almoner is a general practitioner in social healing.
It is the almoner whose job it is to deal with the
personal difficulties and troubles of the patient ...
the constructive side of the social work done by the
almoner seems to know no limits.

(*The Scotsman*, 1937)

From its earliest days as an apothecary, doctors from the Royal Free went out into the community to treat patients who were too ill to leave their homes, or rose in the early hours to meet them at the hospital. 'As there were no telephones,' explained Dr Grace de Courcy, a medical student in 1894, 'if an emergency arose at night and the resident required assistance he would go into the street and take a hansom cab or a growler to the house of the surgeon or physician in charge of the ward to bring him back.'

Dedicated to their patients and uncomfortable with the idea of their private lives being examined, medical staff at the Royal Free had initially been reluctant to share any information with the almoners. For some, the whole idea of conducting financial

assessments on the sick was repugnant. Sir E. H. Currie complained to a reporter for the *London Daily News* in 1904 that
vetting patients using 'special detectives' was 'a scandal'. Currie
'strongly condemned' the use of inquisitorial methods to
'denounce' well-off patients. 'What possible good can one
woman investigator do?' he argued. 'It is ridiculous.'

Mr Rogers, a secretary from the London Hospital, defended
the appointment of an almoner who was to 'watch in the
receiving rooms for cases of imposition'. The secretary stated
that local doctors running private practices had accused the
hospital of 'robbing their profession' by treating patients
who 'they had personally seen ... driving to hospital in their
own carriages'.

Like his predecessors, Dr Peter Harland was another of those
people who subscribed to the view that any sort of surveillance
of the private lives of others was a disagreeable pastime. He was
waiting at the top of the stairs leading to the almoners' basement office when Alice arrived. 'I'm so sorry, doctor. Have you
been waiting long?'

'A minute or so.' There was no reproof in his voice, but his
features were strained.

Alice led the way down the dimly lit stairs, stopping before
a sturdy-looking oak door inset at eye-level with a small barred
window. Dr Harland waited silently as she opened the door to
the office, where arrow-slit windows high up across one wall
overlooked the sodden grey pavement of Gray's Inn Road. The
window sills provided neat cubby holes for reference books and

medical journals, the heavy tomes blocking much of the natural light.

Before the fires were lit by the caretaker each morning, the almoners' office lay silent, the stillness broken only by the rumble of underground trains beneath them. Now, the room was bustling with activity. Frank was seated at the nearest desk, taking ledgers one by one from a small pile and checking them against a list of the hospital's assets. Alexander was kneeling on the floor beside a solid leather trunk and setting a trap for the mice that emerged at night to nibble the edges of his financial reports. He fumbled with the steel mechanism with a harried air, his handsome features twisted and pink with annoyance. In the far corner, Winnie sat behind her typewriter, her habitual anguished frown in place.

At the opposite end of the office, the Lady Almoner, Bess Campbell, was busy preparing lists for a post-New Year party; a get-together for those acquaintances who had missed out on the New Year's celebration that had taken place in her considerable residence in Kensington. Miss Campbell, a woman with a flair for combining dynamic guests with those of a quieter nature so that everyone felt at ease, had a calendar packed with social events, dances and dinner parties.

She was a slim woman in her late forties, with greying shoulder-length hair and sharp but pleasant features. An accomplished and formidable character, she had a love of fine clothes and an air of authority, but she was also possessed of a natural humility, an essential quality in someone working so closely with the poor.

Like the majority of her colleagues, she had been selected from a class superior to those she served, the appointing committee believing that only someone gifted with eloquence could suitably advocate for the working class, who were generally less able to express themselves.

Each member of staff glanced up as Alice entered. At the appearance of Dr Harland, Alexander got to his feet and brushed down his trouser legs. Puffing absently on his pipe, Frank merely jutted out his chin. Miss Campbell beamed. 'Peter, my dear, how are you?'

'Too busy to be here. And you?' The doctor's expression settled as far into solicitousness as it ever went, though his face, all blunt lines and irregular angles, retained its slightly grumpy expression. About six inches taller than Alice, at just under five feet eleven, he was a tall man, sturdy and strong. In his mid-thirties, his square face was framed by a crop of thick curly black hair, his jaw displaying the hint of a beard.

'Well, it's most generous of you to spare some time for us, isn't it, Alice? And I'm splendid, thank you.' Miss Campbell ran the office with a regimen as strict as the fiercest sisters on the wards above her, but there were times when her staff caught a glimpse of the compassion she usually reserved for patients. When Alice had returned to the office after discovering the bodies of Molly and her infant son, Miss Campbell had been the first to her feet, steering Alice with tenderness towards her chair. Within minutes she had pressed a hot, disturbingly sweet cup of tea into one hand and a vinaigrette of smelling salts into the other. Alice was to take her final exam in social work the next day, but after what had happened, she told her boss that she was tempted to withdraw. 'I'm not suited to this sort of work,' she told Miss Campbell mournfully, after everyone else had gone home.

Miss Campbell had reached across the desk and taken Alice's hand in her own. 'If *you're* not suited to it, my dear, I don't think any of us are.'

'If only I'd acted sooner,' Alice had burst out, pulling her hands away to cover her cheeks. She shook her head. 'I knew something wasn't right. I should never have left Molly alone for so long.'

Miss Campbell scoffed gently. 'Would not the world be a finer place if only we were all possessed with blessed foresight?' She paused. Alice dropped her hands and looked at her. The Lady Almoner levelled her gaze. 'Alice, you need to accept that we all have limitations, and that includes you. You're not responsible for every vulnerable waif and stray in London, you know. But you have more empathy and intuition than almost anyone else I know. So you'll go tomorrow and take your exam and then you'll return here to carry on with your work.'

Alice's eyes pooled with tears. 'But I'll fail, just like I failed Molly.'

'Then you shall take it again,' Miss Campbell had said with a note of finality and a short sharp squeeze of Alice's hand.

At her desk, Alice removed her hat and gloves and tucked them into a drawer. 'Would you like a cup of tea before we get started, doctor?'

Dr Harland nodded as he drew up a chair and sat at the end of her desk. From across the office, Frank began to cough theatrically. 'I take it you would like one too, Frank,' Alice said, moving towards the boiler with weary amusement.

'I am parched, now you mention it.'

Winnie got to her feet and made efforts to convince Miss Campbell, who had declined Alice's offer, that it would be wise to keep hydrated. She then hovered behind Alice and warned her of the perils inherent in carrying out any activity involving boiling water. 'I have everything under control, Winnie, thank you,' Alice said with impatience.

The almoner warmed the office teapot using the water bubbling away in a large pot on top of the boiler. After setting a few mismatched cups on top of an empty desk, she swirled the hot water around the pot and emptied the vestiges into the large porcelain sink in the corner of the room. She scooped a caddy spoon of tea leaves inside, the soothing simplicity of the act at odds with the concerns that had been swirling in her mind over the last couple of days, since visiting the Redbournes' house.

Outside, there was a temporary reprieve from the rain. A shaft of winter sunlight shone through the grime-covered, half-blocked windows, temporarily transforming the gloomy office from dungeon to a bright, airy place. The fug of ink, damp paper and coal in the air lifted momentarily, returning less than a minute later when the sun disappeared behind a cloud.

'What have I told you?' Frank roared a minute later, jumping to his feet. 'Milk in last, not first!' He strode towards Alice, pipe in hand, his grizzled features screwed up in mock disgust. 'If you were my wife I'd ask you to tip that away and start again.'

Alice lowered the teapot to the desk and grabbed one of the cups. 'If we were married, Frank,' she said, thrusting the steaming drink towards him, 'it wouldn't be *me* making the tea.' Frank stared at her and took the proffered drink with his habitual hangdog expression. Seconds later, in a huff of smoke and quivering jowls, he bellowed with laughter. A few feet away, Alexander seated himself behind his desk with a look of distaste.

Alice rolled her eyes and passed another of the drinks, this time with more grace, to Dr Harland. After sliding her own cup onto the edge of her desk, she sat beside the doctor and switched on her desk lamp. Light pooled on the slew of beige folders that lay between them, the Redbourne file uppermost in the pile.

As Alice reached out and pulled the folder down in front of her, Winnie appeared. Her handbag was clasped in one arthritic hand, and she picked up Alice's cup with the other. 'Where would you like your tea, dear?'

Alice pushed her chair back and half stood up to retrieve it. 'Where it was,' she said tersely, replacing it on the edge of her desk. Winnie's gaze flicked between Alice and the cup as if trying to communicate the folly of such action, but then she shuffled wordlessly back to her desk.

Before Alice opened the file in front of her, the doctor asked if any progress had been made in securing convalescence for one of his elderly tubercular patients who wasn't well enough to go home.

'Grove House in Eastbourne has reserved a place for the beginning of February. They've booked Mr Hobbs in for at least two weeks.'

Dr Harland grunted his approval, dipped his fountain pen in the inkwell of Alice's desk and scribbled something in his notebook. 'And Mrs Taylor?'

'I saw her just after Christmas. I managed to convince her to apply for a crisis loan from the Samaritan Fund.' Mrs Taylor's husband, Simon, had recently been diagnosed with cancer of the lung, but was struggling to come to terms with the poor prognosis he'd been given. Medical staff had encouraged him to share the burden with his wife, but he continued to reassure her that he'd be back on his feet in a day or two. While it wasn't up to Alice to break patient confidentiality, she had been able to visit Mrs Taylor to make sure that the practicalities of losing the family's sole breadwinner were taken care of. A proud, respectable sort of woman, she had been reluctant to even discuss any form of assistance, but with two weeks' rent arrears and only enough food left to last the week, she eventually conceded that she needed some help. By the time Alice left her, she had been tearfully grateful.

Alice and Peter Harland's discussion turned to the family of a child who had died on the chest ward overnight. Nine-year-old Clara Stewart had been suffering from consumption complicated by pneumonia, and by the time she reached hospital it had been too late for doctors to save her. Clara's parents had never been able to afford to have a family photograph taken and were desperate to take advantage of their one last opportunity to secure a memento mori, something that was certain to become a treasured keepsake, before their daughter's body was buried. 'The poor family,' Alice said softly. 'I'll make an urgent application to the Samaritan Fund. I'm sure the panel won't have any –'

Dr Harland waved his hand. 'That will take time we don't have,' he said. 'I'll take care of the expenses. All I'm asking is that you make the necessary contact with a post-mortem photographer. Not all will take on such a task.'

Alice turned to face him, her expression soft. 'That is very decent of you.'

'It's nothing,' he mumbled gruffly. 'Anything else? I need to get –'

'Just a minute!' Frank piped up from across the room. 'Isn't photography a hobby of yours, Alex? Perhaps you could help them out?'

'I prefer my subjects to have a pulse, but it's terribly good of you to think of me, Frank,' Alexander answered icily, his gaze on the papers in front of him.

'I need to get back to the ward if there's nothing else?' The doctor tapped his fingers on the desk with impatience.

Alice rested her hand on the Redbournes' file, her expression thoughtful. She hesitated for a moment before asking, 'Do you remember tending to a child called Henry Redbourne? He came in at the beginning of the summer. You treated him for pneumonia.'

The doctor gave a small nod. 'Is he unwell again?'

'No, he seems perfectly well. It's just that …' She opened the file in front of her. 'We called in on the family and,' she paused, rolling her lips in on themselves. Across the room, Frank, who had been making notes in a ledger, peered up at her. 'The children seemed quite well, but something wasn't right.'

The doctor looked at Alice, his green eyes cloudy with impatience. 'In what way?'

'I am not sure exactly. Their eldest was upset and … I mean, she didn't say much but she didn't really need to. There was something … I still cannot grasp what it was, but it was unsettling. There was definitely something. I could feel it.'

The doctor raised his heavy brows. 'I prefer to deal with facts, Miss Hudson. Not feelings.'

Alice stared at him for a moment before answering. 'Yes, of course.' She lowered her gaze, returning her attention to the file. She flicked through the papers and then turned back to the doctor. 'A financial assessment was carried out before Henry's admission, and when his siblings were treated before him, but the parents were not forthcoming at the time and –' Her words were left floating in the air.

Dr Harland said nothing, but his lips narrowed into a thin line.

'I wondered if you might shed a little light on the family, if you have memory of them?' Alice pressed.

Dr Harland inched back in his chair, bristling. 'They're fairly respectable, from what I recall. We're talking relatively, of course. But I noticed nothing out of the ordinary.'

Alice chewed on the inside of her cheek. 'But Mrs Red-bourne has been seen the worse for drink on a number of occasions while their children were left home alone,' she persisted, flicking rapidly through the papers again, one way and then the other. 'They've been lying to us about having lodgers, I'm certain of that, and … I realise it's of no medical concern, but I feel that our help is sorely needed.'

The doctor made a face and returned his gaze to the pile of files on the desk. The almoner stared at the pages of the file in front of her for a full half-minute before returning her attention to Dr Harland. 'There was something there,' she repeated insistently. 'Something about the place that just didn't fit. I just cannot yet grasp what it was.' The doctor puffed out his cheeks then returned his gaze to the files.

From across the room, through a cloud of smoke, Frank's eyes were still resting on Alice speculatively.

CHAPTER FOUR

We are all mad when we give way to passion, to prejudice,
to vice, to vanity; but if all the passionate, prejudiced and
vain people were to be locked up as lunatics, who is to
keep the key to the asylum?

(*The Times*, editorial, 1853)

The call of distress from the Redbournes' home came just
before five o'clock that afternoon, as the meeting between
Alice and Dr Harland was drawing to an end.

A quiet but feverish rapping at the door drew everyone's
attention. 'Come in,' Bess Campbell said without looking up.
The tapping stopped but the door remained closed. Alice
turned to meet Frank's gaze. He sat motionless, eyeing her
through a cloud of smoke. She huffed out some air and got to
her feet. When she opened the door her eyes widened in surprised recognition – standing before her was one of the
Redbourne girls, Elsa, wearing nothing more than a thin cotton dress. Soaked through and shivering with cold, the
twelve-year-old looked close to passing out. 'Please, Miss, can
you come?' she cried breathlessly. 'Something awful's going on.'

Alice glanced behind at her colleagues. Miss Campbell and Dr Harland were already on their feet. She turned back and quickly beckoned the girl into the basement. 'Yes, of course, I will come directly, but what is it? What has happened?'

Bess Campbell draped a blanket over Elsa's shoulders and guided her to one of the chairs closest to the hearth, where a fire blazed. The girl refused to sit down. 'We have to go!' she cried, hopping from one foot to the other. 'Mum says you have to come. Charlotte's gone mad and you have to lock her up.'

Alice, Frank and Miss Campbell exchanged glances. 'Why, my dear?' the Lady Almoner asked. 'What on earth has happened?'

'I dunno! They won't let me see her, but Mum says she's lost her mind and the devil's responsible. She said you would take her away.' Elsa began sobbing. Her legs buckled and Alice guided her gently down onto a chair.

Bess Campbell looked expectantly at the doctor. 'I'm about to go off-duty,' he said. After an uncomfortable silence he looked up at the ceiling and added gruffly: 'Right, I'll make a house call then, shall I?'

'Good,' said Miss Campbell. 'Alice?'

The almoner gave a grim nod. 'I'll accompany them,' Frank said, reaching for his hat.

Elsa made a move but Miss Campbell pressed her hands down onto the girl's damp shoulders. 'You'll wait here with me, at least until the storm passes. Once we've established what has happened, then you may return.'

★ ★ ★

Moonlight flickered as Alice, Frank and Dr Harland disembarked from a hackney carriage taxicab at the end of Dock Street. The rain was lashing down, arcs of light from the terraced houses rippling over the surface of the puddles.

Clumps of confetti from the New Year celebrations still littered the pavements, the soggy flakes clinging to the hem of Alice's long cape and the tips of her laced-up boots. A discarded sock trailed over the side of a cattle trough, the wool stiff with cold.

Frank marched purposefully towards the Redbournes' house, his head tilted against the onslaught of rain. Alice wrapped her scarf carefully around her neck and squinted, the doctor following on a few feet behind. Their steps seemed to drag as they followed Frank. Setting out like this gave them all a sense of the likely grimness that lay ahead.

'She was morally flabby right from the off,' Mrs Redbourne proclaimed as soon as she opened the door to the small party. Her jowls quivered as she spoke, her compressed mouth growing so thin that her lips were barely visible. 'Never sat still in church. I knew she'd never amount to much, what with the aggression and the wild ways, but you'd think she'd have learned her lesson after the last time.' She looked angry, but her eyes were shiny with suppressed tears.

'What ails Charlotte, Mrs Redbourne?' Alice asked as she followed Frank into the hall. The doctor stifled a yawn on the shoulder of his coat as he closed the door behind them.

'I don't know what it is, do I? An overflow of blood to the head, George says. I say it's the work of the devil.'

Alice was accustomed to dealing with families who were so mortified by their daughters' behaviour that they claimed they had been inflicted by a sudden onset of insanity. A diagnosis of insanity was seen by some families as a way of ridding themselves of the embarrassment of wayward daughters, a sort of absolution from the stain of it. The affluent sometimes shipped their 'excitable' daughters abroad, or confined them and their offspring to a secluded cottage somewhere in the grounds. There were few appealing options open to most of the Royal Free's patients.

Surprise rippled over the faces of Alice and her colleagues at the apparent spite shown by the woman, quickly followed by distaste. They watched her in silence for a few moments. It was Dr Harland who spoke next. 'If you'll show us the way, then, Mrs Redbourne,' he said quietly, nodding towards the stairs. There was a coldness to his tone and a degree of irritation as well.

Mrs Redbourne pulled her chin in and straightened the apron she was wearing, her neck flushed. When she next spoke, it was with a precision that was uncharacteristic and clearly forced. 'They're in the back parlour. Step this way, won't you?' Her use of the plural pronoun seemed to go unnoticed by the doctor, but Alice and Frank exchanged puzzled glances as they followed Mrs Redbourne along the dim passageway. There was no sign of the other children, but excited mutterings and a distant thud suggested they were shut away in one of the bedrooms upstairs.

Outside the parlour room door, Mrs Redbourne lowered her voice to a loud whisper. 'You'll pardon the smell. I haven't been able to get near the bed to change it and she won't surrender the babe. She's not put it down since delivering.'

Alice turned and looked at Frank with astonished eyes. He grimaced in response, pipe suspended in the air an inch from his mouth. As Mrs Redbourne pushed the door open and went inside, the smells of the enclosed room spilled out onto the hall: damp linen, lochial blood and the sickly sweet smell of colostrum. Frank took a staggering step backwards, folding himself against the wall. Alice sidestepped him. With her eyes fixed on the bed, she raised the coned sleeve of her cape to cover her mouth and stared.

Several dirty blankets formed a makeshift wall along each side of the mattress and just visible above the bedclothes beyond was Charlotte, a tiny infant's head lying in the crook of her left arm. Mother and child were utterly still, their faces alabaster. The bedspread covering them, large with embroidered flowers, was crumpled and heavily stained.

'When did she deliver, Mrs Redbourne?' Alice asked, a slight catch in her throat.

'About an hour or so ago. She's working in the kitchen then all of a sudden she abandons the preparations and goes missing. I heard all the carry-on in the privy.'

Alice closed her eyes momentarily but Mrs Redbourne's face was set, her expression implacable. 'She needs to rest for now,' the almoner said, looking at the woman evenly. 'I shall wait with her while she recovers, and we can examine her when she wakes. The time might be useful for you and your husband to reconcile yourself with events.'

'No, no way,' Mrs Redbourne spat from the foot of the bed. 'You need to get them out of here now. George won't have no product of sin ...' she stopped, gathering her rage. 'A bastard. He'll not have no bastard child in this house, and nor will I!' On speaking the word 'bastard', she crossed herself.

Charlotte stirred then and half-raised her head from the pillow. The baby remained still. The teenager's faintly puzzled frown deepened as she took her unannounced visitors in, then her eyes grew wide. A flush rose up her neck, flooding her cheeks crimson.

For several moments no words were spoken, but a strange uneasiness grew. The seconds stretched out. Charlotte's eyes flitted around the assembled group, analysing their every movement. Slowly, without taking her eyes off her audience, she eased her cradling arm half an inch to the left.

Her mother turned to Frank, eyebrows raised. Taking his cue, he stepped forwards, and then several things happened at once. Charlotte bolted upright and fumbled for her baby, clamping the bundle tightly to her breast. Her thin cotton nightgown shimmered in synchrony with her trembling limbs.

Alice moved then. With one gloved hand outstretched and placating, she edged sideways around a chamber pot half-filled with pink water, blood-soaked rags and something fleshy floating around inside. 'Charlotte, it's all right. We're not going to harm the baby.'

The girl stared at Alice, her eyes wide and fearful. Her lips were almost without colour, the rims of her eyes white. 'When was the last time Charlotte ate or drank anything, Mrs

Redbourne?' Alice asked, without taking her eyes off the young woman. 'She looks terribly weak.'

The woman folded her arms haughtily. 'I've told her. She's getting nothing 'til she recites Our Lord's Prayer.'

'Am I to understand nothing has passed the girl's lips since delivering?' Dr Harland asked quietly from the doorway. Charlotte turned towards the voice, the glaze clearing from her eyes. A shadow passed across her face, one that seemed to pass unnoticed by the others in the room.

Mrs Redbourne shook her head. One of her eyelids flickered, a brief insight into her guilt. She swept it away with a swift wave of her hand.

'Oh for heaven's sake, woman,' the doctor burst out. 'She must have water.'

The woman baulked at that, flattening her hands either side of her substantial breasts. 'I've told her –'

'Water, now please,' the doctor blasted through gritted teeth.

Mrs Redbourne's arms fell to her side and her mouth dropped open, but after a moment's hesitation and an affronted stare she barged past the assembled group and slammed out of the room.

She returned a minute or so later, a cup of water in hand. Without a word she passed it to her daughter, who took a hungry gulp and then choked, the rest of the contents spilling over onto the bed. The infant failed to stir at the disturbance. Alice turned, her features tightened with concern. Dr Harland dropped his Gladstone bag onto a side table near the bed and pulled out his stethoscope. 'I really must examine the child,' he told Charlotte. 'We mustn't delay.'

'Come near me and I'll make you sorry!' Charlotte cried shrilly. She shrank away, tucking herself at the far end, between the head of the bed and the wall. Her arms tightened around the tangle of blankets and towels housing her small, naked infant, her eyes burning manically. Frizzy tendrils of dark hair had escaped the long braid that hung over her shoulder and were standing out from her head, adding to the appearance of madness.

Doctor Harland draped the scope around the back of his neck and lifted his hands up in an exasperated gesture. He glanced at Alice. She hesitated before opening her mouth, but before she could speak, Frank intervened. 'Come now, Charlotte,' he said, easing past the doctor. 'We need to make sure the infant is well, there's a good girl.'

'No!' Charlotte cried out again, this time with a violent lunge across the filthy mattress. Scrambling back out of reach in the far corner of the room, she began screaming incoherently, all the while clutching her still bloodstained baby to her chest.

Fear and grief masqueraded as madness, so that it appeared that the young mother was wildly out of control and in no fit state to take care of her baby. That she was driven to this because three strangers had descended upon her with the intention of tearing her newborn baby away was equally undeniable.

'We had all this last year!' Mrs Redbourne screeched. 'Her being free with herself. There's nothing else for it but to get her brains tested.'

Alice frowned. 'I don't follow.'

'She lost it at five or six months gone, thank the Lord,' the woman continued in explanation. 'You'd think that'd be enough to stop her, but, oh no, she had to go and do it again, didn't she?'

'Perhaps if I spoke to Mr Redbourne?' Alice ventured. 'Sometimes, with support, families are able to –'

'He's disgusted with her,' the woman snapped, though a mild flicker crossed her expression. 'I don't think there's no way you'll talk him round.'

With continuing insistence, Mrs Redbourne acquiesced and asked her husband to come down from his retreat in their bedroom.

'Ain't something you expect, is it?' the porter mumbled grimly when Alice spoke to him in the hall. His dull eyes rested on his wife as he spoke, his fingernails scratching restlessly at the wooden banister. 'Not from your own.'

Mrs Redbourne nodded along with his every word. 'Yes, see, I told you.' She rushed back along the hall towards the parlour, her arm outstretched and beckoning. 'Come on, then, quick. Let's get on with it.'

'Just a moment,' Alice said, unmoving. Mr Redbourne hovered on the bottom stair, looking troubled. The almoner fixed him with a steady look. 'There might be some level of support we can put in place, Mr Redbourne, if you were willing to keep Charlotte here. I cannot promise anything, but if you feel differently to your wife, we can perhaps come to some agreement you would both be –'

'Would you credit it?' the woman roared. 'You're the limit, you really are!' She charged back up the hall and waved her husband away with a flapping hand. 'Trying to come between a woman and her husband!' she said, her hands on her hips. 'We're in agreement, and nothing you can say will change his mind.' Alice's gaze was still resting on Mr Redbourne. He flicked a regretful glance towards his wife and then turned, trudging back up the stairs.

'She's turned into one of those imbeciles you hear about,' Mrs Redbourne shrieked as she led the way back into the parlour. 'She's beyond helping, she's morally corrupt!'

Dr Harland watched helplessly as Charlotte thrashed around, her lips contorting manically. He was a chest specialist with little experience in the field of psychiatrics, but any doctor was allowed to make a diagnosis and confirm a committal to a mental hospital, whatever their speciality. Tears painted white streaks down Charlotte's blood-streaked cheeks. Her eyelashes were wet, her pale cheeks suddenly a bloody crimson.

'Doctor?' Alice said, her tone suggesting impatience.

Her intervention seemed to snap the doctor out of his indecision. He glanced at Frank, who nodded grimly, then turned back to Charlotte. 'Miss Redbourne, I have reason to believe you are suffering from an infliction of the mind.' Charlotte continued to scream and the doctor raised his voice. 'I fear I must commit you to a hospital for your own safety and that of your child.'

He turned to Charlotte's mother. 'Is there insanity or instability elsewhere in the family?' The Mental Deficiency Act provided local authorities with the power to lock away women deemed defective and, although there are no official figures on the number of unmarried women certified for becoming pregnant – most of those unable to support themselves were sent to the workhouse – some unfortunate victims lost their liberty. A repeat offender like Charlotte could be locked up without an official diagnosis, all on the say-so of one of her parents.

Mrs Redbourne reddened with outrage. 'Certainly not! It's nothing to do with us. She's possessed, I tell you. We were willing to put up with her lashing out, destroying property, we even put last year's business behind us, but to do it again? That's just not on. That's madness!'

Alice winced. Motioning Frank with his eyes, Dr Harland strode forwards and made his way around the end of the bed. Frank pocketed his pipe and followed. At the same time, Charlotte lunged over the other end of the bed and slipped off the side nearest the door. Her foot skidded out. A ghastly gurgle followed as the chamber pot upended and the putrid contents spilled out over the floor.

For a moment everyone froze. The room fell silent, the only sound the relentless drum of rain at the window. It was then that Alice grasped the opportunity to take control. 'Charlotte,' she said gently, 'pass the baby to me, dear. I'll be very gentle, I promise you.'

The young woman swung her head from side to side, feverishly checking the position of the others. Frank and the doctor remained still for a full minute, Alice speaking soft platitudes all the while.

After weighing up her options, Charlotte seemed to reach a decision. Locking her eyes on Alice's, she shuffled her feet forwards. There was an oddness to her gait as she rested the infant in the almoner's arms, though she didn't let go of her grip.

Alice made a reassuring noise in her throat. 'There, it's all right, Charlotte. It will be fine.'

Frank crawled over the bed then. Approaching Charlotte from behind, he rested his hands firmly on her shoulders. 'That's it, child, let go.'

Her grip on the infant slackened and she backed away, holding empty hands in front of her. The sodden, meconium-streaked blankets loosened to reveal a tiny baby boy with a painfully thin body and sagging, greyish arms and legs. Alice looked down at him then fixed her gaze on Frank. She pressed her lips together and gave him a sombre, almost imperceptible shake of her head.

Charlotte's chest heaved. A terrible sound escaped her lips then, a mournful, inhuman howl. She sank shakily down onto the bed, put her head in her hands and wept. Her tears fell onto her gown and mingled with the dark splodges of colostrum staining her front. With an awkward manoeuvre, Alice shrugged off her cape and, discarding the filthy swaddling, wrapped the still infant in its soft wool.

'We must get Charlotte to hospital,' Dr Harland said grimly.

The almoners were accustomed to dealing with society's ills, the cases they became involved in so distressing as to sometimes keep them from sleeping soundly in their beds. Charlotte's case was different though, because despite their involvement her immediate future still looked bleak.

And so far there had been no indication that the biggest shock of the evening was yet to come.

CHAPTER FIVE

Sometimes the almoner is called on to find a suitable home
into which young children can be temporarily admitted or
find a foster mother for the baby either herself or through an
outside agency, and probably raise the funds to pay for this.
Her aim, in addition to arranging that the children shall be
satisfactorily looked after, is to secure as far as possible
mental peace for the patient, for worry is a bad bedfellow.

(*The Hospital Almoner: A Brief Study of Hospital
Social Science in Great Britain*, 1910)

At just before 7 o'clock, Peter Harland guided Charlotte down
the front step and onto the street. The rain was still hissing
down in torrents, as if the sky itself were weeping for the small
lifeless body Alice had gently swaddled and left in a drawer in
the parlour. Shadows moved behind the closed curtains of the
adjoining houses. Rainwater overflowed from their gutters,
splashing onto the flagstones below. The young woman's depar-
ture seemed to penetrate Mrs Redbourne's hardened stance.
Watching from the downstairs window, she wept as her daughter shuffled away, a flattened hand clamped over her mouth.

Light spilled onto the pavement as several doors and windows opened along the street, neighbours leaning out to find the source of all the commotion. Once the doctor had settled Charlotte inside the cab he motioned to Alice, who was waiting just inside the hall. Frank held his coat over his colleague as she jogged to the cab, her soiled cape folded over her arm. There was a babble of whispers from the spectators as she climbed hastily inside, Frank's mackintosh flapping noisily in the wind behind her.

When Alice was settled inside, Frank closed the door discreetly and stepped back onto the pavement, watching as the taxicab turned in an arc and disappeared down the rain-drenched street, back the way it came.

Inside the cab, Alice gave instructions for the driver to head towards the Royal Free Hospital.

On the far side, Charlotte was sitting with her forehead pressed against the fogged window, her coat gaping around her still swollen belly. Drops of rain mingled with perspiration and glistened on her cheeks. The napkins Dr Harland had placed beneath her were rapidly turning bright red as she bled out over them, the air in the cab slowly filling with the salty smell of lochia.

Every so often a small whimpering sound escaped her lips. Dr Harland, who was sitting in the rearward-facing seat opposite, considered her quietly. He frowned. 'Are you in pain, Charlotte?' he eventually asked, his habitual gruffness softer than usual. The contents of the chamber pot in the back parlour suggested that the afterbirth had been delivered intact but it had not been confirmed by examination. Alice and the doctor had made several attempts to assess Charlotte – fever, heavy bleeding or even fatal haemorrhaging might occur if part of the placenta remained inside her uterus – but each time she had hissed at them and tried to scratch their arms.

'You can forget about taking me there,' Charlotte groaned after a time. 'I won't go.'

Alice glanced sideways. The teenager shook her head and shrank further into the corner of her seat, moaning loudly. The driver turned his head sharply. 'What the devil's going on back there?'

'We have everything under control,' Alice reassured him firmly, though her eyes lingered on Charlotte for several seconds afterwards. The cab continued along empty streets but, with conditions so hazardous, progress was slow. At the next corner the vehicle slid across the wet road and almost mounted the pavement.

The driver cursed and pulled over. 'I can't get to the Royal. The roads are too bad. I'm not chancing –'

He stopped at another loud groan from Charlotte. With the cab parked up at the side of the road, Alice knelt in front of Charlotte and pressed a hand on her stomach. She turned to the doctor and looked at him. 'There's another baby coming,' she said slowly. Dr Harland's eyes grew wide.

'Well, it's not ruddy coming in here!' the driver shouted. 'I'll not have no strumpet delivering a bastard in my cab!'

Charlotte's hands gripped the seat and gasped as a contraction moved through her. 'They're coming strong,' Alice added with urgency. She brushed Charlotte's dark hair back from her face. 'It's all right, Charlotte. We'll take care of you.' She looked at the doctor. 'What are we going to do?'

He touched his fingertips to his forehead and then raked them down over his bristled face. After a moment he turned to the driver. 'Take us to Fenchurch Street.'

'No way. I want her out!'

'For heaven's sake, man, it's two minutes away.'

The driver groaned and slammed the cab into gear. 'My sister, Elizabeth, lives close by,' the doctor explained. 'We'll take her there.' But within a minute the taxicab had come to a halt. The driver secured the brake. 'I can't go no further,' he said. 'Look.' He pointed ahead.

The doctor wiped the misted window with the back of his hand, peering through the palm-sized clearing. The way ahead was impassable, a deep well of water across the road. He groaned. 'What is it?' Alice asked.

'We'll have to walk.' He dragged his hands over his face again.

'But she's ready to deliver.'

'I know, I know,' he said with an impatient wave of his hand, and then he slapped his legs decisively. 'Right, Charlotte, at the end of the next contraction we'll help you out of the car, all right?'

Gripped by another pain, Charlotte's expression clouded. Alice glanced at the doctor over the young woman's head. They stared at each other for a moment, and then Alice nodded her agreement. Charlotte trembled as the contraction heightened, but she made little noise. Alice took her hand and she gripped the almoner's fingers tightly. She braced herself as Alice spoke soothingly, her feet pressed against the seat in front of her. As the contraction abated and her body began to relax the doctor grabbed his bag and left the cab. After exchanging brisk words and a few coins with the driver, he returned to the back and reached in to help Charlotte out.

With Alice and the doctor either side of her, Charlotte stumbled through the rain a few feet at a time, stopping now and again to press her hand to the small of her back. She cried out when they reached Elizabeth's house, doubling over with a deep rumbling moan. 'I can't,' she sobbed. 'I can't do this no more.'

'It's all right, Charlotte, we're here now.' With his bag dangling from his wrist, the doctor hammered on the door with the side of his fist. Lightning forked jaggedly across the sky above, a loud rumble of thunder following a second or two later. A seagull cried in the distance, closely followed by the clatter of horses' hooves.

Within seconds came the sound of a bolt being released, the door opened by a prim-looking woman in her mid-forties, a shoulder-length wavy bob framing her sharply angled face. Dressed in a figure-hugging gown and intricately woven shawl, she stepped back from the door with slow, restricted movements, her eyes widening in surprise as she took in the unusual party on her doorstep. 'She's close to delivering,' the doctor said in an urgent tone.

The woman's eyes ran over her visitors. There was a pause in which everyone stilled, but then she stood aside. Her eyes dropped to the floor as Alice and the doctor half-guided, half-lifted Charlotte up the front step and into the hall. Her lips curled in distaste at the pool of water appearing beneath the three sets of feet.

'What?' the doctor barked.

Elizabeth dipped her head towards the rug covering the floor. 'Shoes, if you wouldn't mind.'

An agonising moan escaped from deep down in Charlotte's throat. Peter Harland gave his sister a look of disbelief. She rolled her eyes. 'Oh, very well. Go straight through.' She bustled off upstairs as quickly as her gown would allow, returning to the living room with an armful of linen just as her visitors reached her sofa.

'Wait!' she cried, diving between them and the furniture and covering her expensive-looking cushions with several layers of padding.

'Oh, for heaven's sake,' Peter Harland muttered, his forehead glistening with sweat as Charlotte sagged between himself and Alice. As soon as his sister moved away, he dropped his bag onto a sidetable then lifted the girl carefully in his arms and laid her on top of the coverings.

Elizabeth's eyes dropped once more to her visitors' feet. She linked hands in front of her middle and opened her mouth to speak, but another deep groan from Charlotte sent her scurrying from the room. When she returned a minute later, the doctor was standing by the window and Alice was kneeling on the floor at the opposite end of the sofa, its elevation too low for her to attend to Charlotte in a standing position. Her gloves, hat and soiled cape lay on the floor beside her, her reddened and scarred left hand resting on top of Charlotte's splayed knee.

'Would you mind,' Elizabeth said, passing Alice some newspaper and more towels. The almoner gave her a look and then layered the newspapers beneath Charlotte's back, setting a double layer of towels over the top to form a barrier between her and the ornate sofa. In stark contrast to the Redbournes' home, the room was richly decorated, with curtains of thick brocade and a mahogany Victorian dresser.

'Right, I'll be outside if you need me,' Peter Harland said with a brisk rub of his hands. He turned on his heel and headed for the door.

Alice turned sharply. 'Are you not going to deliver the baby?'

He stopped at the threshold and stared at her in mute surprise. When he found his voice he said weakly, 'I'm a chest specialist.'

Alice glared at him. He closed his eyes, let out a breath and sidled back, looking sheepish. Alice lifted Charlotte's shift, removed the long bloomers she had recently helped her into and parted her legs, her face a picture of absorbed concentration. The doctor rummaged around in his pockets, as if he might find some helpful instrument lurking there. 'The head is already crowning,' Alice said, beads of sweat appearing on her forehead. 'Well done, Charlotte, well done!'

The news seemed to have a rallying effect on the doctor. Decided on a course of action, he removed his jacket and rolled back his shirtsleeves. Alice gestured for him to help and together they turned Charlotte onto her side. 'Now, bear down with the next pain, my love,' Alice said, supporting one of Charlotte's legs with her forearm. Peter Harland shifted position so that he was standing behind the sofa. From there he took over the support of Charlotte's leg from Alice, holding it in the crook of one arm. Within seconds Charlotte's stomach tightened with another contraction. With a soft grunt of effort, she began to push. 'Good girl,' Alice said encouragingly at the appearance of a mass of dark hair. 'There, Charlotte. You've done it. The head is born.'

Charlotte's head dropped back. Her bottom lip trembled. 'I want you to pant through the next pain, Charlotte. Here it comes, now pant. That's it, just breathe out.' Charlotte moaned. 'Almost there, my love. The next pain should do it.'

Within a minute Charlotte raised her head and groaned again, chin tucked deep into her chest. In a gush of blood and amniotic fluid the body was born, the baby slipping into Alice's waiting arms. Her eyes brimmed with tears. 'It's a girl,' she told Charlotte, her voice catching. The young mother gave a little sob and sank back, exhausted, onto a cushion. As Alice cleared the infant's mouth, her small features pinked up. The baby gasped and coughed as the almoner worked, then her tiny pink lips pursed and she screamed lustily. Dr Harland reached for his bag and handed it to Alice. She tied off and then clipped the umbilical cord, the faint line of the linea nigra that ran the length of the baby's body mirroring that of her mother and her twin.

At the mahogany dresser, Elizabeth poured steaming water from a floral jug into a large bowl. Alice glanced up at the doctor and their eyes locked, fixed by the intensity of the moment. There were tears on her face. She brushed them aside with the back of her hand and glanced away. When she looked back, he was smiling warmly. The moment was broken as Elizabeth handed Alice the towel she had been warming by the fire. The almoner wrapped the baby up gently and passed her to her mother.

Charlotte gave a cry of joy and cradled her daughter tenderly in the crook of her left arm, where her twin brother had lain barely an hour earlier. She smiled, the earlier parting temporarily forgotten. Another separation remained, but for now the infant lay serenely in her arms.

'She's beautiful, Charlotte,' Alice said gently. The almoner kneeled beside the sofa and rested her hand gently on the towel. Charlotte beamed and gave her a teary smile, but when Dr Harland's shadow brushed over her as he moved towards his sister, a curious flicker passed over her face.

CHAPTER SIX

It is not correct to say that patients in this hostel are,
in every case, suffering from illness incurred as the result
of their own acts. The conditions under which many
girls have worked for the past years involve very
grave and unusual risks of infection.

(Annual Report of the Women's After Care Hostel
in Highbury Quadrant, November 1919)

The murder of illegitimate babies at the hands of their birth mothers frequently featured in the daily newspapers and so, of all their patients, the almoners worried most about mothers who were young, unmarried and alone.

Driven by shame, some went to great lengths to conceal their pregnancies and scurried off when their waters broke, to give birth alone. The women were then faced with a heartbreaking dilemma – what to do with the baby. Panicked and petrified, some attempted to solve the problem by abandoning them. Every year there were cases of newborn babies being found on doorsteps, in churches, on the upper deck of a bus, in shopping bags and sometimes even rubbish bins.

The almoners of the Royal Free kept records of compassionate sympathisers willing to throw a lifeline to society's unfortunates when the need was dire. The Salvation Army (or Sally Bash, as it was known in some parts of London, on account of their marches through the streets ringing out messages of hope with trumpets and drums) and Dr Barnardo's complemented their efforts, working hard to encourage the view of single mothers as victims rather than villains. They offered practical help to lone mothers, seeking out affordable rooms and accommodating employers, as well as issuing regular pleas among congregations for the donation of furnishings, blankets and clothes.

Shortly before midnight, Peter Harland opened the shutters that had been fastened against the storm and peered out of the window. A single leaf twisted through the air and flattened itself against the pane, a reminder that, with a recently delivered girl and her newly born daughter, it would be unwise to venture outside.

A few feet away, Charlotte was dozing, half-parted lips breathing softly onto her baby's head. With a furrowed brow, Alice sank wordlessly into a deep armchair tucked into one of the alcoves near the fireplace, her boots and a large pair of rain-spattered shoes arranged side by side on a folded newspaper beside her. She started at the clink of china against metal as Elizabeth wheeled a silver tea trolley into the room.

'The storm should settle soon,' the older woman said. Her brother mumbled something inaudible above the clutter and clunk of crockery as Elizabeth arranged cups and saucers on an occasional table close to Alice.

'At last,' Alice said in a low tone. She craned her head over her lap and tilted her knees to the side, examining the dark patches on the hem of her skirt.

'Would you like to borrow something of mine?' Elizabeth asked. 'You're still drenched.'

'That's kind, but there's no need, thank you.'

Elizabeth's eyes lingered on the floor, where the damp wool of Alice's skirt was skimming her Persian rug. After a moment she planted an ornate strainer on top of one of the cups, angling her face away from the rising steam as she poured tea from an equally elaborate-looking pot. 'What's to become of them?' she asked, dipping her head towards the sleeping pair. She held out one of the drinks to Alice, a silver spoon carefully balanced on the saucer beside the cup. Her expression faltered when Alice took the drink, her eyes snagging over the scars across the back of the almoner's hand.

Alice rested the drink on her lap, tugged briskly on the cuff of her blouse and then glanced across the room. 'May I speak freely, doctor?'

Peter Harland half-turned and, without meeting her gaze, gave a gruff nod.

Elizabeth piled a couple of logs on the fire and pulled a chair up to the other side of the hearth, opposite Alice. A look of puzzlement was still evident in her expression. Alice cleared her throat and looked at her. 'Anything concerning a patient is confidential, but, well, after the events of the evening, it seems only fitting to share some of what has passed with you.'

Elizabeth blinked. 'I'll certainly not repeat anything.'

Alice nodded and went on to explain the events that had led them to Elizabeth's door. When she'd finished, she sighed and took a sip of her tea. 'I doubt that the poor child will ever be welcome back home, even once the baby has been boarded out.'

Elizabeth clicked her tongue. 'No, well, it's a delicate position the family finds themselves in. She can't surely be left to her own devices though? I read only the other day about a poor young woman who drowned her infant in a dolly tub, through fear of what might become of them both. Can nothing be done for the girl?'

'There may be something we can do,' said Alice after a pause. 'Her parents insist that she has lost her mind, but I question their motivation. I believe we can do better for her.'

The doctor stiffened and mumbled something about 'unqualified' and 'meddling women'. Elizabeth eyed him. 'Why are you being so dour? Has such intimate exposure to a female's travails really proved so terribly alarming for you?' She huffed a laugh and turned to Alice. 'I can't remember the last time my brother courted anyone. He attracts enough interest, always has, though heaven knows, I can't fathom the appeal. No, it's just the retention he struggles with. He's disappointed more girls in the last few years than the Prince of Wales. It's that unfortunate demeanour of yours, isn't it, darling? Leaves them somewhat mystified.'

The doctor turned, his craggy features crumpling still further. 'I mean, just look at that face; it looks like he's been put through the mangle. Not the most comforting sight when you're on your sick bed, I shouldn't think.' She looked at Alice, whose expression remained discreetly non-committal, though her eyes were shining. 'How he ever got through medical school, I can't imagine.'

Peter Harland gave her a long-suffering look. 'Oh, for goodness' sake, take that look off your face and come and have some tea. You look dead on your feet.'

After a moment he walked over and took the proffered cup, still scowling. 'There may be other options we can explore, doctor,' Alice said slowly, looking up at him.

'Call him Peter,' Elizabeth said before taking a sip of tea. He sighed in response to a speculative look from Alice. After flicking his sister a dark look, he returned to the window, the small cup dwarfed in his hands.

'P-Peter,' Alice said uncertainly. She sat up straighter in her chair and gave a small cough. 'I think I may be able to arrange something.' When he didn't turn around, Alice directed her words back to Elizabeth. 'We do have some sympathetic contacts in the community.' She frowned. 'They're few and far between, but I may be able to find someone willing to help.'

'What about the new hostel?' Elizabeth asked. 'I've heard excellent reports of the place.'

Alice had placed several women and girls in the Royal Free Hostel, which had opened in Gloucester Road, Regent's Park in June 1919 to care for expectant and new mothers with venereal disease in the infectious stage.

The girls, often in a state of bewilderment, were invariably greeted on arrival by an indomitable, motherly matron, who guided them through an open hallway brightened with freshly cut flowers, and into their dorm. For most, it was their first experience of structure, cleanliness and the hope of a better life.

The inpatients' next of kin were asked by Alice to pay thirty-five shillings per week towards the cost of housing the girls if at all possible, but most parents washed their hands of errant daughters on admission and robustly refused to make any contribution. Since many of the 'friendless' patients, as the almoners referred to them, were domestic servants who had lost their only source of income once their pregnancy became apparent, the hostel relied heavily on voluntary donations from kindly benefactors.

The girls were encouraged to contribute towards their own keep by learning handicrafts such as toy making, cobbling and needlework, basket weaving and raffia. In light of the reason for their admission, every item produced was disinfected before being sold to members of the public.

'It is full,' Alice said. 'But I don't believe Charlotte would be in need of the sort of care that particular hostel offers. I have another mother and baby home in mind for her, though I don't believe there are any vacancies there either. I shall make enquiries with Matron first thing in the morning.'

'If she is as volatile when she wakes as she was earlier,' said the doctor from the window, 'with all that hissing and scratching, she won't be managed in the community.'

'But Charlotte is restored to calm now,' Alice said, an edge creeping into her tone. The almoners were particularly protective of lone mothers and invariably went out of their way to help them. 'I think she was communicating with us, trying to tell us something.'

'It's telling me she's a menace.'

'How can you say that?'

The doctor huffed out some air, misting the glass of the window. 'I'm back on duty in less than six hours, Miss Hudson,' he said through gritted teeth, his eyes brushing over hers. 'So if you think that an asylum is not the right place for this girl, you need to stop flapping around and decide on an alternative quickly, because at some point tonight I would like to get some sleep.' He turned and walked towards the two women, gulped down the last dregs of tea and then set his cup down on the side table. 'The only other option is the workhouse. Would you rather she ended up there?'

Alice placed her cup gently beside the doctor's and looked up at him. 'Charlotte is capable of reason, I'm certain of it.'

The doctor gave a low growl in his throat and slumped heavily onto a nearby chaise longue. He leaned forward and rested his elbows on splayed knees, his chin cradled in upturned hands, a bored expression on his face. Alice threw Elizabeth a look of exasperation.

'He's impervious to anyone else's point of view, my dear,' the woman said loudly, as if the person to whom she was referring was no longer in the room. 'He'll only ever admit to being wrong if his error is dangled at the end of his nose, and only then if his arm is twisted halfway around his back. And I wouldn't rely on appealing to any sense of compassion that one might expect to receive from a medical man, or you'll be left sadly wanting.' Elizabeth tightened her shawl around her shoulders, the twinkle returning to her eyes. 'Give my brother pustules and bloody lesions and he's as happy as a sand boy. The fact that broken bodies have conscious minds attached to them is nothing but an inconvenience to him.'

Alice stared at Elizabeth for a moment, apparently lost for words, then turned back to the doctor. 'A friendless young mother should not be going to a mental hospital, or the workhouse, Peter. Not in this day and age. We're supposed to have moved on, aren't we?'

Peter Harland's shoulders stiffened, but he said nothing in response. 'Must the poor girl endure more sorrow?' Alice persisted. 'After what she's already been …' her words trailed off as Charlotte began to stir. The almoner sprang to her feet, Elizabeth rising a moment after.

'I ain't parting with her,' Charlotte wailed, before her eyes had even fully opened. She sat bolt upright and hissed again as Alice approached, clasping the baby tight to her chest. 'Get away from me. You're not taking her from me as well.'

'Just for a moment, my love,' Alice insisted. 'I need to see if you're well enough to move.' Without further preamble and ignoring the teenager's warning hisses, the almoner lifted the blanketed infant from Charlotte's arms. As Elizabeth neared,

Alice pressed the small bundle gently against her chest. Almost immediately the baby became fractious and the blanket fell away, her small arms and legs waving around in a distressed, frog-like motion.

The older woman's eyes widened, and for a moment she simply stared at Alice, her arms dangling at her side. 'Just for a moment,' Alice repeated encouragingly, this time to Elizabeth. The almoner's hands remained firm around the now mewing baby. Hesitantly, Elizabeth gathered up the blanket and wrapped her arms around the child. With a look of utter bewilderment, she pivoted cautiously on her heel, as if the package in her arms might explode at any moment. She took slow, shuffling steps back to the armchair, elbows aloft, shoulders stiff and uneven.

After washing her hands in the marble-topped sink located in Elizabeth's bedroom, Alice took up the position at the end of the sofa that she had vacated an hour earlier. Charlotte lowered herself uncertainly back against the cushions. Peter returned to the window, his face angled discreetly away.

'I'm going to try and get you booked into one of the local hostels, Charlotte,' Alice said softly, as she lifted Charlotte's skirt. 'I believe there might be a place coming up in one of them, and you should be able to take the baby along with you. For now though, we shall get you booked into the maternity ward at the Royal Free.' There was a loud gasp and Charlotte snapped her legs closed.

Peter Harland swivelled around as Charlotte threw her nightgown down over her knees and sat up sharply. 'I'm not going there!' she screeched. Her eyes were wide and wild once more, her chest heaving rapidly up and down.

'Charlotte, they'll take good care of you,' Alice said.

'Not there,' the teenager squealed. 'Anywhere but there. Home. Take me home.'

Dr Harland stared at the trembling girl, his brow furrowed. 'There is every chance you can take the baby with you to the Royal, Charlotte,' Alice said soothingly. 'But for now, I do not think that going home is an option for you.'

Charlotte leapt wordlessly from the sofa. As her feet touched the floor, blood trickled down her ankles and onto the rug. From across the room came a strangled groan from Elizabeth. She stared with a pained expression at the red stain expanding at the girl's feet, though she stayed where she was, one of her forefingers finding its way into the tiny palm of the infant in her arms.

Seconds later, Charlotte lurched over and snatched the baby away. Elizabeth gaped up at her in alarm, and then down at the floor, where more red spots were plopping onto the rug. The teenager backed away, narrowly missing the low table behind her. When the backs of her heels had reached the wall near the window at the far end of the room her feet kept on moving, as if she thought she might be able to pass through brick with the sheer strength of effort.

'We'll make our way to Banstead Asylum as soon as we can,' Peter Harland said quietly from a few feet away. 'There are beds free there and for now there's no other option.' Banstead Lunatic Asylum in Surrey had been renamed Banstead Mental

Hospital four years earlier, in 1918, but it was to be a few years before the new name caught on. Thanks to the growing understanding of mental health, asylums throughout the country were being renamed as hospitals, inmates were becoming known as patients and lunatics as 'persons of unsound mind'. 'Insane' and 'incurable' were soon to become words consigned to the past.

Charlotte looked across at him and then down at her baby. 'If I go, I'm taking her with me.'

He shook his head. 'You can't. Let's be realistic, you have nothing to offer the child. She'll be placed in a good Christian home and you can put this unfortunate episode behind you. She won't even register the change.' Alice turned to look at him with eyebrows raised. She shook her head disbelievingly, then returned her attention to Charlotte.

'You're wrong,' Charlotte spat in a tone laden with bitterness. 'She'll know.' She looked beseechingly at Alice, whose eyes flickered as she glanced away. 'You,' Charlotte pressed, staring at the almoner, 'you know, don't you?'

The almoner flicked her tongue over her lips. 'How are we to know what goes on in a tiny mind?' she said, her eyes on the baby. 'But I suspect that the doctor is correct to a degree, in so much as to say that the separation will be far worse for you than for her.'

Charlotte began to weep, the heels of her feet still grinding up and down against the wall. A small whimper emerged from beneath the bundle of blankets, a tiny head just visible above. 'The other day,' she said slowly, her swollen eyes still fixed on Alice, 'the day you came round to ours, I thought you might help us. That's why I followed you upstairs; I felt like –' she stopped, her voice cracking. She looked down at the baby in her arms and when she looked up again, fresh tears were rolling down her cheeks. 'But I was wrong. You're just as bad as all the rest of them.'

Alice stared at her. 'What does that mean? Who are you talking about?'

'All of them,' she wailed, releasing one of her arms and waving it in a sweeping gesture that made the baby's head wobble. 'They're all the same. There ain't no one I can trust.'

'You can trust me and believe what I say, Charlotte,' Alice said soothingly. She shot a warning glance at the doctor, who was beginning to move towards the girl. 'Everything will be all right, but we must stabilise you first.'

'I don't wanna go there!' Charlotte said in a sort of strangled gargle. 'I've heard, you see. First, Molly, then the others. And they all say the same.'

'Molly? You mean Molly Rainham?' Alice demanded sharply, but Charlotte's eyes were fixed on the doctor. 'Charlotte?' she persisted. 'You knew Molly?'

The teenager turned back and gave a small nod. 'She's delusional,' Peter Harland snapped. 'Can't you see?'

'How did you know Molly? What was your connection?' Charlotte blinked rapidly, then her eyes glazed over. 'Charlotte, are you listening? What about Molly? And the others? What do you mean by "the others"?'

Charlotte shivered, her teeth chattering. 'I ain't going there, I won't.'

Alice stared at her. 'Where do you mean? The asylum?'

'No!' Charlotte wailed, closing her eyes and letting out an ear-piercing scream.

Peter Harland whisked the air with broad hands. 'For pity's sake, Miss Hudson, let's stop sentimentalising and procrastinating. The girl is insensible. Beyond reason. She belongs in the asylum.'

Across the room, Elizabeth got to her feet. 'This is dreadful. Can nothing be done to help the girl?'

'I'm going to summon a taxicab,' Alice said calmly, moving towards the door.

When she returned ten minutes later, her eyebrows shot up in surprise. Inside the room, Charlotte was sitting on the sofa, calmly breastfeeding her baby, Elizabeth fastidiously tucking a muslin cloth beneath the baby's chin and another over the cushions beside her. 'We've reached an agreement,' Dr Harland said flatly. 'Charlotte will go to Banstead Asylum voluntarily, and the infant will stay here, with Elizabeth, until she is recovered.'

Alice opened her mouth to speak, but the doctor cut in: 'Charlotte hasn't the means to pay for foster care for the –'

'Daisy,' Charlotte piped up, looking up from her baby for the first time since the almoner reappeared. 'Her name's Daisy.'

'Charlotte, you are in agreement with this?'

The teenager nodded, the glassiness absent from her eyes for the first time since she had woken. 'I'll go to Banstead to get well, but then I have to get home.'

Alice gave her a thoughtful look, then turned to the doctor's sister. 'Elizabeth?'

The older woman looked up at her and nodded. 'I'll do what is necessary, for now.'

The almoner's face fell slack and then she gave a small nod. 'Very well.'

There was a pause, and then Dr Harland said: 'Charlotte has asked that we say nothing about the birth of her second child for now. Our reports of the evening will record the birth of a stillborn child, and nothing more.'

'We cannot do that!' Alice said. 'We have a legal obligation to report the birth –'

'It's been agreed,' the doctor snapped. 'For now.'

Alice stared at him. 'This is most irregular. I cannot understand why you would agree to such a thing.'

'Must you bring drama to every interaction? We've spoken to the girl. She wants the opportunity to repair her relationship with her parents before complicating the issue with a child, and for now our priority is making sure that she gets the treatment she needs. There will be time to register the birth when she recovers. Or would you prefer to drag a hysterical youth gnashing her teeth and spitting through the streets all the way to the hospital?'

Alice sighed. There was a pause, and then she gave a small nod. And so it was with an agreement that the night's events would be discussed with no one, that Charlotte, escorted by Dr Harland and Alice, left the house twenty minutes later, clouds moving briskly across the dark sky above them. As they climbed into the waiting taxicab, Elizabeth stood watching at the window, Charlotte's surviving infant in her arms.

★　★　★

The small party drew up to the gates of Banstead Mental Hospital just after 8 a.m. on Tuesday, 3 January. The rain had passed, leaving a chalky white sky in its wake, one that mirrored Charlotte's sallow cheeks as Alice guided her across a stone track illuminated by lanterns, and over to the gatekeeper's lodge.

The hospital was surrounded by walls ten feet high, designed to protect 'chronic and quiet lunatics' from the harshness of the outside world. A patchwork of outbuildings, the farm manned by patients and a number of workshops were hidden from view, the austere central clock tower above the main entrance perhaps reflective of the torment raging in the minds of those contained within its walls. Female patients like Charlotte who required medical treatment as well as psychiatric care were admitted to the infirmary in Block A, where a view of Banstead Downs could be seen from the wrought-iron bars at the windows.

Peter Harland pulled up the collar of his jacket and held it there with one hand as the porter came out to speak to him. Alice stood next to Charlotte as the young girl chewed her nails, her face creased with concern.

After scribbling his signature in the porter's file, Dr Harland conveyed Charlotte into the grounds, the clang of the gates behind them a signal to other patients that another lost soul had joined their ranks.

CHAPTER SEVEN

No class of the community has a stronger claim than this on public sympathy. These poor girls, enticed from their country homes, seduced, diseased, abandoned, distant from all early and better influences, have no shelter or refuge left to them save within the walls of institutions similar to the Royal Free. It has been objected that this institution receives large masses of the casual poor of this great metropolis; it has done so, and persons who reflect deeply and judge fairly will consider this a recommendation to it and not a drawback from its utility ... While it has accommodation, it takes all it can, and the more wretched they are, and the more diseased, the greater is their claim on this charity.

(Royal Free Hospital Annual Report, 1846)

Nestled beside King's Cross Road, Gray's Inn Road was so named after Gray's Inn, one of the four Inns of Court where barristers lodged and learned their trade. The road stretched away from the hospital to the north and the district of Camden, with Holborn and Chancery Lane tube stations laying to the south.

'Gray's Inn Lane is not the most salubrious, cleanly or pleasantly populated thoroughfare in London,' commented *The Illustrated London News* in 1856.

'The shops are small, filthy and close-smelling – generally devoted to the retail of bad greengrocery, adulterated liquors, vicious newspapers and cagmag-looking meat … All day long [the women] are either shuffling in and out of the courts or standing listlessly at the entrances – unkempt, slipshod, dirty women, clad apparently but in one garment, and even that in most cases unfastened and ragged. The faces of these women are worn and macerated by famine and gin; the bones on their necks and hands seem almost protruding through their skin; their eyes are glassy, their whole demeanour utterly listless and weary. A visit to the gin-palace or the pawn shop, a thrashing from a drunken husband, the wail of a neighbour's child – these are all that ever break the monotony of their lives.'

It was against this harsh backdrop that the almoners conducted their work.

Slick with damp leaves, rainwater and a spill of cabbage leaves from a greengrocer's barrow, the pavements of Gray's Inn Road glittered in the weak morning sunlight as Alice and Dr Harland arrived back at the hospital on the morning of Tuesday, 3 January.

As soon as they left the cab it pulled swiftly away to the north and King's Cross, a sign, perhaps, that the journey from Banstead had been heavy in mood and light on conversation.

It would have been a rare feat indeed; stunning one of London's chatty cab drivers into gloomy, reflective silence.

Falling into step, they passed silently beneath the British Lion mounted over the grand central arched entrance, and into the building. The doctor gave Alice a curt nod at the foot of the stairs leading to the chest clinic. He paused briefly as she walked away, giving her a sidelong glance. The almoner passed through the double doors leading to the nurses' quarters without turning around, then disappeared from view.

Alice left her soiled cape to soak in her room and descended the stairs to the basement just after 9.30 a.m. that morning. She was wearing fresh, dry clothes, hair pins holding her bun securely in place. In the smoky office, Frank glanced up from one of the financial folders he was examining when she walked in. 'Did everything go to plan last night?' he asked.

There was a slight hesitation before the almoner tilted her head. 'Perfectly, thank you,' she said, sitting at her desk and drawing ink into her pen. After writing up a modified version of the previous night's events, she blotted her pad dry, pulled off the top page and stared at it.

Officially, the records of any child that had been boarded out, as it became known in the nineteenth century, belonged in the box marked 'UNWANTED' on one of the high shelves in front of the arrow slit windows in the almoners' basement office.

It wasn't unusual for almoners, doctors or hospital matrons at the hospital to match 'friendless' young patients with foster

carers or adopters without any consultation with the authorities. Other adoptions were arranged by family members and
shrouded in secrecy, with babies farmed out to obliging distant
relatives, friends of the family, even neighbours. Even adoption
societies rarely interviewed adoptive parents; advertisements
were placed in local newspapers, interested parties turned up to
view the children available and, if both parties were happy, they
took the child home. The children were usually placed 'on
approval' for the first eighteen months, so might be returned at
any time.

There had been a number of concerning deaths of infants
placed in foster care over the years. While the majority of children were well taken care of, with their lives transformed by
the care and kindness of their foster parents, a small number
were shut away in attics to starve, quietened with opiates or
deliberately drowned, so that another paying 'customer' could
take their place.

Advertisements regularly appeared in local newspapers
placed by women offering to take in unwanted children for a
one-off lump sum, but mortality rates were high. Alice was
particular about the homes she placed children in, but foster
care was a costly business. In the early to mid-1920s, a weekly
payment of at least twelve shillings and sixpence was expected;
an amount way beyond the means of most of Alice's patients,
and especially a teenager like Charlotte.

'You're in a brown study, dear,' Winnie said after a time. 'Is
everything alright?'

'All is well, thank you, Winnie,' Alice answered briskly.

The typist made a noise in her throat that suggested she believed otherwise. 'You haven't forgotten about our trip to the zoo on Friday, have you, dear?' Winnie was a long-time member of the Women of Westminster Book Club. As well as analysing novels – their latest being P. G. Wodehouse's *Indiscretions of Archie* – they got involved in a variety of projects to improve the lives of disadvantaged children. In partnership with fundraiser Alexander Hargreaves, the club had organised a trip to London Zoo for some of the children identified as vulnerable by the hospital almoners. The trip was one of a number of projects aimed at improving the lives of children in need.

'No, I have it noted, thank you.' The almoner nodded and snatched up some of her post and a sharp letter opener.

Winnie pulled off her glasses and rubbed the inner corners of her eyes with finger and thumb. 'Good, because we don't want to keep them waiting, do we?'

Alice jabbed at an envelope with the sharp instrument. 'I have it firmly fixed in my schedule, Winnie.'

Winnie drew her chin in. Alice sighed and got to her feet. 'I need the key to the records office, Winnie. Do you have it?'

The typist produced a key from a small pot on her desk and handed it to Alice. 'Anything I can help you with?' There was a gleam of interest in her eyes.

'No.' Alice took the key with a curt thank you and crossed to the far side of the basement and the door, partially concealed from view of the main office by a filing cabinet, leading to the medical records store.

There was no electric light in the tunnel leading to the rear entrance of the store, which was usually accessed by a back staircase in the east wing of the hospital. Alice held an oil lamp aloft as she made her way through the narrow passageway, finally emerging into the cavernous store about a minute or so later.

Alice located the main entrance to the store and ran her hand along the stone wall until she reached the light switch. Row upon row of floor-to-ceiling wooden shelves flooded into view under the artificial light. She rested her lantern on the nearest shelf and moved between the sprawling rows, stopping when she reached the register of girls and women receiving treatment for venereal disease at the hospital.

With the advent of penicillin still two decades away into the future, syphilis was one of the venereal diseases most dreaded and feared. An intimate chancre (ulcer) was the first sign of sickness; a lump that appeared a few weeks after exposure. Small and painless, it was a symptom easy to dismiss by those with a strong desire to turn a blind eye. Up to three months after the chancre had healed, the next phase of the infection brought with it blotchy red rashes (over any part of body but usually the soles of feet and the palms of hands), swollen glands and flu-like symptoms, skin growths in the genital area, and, sometimes, hair loss. Symptoms usually cleared with or without treatment within a few weeks, and for a fortunate two-thirds of sufferers the worst was over.

For the remaining third, what had passed was merely an unpleasant warm-up for the main event. Third-stage syphilis could explode any time between three and thirty years after initial infection and once it arrived, the eruption of pustules and foul abscesses meant it was impossible to ignore. A body-eating pathogen, it worked its way through the body voraciously, devouring bones and nerve cells and destroying noses, lips, eyes, mouths and throats.

Since many of the women and young girls suffering from VD lived chaotic lifestyles, the almoners maintained a register to ensure that each and every one of them completed their treatment. From its earliest days the Royal Free Hospital had led the way in treating venereal disease, refusing to stigmatise sufferers who found themselves turned away from other hospitals. A number of the VD clinic's patients were prostitutes; girls who had sought to escape one crisis – the prospect of destitution – by diving headfirst into another.

The almoners tried to seize the small window of opportunity offered by the shock of diagnosis to steer their patients towards more meaningful lives. Whenever a new sufferer turned up at the hospital, the almoners got in touch with rescue and welfare officers, the Sally Army and the clergy, so that action could be taken before desperation turned the girls back to the life from which disease had removed them.

By keeping a close eye on working girls and making sure they completed their treatment, Alice and her colleagues could satisfy themselves that, if all efforts to rehabilitate them failed, at least they would no longer be a source of infection when they returned to their 'work'.

Alice updated the register with details of the patients she had referred to the clinic in the last few days, then moved further into the dimly lit space.

The files relating to the Redbournes were located halfway around the room, on one of the highest shelves in the store. Alice rested a wooden ladder against one of the damp walls, bunched her skirt into one hand, then climbed up and retrieved a manila folder marked 'CHARLOTTE REDBOURNE, DOB 02/10/1906'.

The uppermost page chronicled Charlotte's personal details; her address and next of kin, etc. Alice flicked to the back of the file, where the girl's earliest treatment in the hospital was documented. There was nothing out of the ordinary recorded that mightn't appear in countless other files relating to a child; Charlotte had sustained a gash to the head following a fall downstairs in 1908, which had been repaired by stitches, and had dislocated a toe in 1916 after falling from the wooden bars in the gymnasium at school.

Towards the front of the file was a record relating to an appearance by the teenager in outpatients in December 1920. According to the notes, Charlotte had been brought in by a member of the public after collapsing in the street. Under 'SYMPTOMS', the triage nurse noted that the girl had complained of difficulty breathing and light-headedness. Under the heading 'TREATMENT PLAN', however, the space was blank.

Alice frowned, narrowed her eyes and brought the file closer. She flicked forward and back through the thin file, but there was no other mention of the visit; no referral noted, and no obvious treatment trail. The almoner tapped her fingers on the front of the file thoughtfully. A minute later, the record was back in its place and the oil lamp aloft in front of her. Alice's hand hovered over the light switch at the main entrance, but instead of turning it off, she lowered the lamp to the floor and walked quickly back along the rows of shelves.

About two-thirds across the space she turned down one of the aisles and picked out another file. The corners were dog-eared with damp, the front marked 'MOLLY RAINHAM, DOB 02/04/1900'. Alice flicked through the short medical history. Apart from a short stay in the hospital as a teenager for treatment on a tubercular bone, the deceased had had no other contact with hospital staff prior to her death, according to the file.

The almoner's file relating to Molly in their basement office held records of Alice's post-partum visits to the young mother, as well as a copy of the post-mortem report from the Coroner's Office, which confirmed that Molly had been four months pregnant on her death. An open verdict had been recorded; the suspicion being that Molly had died from shock as a result of a severe haemorrhage after an illegal attempt had been made to remove the foetus.

Back in the almoners' office, Winnie glanced up as Alice walked in and she stared at her over the top of her glasses. 'Well?' she said, restoring the key to the pot on her desk.

'What?'

'Did you find what you were looking for?'

'Yes, thank you.' Alice extinguished the oil lamp, sat behind her desk and chewed her lip. When Winnie's attention returned to her work, Alice slipped the report she had written into the filing cabinet beside her desk.

Charlotte had given birth only a few hours earlier, but the almoner already had several unanswered questions that needed to be resolved. After a quick glance around the room, Alice withdrew a tiny key from the pocket of her skirt and secured the lock.

CHAPTER EIGHT

It is heartrending to refuse help to a woman in her
confinement because her husband is a drunkard or a
loafer … But if the husband is able-bodied and can work,
it is clearly inadvisable to remove the impetus that might
rouse him in his duty, and if a man spends half his earnings in
the public house, it is clearly wrong to support his wife and
thus remove the responsibility from his shoulders.

(St Thomas's Hospital Almoner, Anne Cummins)

Besides keeping their own files and financial reports updated, the almoners devoted some of their time to helping patients who were illiterate or out of practice when it came to writing. They regularly found themselves filling in forms, responding to official letters, even sometimes writing to patients' loved ones. One of Alice's tasks on the afternoon of 4 January 1922, just over twenty-four hours after Charlotte Redbourne had been admitted into Banstead Hospital, was to assist a soldier in making an application for extended leave so that he could care for his children while his wife came into the hospital for an operation.

Alice sent off the relevant forms to the Ministry of Defence and then embarked on one of the most challenging tasks she faced as almoner; convincing a room full of East End housewives that beans and pulses were a delicious alternative to one of the staples of their diet: bread and dripping.

The war had highlighted in stark terms the impact of deprivation on health and the almoners were expected to play their part in educating the public on the benefits of eating well.

Twelve women in all had been cajoled into observing Alice's cooking demonstration in one of the side rooms of the outpatients department. Her audience's initial suspicion, she later recorded in her notes, turned to interest as they watched her weighing out and mixing the unfamiliar ingredients, though she added that when she had handed each of them a bowl of fresh lentil soup and assured them their husbands would find the dish wholly satisfying, she was met with shrieks of baying laughter.

After handing out small samples of haricot beans for the women to take home, Alice made the short walk from Gray's Inn Road to Chancery Lane station. There she paid the 2 d. fare and rode the tube to Liverpool Street, arriving at the home of Tilda Simpkins, daughter of Ted and Hetty Woods, the couple who had made outpatients their temporary home, at just after 4 p.m.

Two horses were tethered to an iron ring at the end of the street, their heads dipped over a drinking trough. One of them lifted its head as Alice passed by, its soft whinny accompanying the tapping sound as she knocked on the door of a narrow house at the end of a row of terraces.

A harassed-looking pregnant woman with a young baby balanced on her hip answered the door. The bruise on the delicate skin below the woman's right eye and the crusted gash on her chin gave clues as to the nature of her home life. 'Tilda? I'm Alice Hudson, an almoner from the Royal Free Hospital. May I come in?'

The woman claimed that she was too busy catching up with laundry left over from the previous day. Alice persisted, telling her that it was her duty to ensure that all parents of children under the age of one were furnished with the latest recommended feeding advice.

Armed with the knowledge that nourishing food, fresh air and sanitary living conditions could improve overall health, social reformers hoped to make a rapid difference in the health of their patients in the years following the war by going out into the community and educating them.

Besides harnessing goodwill and linking arms with the socially minded, proactive clergy, Alice worked hard to try and improve the nutrition of babies and young children. The Maternal and Child Welfare Act of 1918 saw the arrival of mother and baby clinics around the country, but with word spreading that staff in the centres were on the lookout for cases of neglect and abuse, they were not utilised by those who were most in need. The almoners regularly picked up the slack, visiting mothers in the most deprived areas of the capital and

offering leaflets, encouragement and advice. It was a convenient ruse to use if they wanted to check on particular children
they held concerns about.

The woman peered over Alice's shoulder onto the street.
'We'll have to be quick.'

Alice followed Tilda down a narrow hallway and into a small
scullery at the rear of the house, where most of the bare stone
floor was taken up by tubs of soapy grey water and piles of
clothes. Wash day was almost universally on a Monday in the
pre-washing machine era, with ironing of the almost-dry
clothes usually swallowing up most of the next day.

A boy of around ten years old was sitting at a pock-marked
table on the far side of the kitchen, his grubby flannel shorts
revealing dirty knees and calves that were far too thin. His face
was almost as grey as the water at his feet. 'This is Billy,' Tilda
said, pulling out another of the chairs. The wicker seat was
almost entirely missing. She pushed it hastily back, pulling out
another for Alice to sit down.

Tilda lowered the baby she was holding, a boy of around
nine months, to the stone tiles and gave him a pair of wooden
tongs to hold. He grinned, sucked on the metal tip then banged
the soggy end on the floor with a loud babble. 'You wouldn't
usually find us in such a mess,' Tilda said, holding the back of
one hand to her forehead. She blew stray mousy tendrils of hair
from her eyes and related how she had been unable to get
through all the washing yesterday on account of Billy being
poorly. Slight of build and thin in the face, it appeared as if
her bulging stomach didn't belong to her body, but had been

fastened on. She spoke wearily, as if all her vitality had been drained away.

'Is it your chest, Billy?' Alice asked the older boy.

He nodded breathlessly, his shoulders hunched in the pose of a suffering asthmatic.

'Has he seen a doctor, Tilda?'

'Heavens, no! We can't afford that.'

'Well, you may qualify for free treatment,' Alice said, her eyes still resting on the young boy. 'We can complete an assessment straight away, if you'd like?'

There was hesitancy in Tilda's stance. 'I-I'm not sure. I think he's over the worst. It's always bad in the damp.'

After a pause, Alice enquired whether the baby was getting all the milk he needed. Tilda returned her attention to her washing. 'I try, but it's so expensive,' she said, heaving a heavy sheet from one of the buckets and wringing it out. The cost of a quart of milk was only around 5d. in 1922, but it was still unaffordable for some families. Common alternatives used at the time – weak tea, vegetable stock thickened with cornflour, or condensed and evaporated milk – were low in calcium and other nutrients, and children in poorer families were in constant danger of wasting away.

'He really needs cow's milk, if you're not feeding him yourself, Tilda. We can go through an assessment if you would like, and see if we can get you some relief. There is assistance available in some circumstances, for milk and extra nutrition, as well as medical attention.' She looked at her. 'What does your husband do?'

Out of breath, Tilda draped the still-dripping sheet over the back of one of the chairs and dried her reddened hands on her apron. 'He's a labourer.'

'And how much does he bring home?'

Billy gripped the table, his knuckles a pale white. Tilda hesitated and then said: 'I wouldn't like to say.'

'You would rather not say, or you do not know?'

'I don't know.'

'Can you find out?'

Tilda folded her arms and ran her hands up and down her arms. 'It's not my place to ask.'

Alice pulled a notepad and a pencil from her bag. 'Well, I would estimate a reasonable wage for building work. What are you paying in rent? We can help you find cheaper lodgings if you would like, to make things a little easier.' The almoners encouraged thrift wherever possible and often suggested ways of cutting outgoings to help struggling families to make ends meet.

'Rich won't want nothing smaller.'

Alice's pencil hovered over the pad. 'But your little one's needs must come first, Tilda, and milk is a necessity if he is to stay well.'

'We're doing alright, really. Now, I got to get this lot cleared away before Rich comes home or –'

Alice lowered the pencil to the table and gave the woman a keen look. Tilda stiffened and turned away. As she did so, the pocket of her apron caught the handle of a pot balanced on the stove. Alice lunged to prevent the spinning pan from clattering down onto the baby's head, and Tilda, a woman primed for the unexpected, gasped and threw her arms up to her face in defence. Alice stilled with the pot in her hand, her eyes on Tilda, then turned and placed it slowly back on the stove. Billy's eyes, the size of saucers, flicked between the almoner and his mother.

'Tilda,' Alice said quietly, taking a step towards the young mother. Tilda made a noise of acknowledgement in her throat but turned and busied herself with the washing. She transferred some small vests from a sink full of soap suds to a pot of clean water, keeping her face angled away. 'We're here to help. If you're having some difficulties ...'

Tilda took a deep breath, patted her hands on her apron again and then sank into a nearby chair. Alice sat beside her and anchored the woman with her eyes. 'I know that Ted and Hetty would love to offer a hand, if you'd let them.'

'You know my parents?'

'We are acquainted.'

Tilda's shoulders sagged and her bottom lip trembled. 'I know. I miss them so much, but Rich thinks they interfere too much. They exchanged words a few months back and now he won't let them anywhere near. He made me swear not to contact them. He wants us to make a clean breast of it, just me and the kids.'

'And what about you? What do you want?'

One of Tilda's hands skittered to her hair. She opened her mouth to speak, but a noise in the hallway stilled her. She was off her seat within a second. Billy's hands fell away from the table and shrank back into his chair.

A tall man with a flattened nose and stocky shoulders walked into the kitchen. His infant son lowered the tongs he was holding to the floor and peered up at him silently. 'What's all this?'

'Oh, this is Miss Hudson, Rich,' Tilda said with a note of hysteria creeping into her tone. 'She reckons Billy might qualify to see a doctor. Wouldn't necessarily cost us nothing either.'

Her husband scoffed a laugh. 'Oh she does, does she?' he said in a mocking tone. 'She thinks we're a case for charity then?'

'Not charity, no,' Alice began in an emollient tone. She angled herself around in her chair, turning her full attention to him. 'It's a case of everyone contributing according to their means, Mr Simpkins. Naturally, those with the broadest shoulders bear the greatest responsibility. It's the fairest way.' She got to her feet. 'Perhaps you would care to come along to our information evening for expectant fathers at the Royal Free? They run every fortnight on a Tuesday evening, and while you are with us we could explain a little more about who qualifies for free treatment.'

'Why would I wanna do that?' The man's eyes were shiny, his voice slightly slurred. Perhaps responding to a sharpening of the air in the room, Billy's chest began to heave rapidly, a whistle accompanying each of his breaths.

Alice glanced in the boy's direction. 'We should discuss this another time, when the children are not around. For now I think it is a priority for Billy to get the treatment he needs.'

'Oh, a priority is it?' Richard Simpkins sneered, before turning to his son. 'Come here,' he said quietly. Billy flushed but didn't move. His father grabbed him by the ear and hauled him to his feet. The boy screwed up his face in pain and bit his lip to stop himself from crying out. 'Leave us to it, laddie, so the nice lady can say what she must.' The young boy took advantage of the opportunity to escape and scuttled from the room.

Alice gave the labourer a cold glance. The sights and sounds of the battlefield still resonated with her, but back at home it was the viciousness towards children she had encountered since becoming an almoner that was most disturbing to her. This was a war utterly without cause or justification.

The physical punishment of children was commonplace at the time, expected even. Great store was placed in the Bible's warning 'spare the rod, spoil the child', and few households with children in them were without the customary strap or poker handy to keep them in line. Hearsay told of the punishments being doled out by nuns in some of the local children's homes – the flagrant beatings, the punitive bathing of youngsters in scalding water, the use of hot pokers to 'imprint' the importance of Bible study in their minds. But what was most shocking of all was the deliberate and callous abuse meted out by those who were supposed to love children most: their own parents.

In the last few months alone a newborn baby had been abandoned in a ditch, a toddler had been poisoned with two pennyworth of salt and a child of three months had been thrust head first into a pail of water by its own mother. Had it not been for the speedy actions of a concerned neighbour, who rushed in and revived the blue-faced infant, she might have drowned.

'Perhaps it would be better if I returned another time,' Alice said, levelling her gaze. 'When you're sober.'

Mr Simpkins' face flooded with colour, his chin stiffening. Perhaps realising that it wasn't wise to expose his family to further scrutiny, he took a breath and moderated his attitude. 'We don't need any more calls or advice from outsiders.' He thumped his own chest with a closed fist. 'My family is my business,' he said quietly. 'And nothing to do with no one else.'

The almoners regularly issued stern warnings to heavy drinkers, and Alice was no less forthright when she told Richard Simpkins that the welfare of his children was, as a matter of fact, her concern. And then, with no trace of judgement or condemnation in her tone, she said: 'But we can only give our help to those who do their utmost to help themselves.'

Alice and her colleagues' commitment to social change would eventually lead to the creation of the welfare state, but like many reformers they strongly believed that people should be encouraged to help themselves. The provision of charity was not to be regarded as a permanent arrangement, as far as Alice and her colleagues were concerned. The motto 'heaven helps those who help themselves' was one well used in the almoners' office. It was strongly felt that material assistance could corrupt and encourage those with a tendency towards vice to indulge themselves more.

'We don't need nothing from you, thanks very much.'

If the ice in Mr Simpkins' tone had been intended to intimidate Alice, then he had certainly failed, but his wife whipped her youngest son up from the floor and shrank back against the furthest wall. Alice's gaze lingered on the man's face and then she dipped her head. 'Very well. Tilda, it was nice talking to you,' she said, keeping her eyes on Tilda's husband. 'If your son's condition deteriorates any further, it's imperative that you bring him to the hospital without delay. Good day, Mr Simpkins.'

Outside, Alice made note of Tilda's nervous disposition and the condition of her ashen-faced son – *Tilda Simpkins, battered wife? Richard Simpkins, drunkard, not suitable for material assistance. Billy Simpkins, asthmatic. Will return with further words of advice.* She heaved a sigh, closed the pad and slipped it into her bag.

Unless Tilda took the decision to take a stand against her husband, there was little that Alice would be permitted to do. Until then, the woman was in the dangerous position of being at the mercy of a violent husband. And if there was one thing the almoners learned early on in their careers, it was that some people were capable of anything.

Alice's shift officially ended at 5 p.m., but it was almost quarter past six by the time she descended the stairs to the basement. The sound of lowered voices could be heard outside the office, but they fell abruptly silent when she opened the door.

'Ah, Alice,' Bess Campbell said, a frozen smile on her face. 'I didn't expect you back so late.' Frank, who had been seated opposite the Lady Almoner with his elbows resting on her desk, got to his feet. There was a pause, and then Bess cleared her throat. 'But now you're here, I'd like to talk to you about the upcoming medical social work conference at High Leigh.'

Alice took the seat that Frank had just vacated. 'We're to make a presentation on the benefits of social intervention in improving overall health,' Bess continued, 'and I need you to sort out some cases that best highlight our success.'

Alice nodded quietly, her gaze following Frank as he retrieved his umbrella from the coat stand in the corner of the room.

CHAPTER NINE

This is no case of a 'chateau en Espagne' – a castle in the air
– there it stands in solid bricks and mortar. It is as real as the
poor suffering creature who lies at your feet at the doorstep,
as you pass home in the dark ... I believe there are in this
great town hundreds of well disposed people so struck to
the heart by the spectacles which the streets of this great city
present that they would gladly do anything to set those
things right if only they knew how.

(Charles Dickens' fundraising speech on behalf of
the Royal Free Hospital, 6 May 1863)

In the spring of 1828 a small apothecary in Greville Street,
Hatton Garden, opened its doors to the poor. 'Persons not able
to pay for medicines will be furnished with them free' promised its founder, William Marsden, a young surgeon from
Yorkshire. Marsden also declared that the only necessary qual-
ifications for being seen by the three voluntary physicians
working there were 'poverty and disease'.

It was a revolutionary idea. Until the arrival of the apothecary, which was originally known as the London General

Institution for the Gratuitous Cure of Malignant Diseases, there had been few appealing options for London's ailing poor. A few hospitals admitted patients on an emergency basis, but only at the discretion of the doctor on duty.

William Marsden had been moved to take drastic action to improve the dire situation after encountering 'in the street at a winter's dawn a desperately ill girl whom,' reported the *Daily Chronicle* in 1902, 'having no influence with governors, he could not get into any existing hospital'.

It was shortly before Christmas in 1827, and despite her being accompanied by a respectable gentleman, the local hospitals refused to admit her, it is thought, because they suspected that she was a prostitute in the grip of venereal disease. Marsden, a newly qualified doctor, carried the girl to his personal lodgings and cared for her himself. When she died, two days later, he vowed to open a hospital that was free for all and discriminatory against none.

Plans were drawn up on a late winter's day in February 1828, in a little coffee shop in Gray's Inn Road. Within two months the apothecary was up and running, the poor of London streaming in through its doors. Just under a thousand patients were treated in the apothecary in its first year, with almost four times as many on the receiving end of its charity four years later.

William Marsden perhaps could not ever have imagined that almost two centuries after the small apothecary was established, a quarter of a million outpatients would pass annually through the Royal Free Hospital's doors.

★ ★ ★

The outpatients department of the Royal Free was one of the busiest in London in 1922, and it was in full swing when Alice Hudson crossed the atrium the next morning, on Thursday, 5 January.

It was 9 a.m., just over forty-eight hours since the almoner had overseen Charlotte Redbourne's committal into hospital. The notes on her desk revealed her eagerness to return to Banstead to check on the teenager, but there was little flexibility in her schedule to allow for a time-consuming journey out of town.

The Woods had already made themselves comfortable, a horsehair blanket draped over Ted's knees. A half-finished knitted shawl was spread over Hetty's lap, one of many she was making to donate to the abandoned babies on the wards upstairs. 'I'm not sure there is much I can do for your daughter at the moment, I'm afraid,' Alice said quietly as she eased herself into the narrow space on the bench beside Hetty.

The stale smell that pervaded the air in the department intensified. Alice stilled for a moment and frowned. There was a pause and then she said: 'How Mr Simpkins manages his money is only something I can involve myself in if invited, but I suspect –'

'Oh yes, we know most of his income ends up in the tills of the Red Lion, duck,' Hetty said, lowering her knitting needles to her lap. 'No, you don't want to be involving yourself with him. He'd thrash you soon as look at you. Poor Billy's been on the wrong side of his fist many a time, I'm sad to say. Isn't that right, Ted?'

Her husband leaned around her and nodded ruefully, his jaw stiff. 'Thanks for trying, Miss Alice,' he said softly. 'It's much appreciated.'

Alice pressed her lips together and squeezed Hetty's hand. 'I am going to have a word with one of the doctors here, to see if I can arrange a house call to Billy. I will let you know if –'

She stopped abruptly as Hetty winced and clamped a hand to her chest. Alice peered at her. 'Are you alright, Hetty?'

The woman closed her eyes briefly, her hands closing tight around one of the knitting needles on her lap. 'Yes, duck, not too bad. I'm just worried about Billy. Is it his chest again?'

'You must try not to worry,' Alice said slowly, her eyes still fixed on the elderly woman. 'I'll see what I can do to help. In the meantime, I think we should get the doctor to have a little look at you, Hetty.'

'Oh, there's nothing wrong with me, duck.' Hetty made a shooing motion with her hand. The fetid smell in the air turned rancid.

The almoner leaned forward again and looked at Ted, her eyebrows raised. Even almoners without previous nursing experience had a knack for spotting serious problems, their everyday exposure to all sorts of suffering helping them to develop a practised eye. Ted shifted in his seat, looking between the almoner and his wife, and then he seemed to reach a decision. He turned to his wife. 'She's right, love, I think you should do what she says. It's gone on long enough.' Hetty shot him an angry look. He reached for her hand and patted it, though his eyes were on Alice. 'She's been in pain for a while now, Miss, but all she can think about is getting Tilda sorted.'

The woman gave her husband another irritated look. 'I don't want any fuss made,' she told the almoner. 'I'd rather you spent your time trying to help Tilda get straight.'

Alice reached for her other hand. 'We can do both, Mrs Woods. Don't you worry, I will see to it that we do both.'

The nurse in charge of the chest ward and associated clinic, Sister Nell Smith, was a formidable member of the Royal Free Hospital's staff. A skinny-framed woman with delicate, bird-like features, she was on her feet as soon as the double doors to the department swung open, her sharp eyes trained on Alice as the almoner approached the main reception.

'Ah, please tell me you're here to sort this mess out, Miss Hudson. It's been like Casey's Court up here.'

Alice frowned. 'I don't know anything about any mess. I would like to speak with Dr Harland, please.'

Nell scoffed. 'Yes, you and me both. I'm afraid the good doctor's done one of his disappearing acts again. Anyway, some-one's got to sort this charade out.' She folded her arms across her flat chest. 'I'm short on beds, long on admissions and run-ning out of patience.'

'I'm afraid I'm not following, Nell. I'm here to book a patient in for an urgent appointment.'

The nurse dipped her head towards the male ward on the left-hand side of reception. 'Not before you've sorted out old lover boy in there,' she said. 'I've had just about enough of it.

Two of them we've had up here since yesterday, all in varying stages of confinement. I've never known anything like it. And I'm still waiting on those two convalescence places you promised me last week.'

Alice took her hat off and rested it on the high desk. She scratched her head. 'Are we talking about Jimmy Rose, by any chance?'

The nurse nodded. 'One and the same. If he can't keep his women under control he'll have to go elsewhere. I'll not have my department made into a harem for the likes of him.'

Alice took a long breath in. 'I'll have a word.'

'Cup of tea when you're done?' Nell called out as Alice walked away.

'I would love to,' Alice said over her shoulder, 'but I have to make some house calls today, and I have several convalescences to organise, remember?'

The newly washed tiled floor gleamed under the bright lights overhead as Alice made her way past the unmanned nurses' station at the head of the male ward. There were twenty beds on the ward: ten at evenly spaced intervals along one side, another ten mirroring those on the opposite wall. Beside each bed was a side table with a jug and basin on top, and a cup for water.

Locating Jimmy wasn't a difficult task. Several beds along the ward were empty, the nightgown-clad occupants gathered around a bed at the far end of the ward, where faint plumes of smoke were rising into the air. 'Ahh, hello, my darling,' Jimmy said jovially on sight of the almoner, his teeth clamped around

120

the end of a cigarette. It jiggled as he spoke, particles of ash escaping and dropping onto the starched sheets. 'What a treat for the eyes, so you are.'

The other patients, each holding a set of cards in one hand and a cigarette in the other, exchanged glances and grinned. 'I would like to have a word with you, Jimmy,' the almoner said authoritatively.

'Nothing would give me more pleasure, my darling.'

'In private, please,' Alice said, with a fierce glance around the assembled group.

'Later then, gentlemen.' Jimmy dismissed his guests with a wave of his nicotine stained fingers and then gathered up the coins that were piled up in the middle of his bed.

Once the other patients had returned to their beds, Alice sat on the chair closest to Jimmy's. 'It has been reported that you have had a number of unexpected visitors, Jimmy,' she began. 'Intimate associates of yours, so it would seem?'

'Ah, that. Yeah, I have no idea why they're targeting me, Miss Hudson, so I don't. I suppose it's because I'm such a nice fella.' He ran his fingers through his dark curls. 'They get themselves into trouble and think that I'm too soft-hearted to turn them away in their hour of need.'

Alice shook her head and pursed her lips. The almoners were accustomed to unravelling emotional tangles. After only a short time in the job, there was very little that shocked them. 'You need to sort it out, Jimmy. We cannot have the ward turned into a poker den, and most certainly not a harem. Sister will not allow it.'

'Oh I will, darling, don't worry your pretty little head about that.'

Alice rolled her eyes and then informed him that she would be turning her attention to his case in the next few days. 'Before I go, I shall note down the name of your employer.'

The twinkle in Jimmy's blue eyes faded. After a pause he said: 'What do you want that for?'

'I need to make sure you have somewhere dry to sleep, Jimmy, before you are discharged. You have a diagnosis of acute bronchitis, I believe. We cannot have you returning to the same dreadful conditions from which you came, or you will end up back here in no time.' Alice worked hard to educate her patients on the prevention of disease as well as its cure. She discouraged spitting in public to try and contain the tuberculosis epidemic, threw open windows when visiting festering, bug-ridden homes and badgered landlords into improving the state of their properties' repair.

She also made attempts to educate employers about the conditions endured by homeless employees; the railwaymen living in empty coaches with their fellow workers and going to bed in damp clothes because there was no way of drying them, and builders and labourers who slept in half-built structures that offered little protection on the cold winter nights. The almoners sometimes arranged the construction of on-site huts similar to the Morrison shelters that would offer sanctuary to Londoners during the Second World War, to provide protection from the elements and help to improve the health of homeless workers.

Jimmy coughed and snuffed out his cigarette on an ashtray on his bedside cabinet. 'Ah, that's good of you, Miss, so it is, but there's no need to go to all that trouble for me, m'darling. I don't want to go causing any aggravation for the boss. I need my job, so I do. I can't risk losing it.'

'It is no trouble at all, Jimmy. It is what I am paid for.'

Jimmy raised copious objections, each summarily dismissed by the almoner. 'But a man has to sort out his own troubles, or he's not fit to call himself one.'

'Jimmy,' Alice said sternly, 'do not make this difficult.'

Jimmy's shoulders sagged. 'Ah, I can't remember the boss's name and that's the God's honest truth, darling, I swear.'

Alice pre-empted any further argument by snapping her notepad to a close and springing to her feet. 'Very well. I shall make my own enquiries.'

'You're a persistent woman, so you are,' Jimmy said as she prepared to leave. 'But no less beautiful for it.'

Alice threw a mock chiding look his way. As she emerged from the ward, Dr Harland appeared at the opposite end of the corridor, his curly hair unkempt. Their eyes locked. Harland slowed, shoulders stiffening, then turned towards a side room. 'Doctor?' Alice called out. 'May I have a word with you?'

Harland stopped. He dropped his head back and closed his eyes briefly, turning slowly as Alice approached. 'What now?'

Alice blinked and pulled her chin in. 'There is someone I am concerned about. But first, I need to ask you … when did you first meet Charlotte Redbourne?'

The doctor scowled. 'You know very well when I first met

her; when you dragged me along on one of your mercy missions, that's when.'

'So you had no previous knowledge of her before that day?'

Dr Harland's eyes hardened. 'No. Although what authority you think you have to question me ...'

'Charlotte was brought into hospital suffering with breathing difficulties just over a year ago, but there is no record of the treatment she was given.' Alice paused, keeping her gaze fixed on him. 'I presume that with those symptoms, she would have been referred to the chest clinic.' The doctor gave a small shrug. After another pause Alice asked: 'So you are certain that you did not treat her?'

'If I had,' the doctor said, his jaw stiff, 'the records would reflect it. I'm not the only doctor who works in this department, as well you know.'

Alice gave a small nod. After a moment she said: 'I'm concerned about an elderly woman. I would like you to see her urgently, if you can manage it. And I also think a house call might be in order for her grandson. A young boy with –'

Harland groaned. 'Not another one of your –' he stopped and bit his lip, most likely in an effort to prevent himself from verbalising his frustration. 'I've spent most of the morning dealing with *your* patients, Miss Hudson.'

Alice glared at the doctor. '*My* patients?'

'Yes! The troublesome ones that you insist on sending up here!'

Alice's nostrils flared. 'What do you expect me to do with them, then?'

'I thought your job was to ensure the smooth running of the hospital,' the doctor snapped. '*You* seem to create a commotion wherever you go.'

The flush rising from Alice's neck and up to her cheeks evidenced her fury. 'First and foremost my duty is to ensure that patients have the best possible chance of making a full recovery, doctor. It is not, as you seem to believe, to make your life more convenient. And if you think –'

Dr Harland held up a flattened hand in front of her. 'Please stop speaking,' he said. 'If you have an urgent case, bring them up in one hour.' He turned on his heel and dived into his office, slamming the door loudly behind him. The almoner stared at the door with a look of disbelief. After a moment she returned to Nell at the main reception and shook her head silently. The nurse returned her exasperated look. 'Our lord and master's finally graced us with his presence then, I see.'

Alice nodded then looked at her thoughtfully. 'You mentioned that the doctor often goes AWOL,' she said slowly, leaning close to the counter. 'Do you have any idea where he goes?'

'You might well ask,' the nurse said, and then she gave the almoner a meaningful look. 'Perhaps Mr Jimmy Rose isn't the only one with secret lady friends around here. Although why the doctor would feel the need to leave the hospital to find one I have no inkling. Lord knows there are enough simpering, silly nurses up here throwing themselves at him.'

Alice pursed her lips, then nodded to the nurse and reached for her hat.

'Come back for a cuppa when you've got more time,' Nell said, as Alice walked away. 'And make sure you bring news of that convalescence home along with you. Something's got to give sooner or later.' She leaned over her desk as Alice pushed on the doors leading to the stairs. 'I'm not a miracle worker, you know.'

CHAPTER TEN

It is the stoutest, not the kindest, heart that is wanted ... all
we have to do is weather the storm as well as we are able,
taking additional care to be vigilant and strict in keeping all
members of the community within the bounds of duty.

(Quoted by Mr Longley in his Report to the Local Government
Board on Poor Law Administration in London, 1874)

As each year passed, Alice and her colleagues' 'people' skills
were to be increasingly drawn upon by the medical staff, the
frontiers of their work creeping ever more forward. It wasn't
until the Second World War that their contribution would be
fully appreciated, however, and then officially recognised.

During the nightly bombing raids over London, the almoners were the ones who cushioned the trauma for patients
bunkering down in shelters specifically built by the Ministry of
Health. They helped to fill the sandbags that were to be piled
up around the entrances to the hospital and taped up its many
windows with blackout curtains. They were the ones providing
the sick with hot tea from thermos flasks, extra blankets and
words of reassurance, and reuniting lost children with frantic

parents. And then, in the aftermath of the raids, they shouldered the task of salvaging what they could from the ruins of bombed-out homes, liaising with the authorities and charitable bodies to help rebuild devastated lives.

Rotas were reorganised through the war years to ensure that the almoners' office was always manned, so that the public could be reassured that, whatever time of the day or night, they could always count on finding a friendly face in the hospital, someone ready to offer a helping hand.

Half past ten on the morning of 5 January, three days after the birth of Charlotte's infant daughter, found Alice escorting a reluctant Hetty Woods up to the chest ward.

After booking her in with Nell at the main reception desk, the almoner led her along the corridor to a small, tucked-away waiting area, its rows of benches packed with other patients. Several glanced up, their faces glum. Alice guided Hetty to the end of one of the nearest benches and supported her arm as she lowered herself between an elderly gentleman with a hacking cough and a younger woman in a wheelchair. Hetty wrung her hands in her lap and looked up anxiously at Alice. 'Are you sure you don't want your husband with you, Mrs Woods? I'm happy to fetch him for you before I head off.'

The woman waved the suggestion away with a flap of her hand. 'No, he'll only fuss and make it worse. And please, call me Hetty.'

Several patients turned in unison at the sound of approaching footsteps. At the appearance of Dr Harland, one or two gathered their belongings and gave him a hopeful look. He scowled when he caught sight of Alice. 'Right, come this way,' he said, exhaling loudly before striding off. One of the women clucked in annoyance as Alice helped Hetty to her feet, another mumbling something about jumping the queue.

'Well, I'll leave you with the doctor now, Hetty,' Alice said when they reached the examination cubicle where Dr Harland was waiting.

The elderly woman gave her an anxious look. 'Actually, duck, I wouldn't mind a bit of company, if you can spare the time?'

The almoner looked at the doctor, who sighed in reply and said: 'You won't mind if a few students sit in on this, will you?' It was a statement rather than a question, and as Alice guided a pale-faced Hetty up onto a couch and into a half-reclined position, five white-coated men and one woman formed a semi-circle around them.

The doctor expanded a moveable screen across the opening to the cubicle and waved Alice out of his way with an impatient nod. She edged around the examination table and stood to Hetty's right. Without preamble the doctor asked: 'What are your symptoms, Madam?'

Hetty glanced at Alice, who gave her a reassuring smile. She turned back to the doctor. 'I-I've … it's my chest, doctor. I have a sore chest.'

Dr Harland pressed his fingers to Hetty's wrist. He kept them there and stared into the middle distance. After half a minute he asked: 'How long for?'

'A few months now, though it's been a bit worse lately.'

The doctor shone a light in Hetty's eyes. 'When you say soreness, do you mean chest pains? Light-headedness?'

'Not exactly,' Hetty said evasively, looking back at Alice. The almoner reached for her hand and gave it a quick squeeze. Dr Harland pulled the stethoscope from around his neck and fitted the ear-tips in his ears. Wordlessly, he sought permission to listen to Hetty's chest by raising the silver chest-piece and glancing at her from beneath his brow. She nodded hesitantly, biting down on her lip and closing her eyes as he parted the cardigan she was wearing and slipped the scope under her top.

A sour smell wafted into the air. Almost immediately, the doctor's expression changed. Slowly, he withdrew the scope and looked at her. 'Please undress,' he said, his tone marginally softer than before. Alice's puzzled gaze flitted from the woman to the doctor and back again. The doctor turned to a silver trolley, handed Hetty a blanket and then motioned for the students to leave. 'We'll return in a moment.'

When he came back, Hetty was sitting bare shouldered with her feet dangling over the side of the couch, a grey blanket clamped to her chest. 'Come on, Hetty,' Alice said, her cheeks drained of colour. She rested her hands gently on the woman's shoulders. 'It will be alright,' she said as the woman shuffled back and leaned against some pillows, the blanket pulled up to her neck.

Alice gave the doctor a grim nod. Gently, he eased the blanket down to Hetty's waist, exposing one pale, sagging breast, the other shrivelled up and pitted with fungating wounds that oozed bright yellow fat and a pus-like fluid. The distinctive smell of rotting flesh immediately invaded the air. One of the male medical students gasped and took a stumbling step back-wards. Another lifted his hand to cover his nose and mouth. A small whimper escaped Hetty's lips. 'It's alright, Hetty,' Alice said, stroking the older woman's arm. 'You are being very brave.'

Another medical student decided he had seen enough and averted his gaze, but Dr Harland made a contemplative noise in his throat and leaned closer to examine the wounds. 'Gentlemen,' he said as he straightened. 'And ladies,' he added as an afterthought, his gaze sweeping over the assembled group. 'This is actually very rare to witness,' he said in a tone that revealed an interested fascination. 'A tumour of the breast has clearly broken out onto the skin.' He turned and leaned over again to get a closer look. 'You'll notice how the nodules have coalesced to form a mass of rotting tissue, some of it already turning necrotic.'

Several of the students shifted from foot to foot. 'Doctor,' Alice snapped, glaring at him. Peter Harland looked up. She tilted her head meaningfully towards Hetty.

He cleared his throat, straightened and pulled Hetty's blanket back in place. 'Madam, your condition is not one I'm able to deal with here on the chest ward. I'll ask one of the nurses to dress the wound and then you will be referred to one of my colleagues.'

'Thank you very much, doctor,' Hetty said reverentially, but when he left, the students filing out obediently after him, her careworn features crumpled further. 'I thought he was a chest doctor? I don't want to go showing this monstrosity to someone else as well.'

'It's not his field, I'm afraid, Hetty,' Alice said gently. 'You need to see a specialist.'

The woman chewed her bottom lip. 'It's bad, isn't it?'

Alice patted her hand. There was a pause, and then she said: 'It has reached a difficult stage, but there are things that can be done to ease your discomfort.' She levelled her gaze. 'What prevented you from seeking help before now? You must have been suffering for quite some time.'

Hetty's rheumy eyes filled with tears. 'I tried to push it out of my mind, I think, duck. I thought if I kept applying the poultices, it would sort itself out. Truth be told, I was too ashamed to tell anyone.' There was another pause. 'What can be done, do you think?'

Alice looked at her. 'The breast will have to be removed, and then some radium therapy perhaps. We will have to see.'

The almoner sat with Hetty while one of the nurses applied liniment and dressings to the wound, then supported her as she made her way back to Ted, who was still waiting in outpatients. Since Hetty sat down without a word and took up her knitting, the task of explaining to Ted that his wife would need extensive surgery fell to Alice.

Alice regularly found herself called upon to speak to patients by doctors who recognised that their bedside manner wasn't quite what it might be. Ill at ease with breaking bad news and dealing with the subsequent emotional fall-out, they often called for an almoner to be present in the relatives' rooms, sometimes even scarpering before the deed was done.

The almoner finally resumed her office duties at half past eleven. With a pile of paperwork weighing down her desk, it was another half an hour before she had managed to extract herself to make her first house call of the day.

The skies over the capital that morning were a cloudy, gunmetal grey, the wind that had dominated throughout the early part of the month persisting as the almoner made her way to Dr Harland's sister's house on Fenchurch Street.

The clock on the mantelpiece in the living room struck 1 p.m. as Elizabeth Harland ushered Alice inside. In stark contrast to the smart, immaculately turned-out woman they had called on at the beginning of the year, her long gown was covered in damp patches across the chest, her shoulder-length hair hanging in uncombed tendrils around her face.

The room was warm, the fire in the hearth emitting a comforting amber glow. The logs piled up beside it were the most ordered objects in the space. Almost every other surface was covered with badly folded piles of linen and soiled clothing, where before they had been adorned with highly polished ornaments and neatly stacked china.

'I hope you do not mind my descending on you unannounced,' Alice said as she rested her bag and folded cape on one of the few uncluttered spaces left on the sideboard. 'But I plan to visit Charlotte as soon as I am able and I would like to give her some news of the infant.'

Before Elizabeth could respond, a small mewing sound from across the room drew her attention. Alice followed her to the sofa, where Charlotte's baby lay tucked up in a wooden drawer padded with blankets. Tightly swaddled, she blinked up at the almoner and emitted another contented coo. 'May I?' Alice asked, inclining her head towards the makeshift cot.

Elizabeth nodded. The almoner removed her gloves and lifted the small bundle into her arms. 'I was about to give her a wash, but we can take tea first if you'd like?' the doctor's sister said, after gesturing for Alice to take a seat.

'Oh, no, you go ahead,' Alice said, sitting down next to the drawer. She smiled down at the baby and slipped her forefinger into her tiny palm. 'Do not worry about tea for me.'

Elizabeth bustled out of the room. She returned a few minutes later, carrying some linen and a jug of water. 'Come on,' she said briskly, taking Daisy from Alice. Immediately the baby vomited on her shoulder.

Elizabeth's arms shot out, her face reddened in alarm. The baby hovered at arm's length, her legs dangling below the unravelling blanket. A moment later, the woman recovered. She dabbed at her dress with a cloth, mumbled something in a mildly chastising tone then sat on a stool by the fire. She settled the baby on her lap so that the small head was resting on her knees, her tiny feet nestled against Elizabeth's plump middle. With fingers that were still slightly clumsy, she fumbled at length with the baby's nightgown and lifted the tiny body up. The skin on the soft limbs protruding from her cloth napkin was already less saggy than it had been a few days earlier, a healthy pink glow replacing the grey.

'Is she all right?' Alice asked. 'She's terribly small.'

'You're perfectly fine, aren't you?' Elizabeth answered, directing her answer to the infant. 'She's a hungry little madam. She takes a whole three ounces a time, and she cries for it before her four hours are up. I'm feeding her with Nestlé.' Condensed and evaporated milk were widely used for babies in the early twentieth century, with Nestlé promoting their products as 'safe and nutritious'.

Elizabeth frowned in concentration as she wrapped the baby in a towel and cleansed her skin from top to bottom with a soft linen cloth. The baby watched her with silent, sleepy interest, as if she knew that she was in a safe, albeit awkward, pair of hands.

When she was back in a nappy, dressed in nightgown, bootees and bonnet and wrapped in a woollen shawl, Elizabeth leaned down and gave the baby's minuscule fingernails a brief kiss. 'So, you may tell the young lady that Daisy is quite well, thank you.'

'I will. Thank you so much for what you're doing, Elizabeth. Charlotte will owe you a great debt of gratitude when she's reunited with her little one.'

Elizabeth gave a curt nod as she shifted the baby upright against her chest. 'Well, if that's all?'

Alice nodded and got to her feet. She gathered up her cape and bag and turned in the direction of the door, but then she stopped mid-step. 'May I just ask, Elizabeth, whether your brother ever treats patients in a private capacity? I forgot to enquire with him when we last met.'

'I don't believe so,' came the curt reply. 'He spends every waking moment on duty at the hospital, as far as I'm concerned. The only time I'm honoured with a visit is when some imminent disaster is afoot, as you witnessed only a few days ago.' She placed a hand on the infant's back and got to her feet. The baby's tiny head lolled sleepily over her shoulder, her small hands clasped, one at each cheek. The woman turned and looked at her. 'But surely that's something you should be asking him yourself?'

CHAPTER ELEVEN

I have never smelt such a stench in my life. The stench was so
great I felt almost suffocated; and for hours after, if I ate
anything, I still retained the same smell; I could not get rid
of it; and it should be remembered that these cells had
been washed out that morning, and the doors had been
opened some hours previous.

(The banker Henry Alexander, on his visit to the lunatic ward
of a nineteenth-century workhouse in Devon)

It was another four days before the opportunity arose for Alice
to visit Charlotte Redbourne.

The almoner took a taxicab from the Royal Free Hospital
on Monday, 9 January, arriving at Banstead Mental Hospital at
11.15 a.m. Two stray dogs circled her feet as the porter emerged
from his lodge and fumbled with the keys at his leather belt.
They tried to barge through the gap when he opened the
tall wrought-iron gates and yapped at the drizzle in the air
as he eased them away with one foot and slipped a heavy iron
key back in the lock.

The almoner followed a horse-drawn cart as it wobbled its

way down the narrow track beyond the gates towards the main hospital building. The panes of the windows of Block A reflected the weather, perhaps giving visitors the impression that it was raining inside the wards as well as outside.

The care afforded to Banstead Mental Hospital's patients was a world away from the beatings, purges and rapes doled out by attendants in the madhouses of the past. Advertisements of staff vacancies placed in local Surrey newspapers sought those of a kind and caring disposition, possessed with the nurturing qualities that would allow them to converse with patients as well as to firmly guide them.

Nurses in mental hospitals were generally afforded less respect than those in the medical sector, as well as less pay. The nursing of mentally ill patients was considered in some circles to be a profession that might appeal to those from the lowlier classes. It was almost as if asylum staff were tainted with the same stigma that clung to those they treated.

Regularly scrubbed by patients on their hands and knees, the tiles covering the internal passageways of the hospital glimmered faintly under the dim gas lights fixed to the wall as Alice followed one of the nurses to Block A's day room. The sound of weeping and the smell of wax and polish accompanied their footsteps, punctuated every so often by a loud wail.

They passed several wards along their way, the interior of each almost entirely white, but for the black iron bars at the windows, the coarse grey blankets and the leather-bound Bibles at the side of each bed. The nurses wore starched white uniforms with white aprons on top, even the colour of their hair hidden from view beneath stiff white caps.

Alice's guide, a plump nurse wearing steel-framed glasses with thick lenses that magnified her eyes, stopped in the doorway to the day room. 'She's still a bit delusional,' said the nurse in a loud whisper. 'She's been diagnosed with hysterical neurosis, but there's a bit of paranoia in the mix as well, if you ask me. Still, who am I to venture an opinion, eh?'

The day room smelled of cigarette smoke and something sharply antiseptic. There were French doors on the far side of the room, with a view of a courtyard garden beyond the glass. Cream and brown striped wallpaper gave the space a more homely feel than the wards, the fireplace at the far wall and the deep armchairs arranged around it adding to the sense of warmth.

Charlotte was sitting on one of the armchairs, staring into the distance with unseeing eyes. She started when the nurse touched her shoulder. 'Now, don't start working yourself up, there's a good girl,' she said in a tone that, in the outside world, would pass as heavily patronising. She grabbed Charlotte's upper arm, pulled her forward and tucked a pillow briskly behind her. 'You've got a visitor, pet.'

Charlotte blinked between the nurse and Alice. 'Ten minutes, no more,' the nurse said, with a stern, short-sighted nod at the almoner. 'I'll not have her wearing herself out,' she added, before bustling to the door.

A woman in a shapeless long smock trudged slowly through the same door seconds later. The smocks issued to patients were heavy and unforgiving, especially designed to be resistant to tearing. Supported by a uniformed porter, the woman's feet slid along robotically without any part of the soles leaving the floor. She sank with sloped shoulders into a chair by one of the windows and began rocking silently back and forth.

Alice's gaze lingered on her for a moment and then she stepped forward and leaned down in front of Charlotte. 'Hello, Charlotte. It's Alice.'

'Alice,' the teenager repeated croakily, as if she hadn't spoken in a long time. She winced and touched her hand to her slightly swollen stomach.

Alice tucked her bag under the armchair opposite. She took a seat, draped her cape over her lap and asked: 'How are you feeling?'

The girl peered over her shoulder at the door, rubbed a hand over her forehead and then focussed her eyes on the almoner. 'It ain't safe to talk here,' she said in an urgent whisper. 'Just tell me, is she alright?'

'She's quite well,' the almoner said. 'She's putting on weight and coming on nicely.'

'What about Elsa and the others? They alright?'

When Alice reassured her that she would call in on her family to check on their welfare, Charlotte's face lost its pinched expression. She nodded, then frowned again. 'What day is it?'

'Monday.'

'So I've only been here a week? It feels like so much longer.'

Alice leaned forward and patted her hand. 'You've had a difficult time, Charlotte. But there is hope. I will find a place for you, I promise. You must try not to worry.' In an effort to demonstrate their worth, but perhaps also to encourage and motivate their colleagues, the almoners' year-end reports high-lighted many cases they had been involved in that had been resolved with happy endings.

Alice was aware, she told Charlotte, of several cottagers in the north of the country who were open to offering board to young mothers in exchange for help on their farms, as well as several Londoners who might come to her aid.

Charlotte's blunt fingernails worked nervously on her lap. 'You can't pack me off to the country! I've got to get home as soon as I can. Have you spoken to me mum and dad? I need them to let me back.'

The almoner shook her head. 'I do not think home is an option, at least not for now.'

Charlotte made a growling noise and slapped her hands down on her lap. 'I've been so stupid. I'll never manage it now.'

Asked by Alice to explain what she meant, the teenager said: 'It was a dream. I shoulda known it wouldn't happen.'

'What was a dream?' Alice leaned forward but Charlotte closed her eyes. The almoner touched a hand to her leg again. 'Charlotte, what was a dream?'

The teenager blinked several times. She gave her head a little shake, leaned forward conspiratorially and whispered: 'Me, being on the stage. I thought I could save us all. I shoulda known it would never happen. I shoulda known it weren't safe.'

'Not safe? Charlotte, whatever do you mean?'

The teenager groaned impatiently. 'I told you before. Bad people. They pretend they want to help, but none of them

141

mean it. There's no getting away from them either. They're everywhere.'

Alice fixed her gaze on the girl. Eventually she said: 'Would you like me to make contact with –' she paused, rolling her lips in on themselves '– your baby's father?'

Roused into sudden alertness, Charlotte reeled back in her chair. 'No!'

'But surely he should be told?' Alice persisted. 'If only so that we can secure some support for you, for when you leave here.' The almoners did what they could to encourage fathers to do their duty and support their offspring, whether they were 'born on the wrong side of the blanket' or not.

The girl made no answer, but shook her head, still agitated.

'How would you describe your relationship with the child's father?'

Charlotte nibbled the ends of her fingers and shot Alice an angry look: 'It's hard to explain.'

'Well, can you tell me what terms your relationship was on?' Accustomed to interviewing patients, Alice would have been careful with her phrasing, so as not to lead or plant ideas in Charlotte's head. When no answer was forthcoming, the almoner pressed on: 'Were you even in a relationship?'

The teenager flushed. 'Not exactly.'

'Friends, then?'

Her head snapped up. 'Definitely not.'

The almoner nodded. She considered the girl for a moment and then asked: 'How old is the gentleman concerned?' The teenager shrugged. 'Older than you?'

Charlotte gave a small nod at this. There was a pause, and then Alice said: 'How did you come to know Molly Rainham, Charlotte?'

'I – *said* – I – mustn't talk about it.'

Alice stared at her. There was another pause and then she asked: 'Is there ill feeling between you and Dr Harland? Anything untoward in –'

Charlotte sprang to her feet and backed away. The woman in the nearby armchair stopped rocking suddenly. Her lips began moving quickly as she stared at the teenager, though no words came out. Alice stood slowly, her movements calm and measured. 'It's alright, don't fret, Charlotte, please. There is so much more I need to ask you.'

The teenager gave a small wail. Within seconds, the short-sighted nurse who had accompanied Alice to the day room appeared at the door. Her eyes widened as Charlotte's howls grew more desperate, then she withdrew a whistle from her pocket and blew it. 'No, please, it's alright,' Alice said, at the appearance of two other attendants. The nurse gave her an icy stare and shooed her away. There was a burst of activity, a struggle, and then the nurse was left to settle Charlotte back in her chair.

'What have I told you, lovey?' she said, tucking a sack–like blanket around the teenager's legs and tutting. 'You mustn't take on like that. Getting all het up won't do you any good, you know. No good at all.' To Alice she said: 'She'd do well to go without visitors for a while. She really isn't up to it yet.' And then to Charlotte: 'Are you, my pet?'

'You don't realise what you're getting into,' the teenager mumbled feverishly, as Alice gathered her bag and cape. 'There's people in on it,' she whispered. 'People everywhere.'

CHAPTER TWELVE

When a bastard child becomes chargeable to a union
or parish ... justices may summon the man alleged to be
the father of the child to appear before any two justices ...
to show cause why an order should not be made upon
him to contribute towards the relief of the child.

(Secretary of the Charity Organisation Society, C. S. Loch,
in his reference book for almoners published in 1895,
How to Help Cases of Distress)

There were a number of increasingly urgent duties awaiting
Alice, back at her basement office in the Royal Free.

A priority highlighted by the Head Almoner was the search
for unskilled light work for soldiers who had been injured in
the Great War. More than 2 million were physically wounded
in battle, with many more bearing the less obvious scars of
'shell shock' or, in modern terminology, post-traumatic stress
disorder (PTSD). Finding work for men who might shake
uncontrollably, or weep without warning, was a task that
almoners across London were happy to take on, despite the
odds being stacked against them; unemployment had doubled

from 1 to 2 million in the first six months of 1921, and was to hit 2.5 million by mid–1922. Many hours were spent helping returning servicemen to adjust to the emotional turmoil and practical difficulties of life as a disabled citizen, as well as making the transition from conquering hero to unskilled civilian.

As well as the search for compassionate employers, Alice needed to arrange convalescence for recovering patients to free up some beds for new admissions and pen several applications to the Samaritan Fund for newly bereaved families. On top of that, she still hadn't managed to persuade Dr Harland to carry out a home visit to Billy Simpkins, the Woods' eldest grandchild.

Nevertheless, the almoner made a detour after visiting Charlotte at Banstead Mental Hospital, arriving at Dock Street in east London at ten minutes past one.

The notes Alice had scribbled in the pad tucked away in her bag revealed her commitment to uncovering the identity of Daisy Redbourne's father during the visit, so that a contribution towards her upkeep could be secured. However good her intentions may have been, George Redbourne was distinctly underwhelmed when he saw her.

The porter was standing in the front yard fishing a handkerchief out of his pocket. He spun around at the sound of footsteps, his head jerking up. On sight of the almoner he pulled a face and glanced nervously behind him, towards the house. 'The wife'll be none too pleased to see you back,' he said in a low voice of warning.

Alice joined him in the yard. 'No, I expect not. But there are a few loose ends that must be tied.'

The porter blew his nose and stuffed the hanky back in his pocket. 'Ah.'

'Nothing to worry about. I just have some brief questions for Mrs Redbourne.' She looked at him. 'Although, perhaps you can help?'

Dressed in his uniform, he drew the sleeve of his jacket across his shiny forehead and then scratched his pot belly. 'I'll do my best, as long as you're quick.'

The almoner opened with a 'soft' question, asking the porter about Charlotte's interest in acting.

He gave her a sad smile. 'Ah yes. That was seeing Marion Davies at the pictures a few years ago what got her started on that. Sparked some fanciful ideas in her, it did. I tried to take her as much as I could after that but, well, you know what it's like. We couldn't go as often as she wanted. I wish now I'd made more of an effort.' A bead of sweat dropped from his eyebrow and made his eye twitch. He blinked and sighed heavily then began tapping nervously on the gatepost with his fingers. 'Look, if that's all, I gotta get to work.'

'Yes, of course, but before you go … could you tell me, what was Charlotte's relationship with Molly Rainham?'

He sniffed and grabbed his cap from his head. 'I ain't sure I know too much about it. You know what teenagers are like. Secretive, ain't they?'

'But the name is familiar to you?'

He nodded. 'Charlotte might of mentioned her once or twice.' He rubbed his cheek with the brim of his cap, wariness telling in the pulse that throbbed in his temple. 'How is she, anyway?'

'She is in an anxious state, naturally, but she is being taken care of.'

The porter nodded grimly. His eyes flicked to the window again then he leaned in and said in a low tone: 'I tried my best to convince —' He stopped and spun around nervously at the sound of tapping.

Behind him, Mrs Redbourne's face was pressed close to the glass. Seconds later she hauled the window open. 'Haven't you got a job to go to, George? Or is she trying to get you sacked?' After an icy glance in the almoner's direction, the woman slammed the window but continued to glare at them.

The porter grimaced and fumbled with the latch on the gate. 'Mr Redbourne?' Alice called after him.

He half-turned around. 'Look, I can't,' he hissed. 'She's got her dander up. I'll have to go.'

The almoner closed the gap between them and asked in a hushed tone: 'I just need to ask … were you aware that your daughter was involved with anyone?'

The man put his cap back in place on his head and, after another glimpse towards the house, pulled the brim down over his eyes. 'Nope.'

'Are you able to make a guess as to whom this person might have been?'

'I'm afraid I can't help you,' he said in a nasal tone, before turning hastily away.

Alice knocked at the house several times before Mrs Redbourne answered. The almoner removed her hat with a stiff smile when she eventually opened the door. 'May I come in?'

'I've got nothing to say to you that can't be said on the doorstep.'

Alice's eyes flicked to the neighbouring house. 'I suspect that what I have to say, Mrs Redbourne, you may prefer to hear in private.'

The woman smacked her lips then turned away, leaving the door open. As Alice stepped into the hall, she rushed ahead into the living room. Dozens of shirts were hanging from the picture rail inside the room, and a fire blazed in the hearth. On the floor were two baskets full of balled-up clothes, a plank of towel-covered wood resting between two chairs above them. The surface of a sideboard at the far end of the room was covered with dust, all except one corner, which was spotless, as if something had just been removed. When Alice arrived at the doorway, Mrs Redbourne was stuffing something hurriedly into the pocket of her apron. 'What is it you want?' she asked abruptly as she positioned herself behind the makeshift ironing board. There was no trace of the coyness Frank had elicited on their visit over a week earlier, but her face was flushed, two bright red spots high up on her cheeks. 'I've got to get this lot finished before Elsa collects the rabble.'

Alice ran her eyes around the room. 'Such a lot of shirts,' she remarked. There was an edge to her tone.

'So?' the woman snapped. 'There's a lot of us living here, ain't there?'

Alice gave a curt, disbelieving nod. After a moment she said: 'I thought you might wish to hear news of Charlotte.'

'Did you now?' Mrs Redbourne said. She folded a cloth, wrapped it around the wooden handle of the iron that was resting over the fire and picked it up. There was a sizzle as she spat on the underside, then a thump as she slammed it down onto another shirt. 'Well, you can think again, because I've no desire to hear about her at all, thanks very much. She's caused quite enough trouble for this family.'

Alice stared. 'Surely you must be concerned?'

The woman carefully draped the shirt over a hanger then turned around to place the iron back on its rest in the fire. When she turned back, she pressed her hands down on the board and glared at Alice. 'Have you any idea what it was like, dealing with that – that thing she left behind?' She ran her eyes over the almoner. 'No,' she said venomously. 'People like you think you're the cat's particulars. I know exactly what you're about. I don't suppose you've known a moment's hardship in your life, have you?'

The almoner didn't react. After a pause she said: 'So the burial has been arranged?' Funerals were an expensive burden for poor families. There had been several cases of women dressing their infants in death robes, packaging up their bodies and sending them off by train to convents or other institutions in the hope that the recipient might perform a proper burial.

Mrs Redbourne turned and raked the fire, stabbing at it aggressively with the poker. When Alice repeated the question she dropped the poker and grabbed the iron and another shirt, attacking it with increased vigour. 'It's been dealt with, it's in the yard,' she said through gritted teeth, her eyes focussed on her work. 'My George won't forget having to do that in a hurry, I don't mind telling you. The man was beside himself.'

'He seems restored to reasonable spirits now. In fact, I found him to be a little more talkative than previously.' The almoner levelled her gaze on the woman before adding: 'If a little nervous.'

Mrs Redbourne gave her a curious look and then made a scoffing noise in her throat. Alice's eyes drifted to the door and back again. 'I imagine it has been a traumatic time for the whole family.'

The woman nodded grimly. 'You can say that again.'

There was another pause, then Alice said: 'Charlotte is refusing to name the father.'

'I told you, I don't want to hear no more about it. She's made our lives a misery these last couple of years. No, I've washed my hands of her.'

Alice clasped her gloved hands in front of her. 'It is not possible for you to wash your hands of her entirely, Mrs Redbourne. You are financially responsible for her, for the time being, at least.'

There was a strong belief, even among the most charitably minded citizens, that parents should not be allowed to shirk their responsibilities, only to reclaim their children when they were old enough to work.

In response to a considerable amount of bristling from Mrs Redbourne, Alice continued: 'Of course, if I were able to make contact with the gentleman who led Charlotte astray, he may be persuaded to make some recompense, thus relieving you of the burden.'

The woman looked up with interest at that, but then her expression clouded over. She hung another shirt on a hanger and muttered: 'Can't you get it into your head? We just want to put it behind us.'

Alice stared at her back as she shifted the shirts hanging from the rail around to make room for another one. 'Were you aware that Charlotte was involved with anyone?'

Mrs Redbourne leaned down and snatched another shirt from the basket. She slung it over the ironing board and then said: 'Course not.'

Alice expressed surprise that a relationship of such an intimate nature could be concealed by someone of Charlotte's tender age, but Mrs Redbourne merely shrugged her shoulders and reached for the iron again.

'Do you think that the man who fathered the baby that Charlotte lost last year is also the father of the tw –' Alice stopped. She bit her bottom lip and then continued: 'Is also the father of the recently deceased infant?'

'I wouldn't know.'

'Did you not discuss the incident?'

'What incident?'

'Charlotte's previous miscarriage.'

Mrs Redbourne, keeping her eyes on the task in front of her, mumbled: 'No.'

'And the first you knew about the latest pregnancy was when Charlotte gave birth in the privy?'

The woman nodded frostily, her lips pressed tightly together. Alice allowed another moment to pass and then asked the date of Charlotte's miscarriage.

'I can't say as I remember.'

'Was it not December just gone but the one before?'

Mrs Redbourne stopped what she was doing for a moment and cocked her head. 'I believe so.'

Alice nodded. 'And she lost the baby here, at home?'

'No. She came home and it was already gone.'

'She miscarried in hospital, or alone somewhere?'

The woman expelled some air, the iron held aloft in front of her. 'Oh, I dunno, do I? I was just glad it was over. Why all the questions? It's not unheard of, is it, to lose one? Happens to the best of us.'

Alice gave a small nod. 'Did Charlotte receive treatment in hospital for breathing difficulties around the same time?'

'What? No. Why d'you ask that?'

The almoner swiftly changed direction; a ploy that was sometimes used to disorientate, when a case of fraud was suspected. 'What was Charlotte's demeanour after the pregnancy ended?'

'I dunno. A bit sulky, I suppose. That's right, I remember because she moped around the place, making everyone's Christmas miserable. Wouldn't talk about it. Rewarded with some filthy words and worse I was, if ever I brought it up.'

'Were you not concerned that she might continue in her reckless behaviour?'

'I wouldn't say so, not particularly. Her father gave her a good hiding. We thought she'd learned her lesson, didn't we?' The woman slammed the iron down on its rest and turned back to Alice. 'Look, I'm sick of this. If it's not people like you, it's the Sally Bash, sticking their noses in where they're not wanted. Now, tell me, are you just here to criticise, or do you actually want something?'

Alice took a breath. 'When I was last here I noticed that John had a rash.'

The woman shrugged. 'If you say so.'

'I suspect it may be a scabies infection. If that is the case, every one of you will need treatment.' She glanced behind her and peered into the hall. 'Where are the children?'

'Elsa's upstairs. Henry and John are across the road. Jack's next door. No one can manage him unless he's on his own.'

Alice raised an eyebrow. 'You have accommodating neighbours.'

Mrs Redbourne sniffed. 'It's not all one way. We do for them, they do for us.'

'The children are not in school?'

'They're not hopping the wag, if that's what you're suggesting.'

There were occasions when the almoners stepped in to lighten the load from parents who were struggling to manage their large families. Alice had arranged placements in industrial school for several children in the last few months, to free up some living space and relieve some of the burden from the shoulders of overstretched parents. She had also authorised the purchase of clothes for parents who wanted to search for work but had nothing suitable to wear to attend interviews.

'I am going to try and arrange a placement to dovetail with Charlotte's release from hospital, either in one of our hostels or in industrial school. A final decision will be made on the level of contribution you need to make on completion of a financial assessment.'

Mrs Redbourne's jaw slackened. 'Oh, don't start on about that again! You come here criticising, then ask me for money! We can barely afford to put a crust on the table as it is. You've got some gall, lady!'

Alice put it to the woman that she was concealing an income from taking in laundry, as well as from the sub-letting of the attic space. Mrs Redbourne refuted the claim, muttering aggressively under her breath as she slung another shirt over the board. 'Are you asking me to believe that your husband gets through thirty-six starched shirts in a week, Mrs Redbourne? More than five shirts every day, working on the railways?'

Mrs Redbourne made no answer. Alice continued to stare at her, but she refused to meet the almoner's gaze. 'Do you wish to see your daughter in the workhouse, Mrs Redbourne?'

'I don't give a fig where she goes, so long as it's not back here.' Mrs Redbourne abandoned the iron she was holding and folded her arms. 'And don't you go thinking I want relieving of any of the other kids, thank you very much. I know what you lot are like once you start poking your nose where it ain't wanted. We might not be what you lot think's up to scratch, but we're muddling along as best we can.'

Perhaps recognising that she had little to gain in continuing, Alice made arrangements to treat the family's scabies outbreak and then Mrs Redbourne showed her to the door. The almoner paused on the front step and turned around, just as Mrs Redbourne was preparing to close the door. 'There is just one more thing. Was Charlotte engaged in any activities outside of the home?'

The woman huffed out some air. 'What you on about now?'

'Was Charlotte in employment outside of the house?'

The woman smoothed her apron and folded her arms beneath her bosom, her eyes cast downwards. 'Nope.'

'Training then? I believe she was nursing an ambition to become an actress?'

Mrs Redbourne looked up at that and cackled a laugh. 'Her, an actress?! Not likely! She's a little liar, I'll give you that, but not a professional one!'

Alice expressed surprise at the apparent contradiction of her husband's words, but Mrs Redbourne looked unabashed. 'Him? He can't hold nothing in his head for longer than two minutes. It's –' she stopped, pressed her lips together and then slammed the door.

156

Alice sighed and crossed the road, but the sound of heavy footsteps drew her back to the house. 'Excuse me,' she called out, quickening her step until she was standing about a foot away from a long-coated, bearded gentleman who was about to turn into the Redbournes' front yard. 'May I speak with you for a moment?'

'Why certainly, Madam,' the man answered in a heavy Russian accent. 'What is it may I help you with?'

'Do you live here, Mr –?'

'Sokolov.' He dipped his head when Alice repeated his name. There was a pause and then he said: 'And no, I do not live here.'

'And yet I believe that when I saw you last, it was on the upstairs landing of this house.' Her eyes dropped to his hand. 'And you appear to have a key.'

Mr Sokolov inclined his head politely, but appeared somewhat bemused. 'What is it would you like from me, Madam?' he said softly. 'I do not know why you ask me these questions.'

'I beg your pardon, Sir, I should have introduced myself. I am an almoner from the Royal Free Hospital. I –'

'*Zloebuchii hui, mne vse ravno!*' he shouted, flapping his hand at her. '*Uhodi ot menya!*'

Alice backed away, her eyes widened in alarm. She crossed the road, the Russian shouting indecipherable expletives behind her.

'Where have you been?!' Winnie demanded, as soon as Alice arrived back at the basement. 'Sister Smith has been asking for you on the chest ward.' She dipped her head towards Frank, who was sitting at Bess Campbell's unoccupied desk, examining a file. 'There's been more trouble up there. Frank had to go up and sort it out in the end, and it's not what he's here for.'

'What exactly are you here for, Frank?' Alice said, removing her gloves and dropping them onto her desk. There was a note of challenge in her tone, but a playful twinkle in her eyes as well. She picked up the small pile of post on her desk, ran a cursory eye over each envelope then fixed her gaze back on Frank. 'It certainly isn't to make our lives any easier, is it?'

The COS representative, usually effusive in nature, merely lifted a bushy brow then returned to his work. Alice stared at him for a moment then sat behind her desk and began working her way methodically through the post. The first two letters went into the waste paper basket beside her desk, but when Alice opened the third she froze, her eyes fixed on the small black script in front of her – 'I KNOW WHAT YOU DID'.

The almoner stared at the note for another half a second, her breath held, then folded it hurriedly and stuffed it in her bag. She ran her eyes around the room. Winnie was absorbed in the task of replacing the ribbon on her typewriter. As the typist muttered, huffed and groaned, Alice glanced at Frank. He looked up briefly, met her gaze, then returned his attention to his work.

CHAPTER THIRTEEN

What more glaring picture of charitable impotence is
there than that destitute persons should constantly
apply to a free dispensary for drugs which cannot
benefit them if they lack necessary food?

(C. S. Loch, *The Confusion in*
Medical Charities, 1892)

At the request of Bess Campbell, Alice went to the Mary Ward
Settlement in Holborn at 9 a.m. on Friday, 13 January. There,
she met Winnie Bertram and several other members of the
Westminster Book Club, the women in the throes of trying to
secure an accurate count of twenty unruly children.

Alice was no stranger to the settlement, having completed
part of her social work training there in 1921. It was a place
where the poor gained a chance to enjoy pastimes that were
previously out of their reach. As well as socialising together,
visitors could listen to music or take part in debating or chess
clubs. There were mother and toddler groups and an after-
school club, as well as training sessions for the unemployed and
a 'poor man's lawyer' service.

'Who would like a barley sugar when we get to the zoo?' Winnie asked, a few of her book-loving companions beginning to look a little rough around the edges nearby. Twenty bright grubby faces spun around, their eyes wide. From her pocket she withdrew one of the covetous sweets and held it up in the air to rapturous shouts and cheers. 'Against the wall then, all of you,' Winnie commanded, her habitual careworn expression momentarily absent.

Alice clasped a hand to her hat as they left the main building, the gusty wind that had dominated London in the last few days threatening to whip it away. Despite temperatures being close to zero, most of the children were inadequately dressed. The knees of some of the younger ones were so red and chafed it appeared they might, at some point, burst out of their skin. Perhaps that was one of the reasons Alice removed her cape and draped it across her arm.

'It's windy enough to blow the feathers off a goose,' Winnie trilled as she led the crocodile of children along Kingsway towards High Holborn. 'Isn't it wonderful?!'

Alice, bringing up the rear, eyed her colleague with an amused, slightly puzzled frown. The dour typist was brightly animated in her interactions with the children, who varied in age from the youngest at four, up to around eleven. There was no trace of the stubborn, bloody-minded awkwardness she often displayed at work.

The last few days in the almoners' office had been manic as preparations were made for the forthcoming social work conference at High Leigh. Besides booking their accommodation and making the travel arrangements, Alice had spent hours trawling through the files to identify cases that adequately represented the value of the almoners' work, in accordance with Miss Campbell's request. Her efforts to find a placement for Charlotte had been limited to a few handwritten letters and an enquiry with the matrons of the local mother and baby hostels, who confirmed that, for the foreseeable future, every bed was spoken for. She had tried to persuade Winnie to type up a standard letter so that she could send it out wholesale, but the typist had frustrated her efforts at every turn.

It was as if the typist's basement persona had been chased away by the children's shouts of excitement and the high winds.

The party arrived at the north end of Regent's Park shortly before 10 a.m., the pungent scent of the wild, of animals and straw all around them. The oldest scientific zoo in the world, London Zoo opened its doors to the public in 1847. It was a popular choice for charities organising day trips for disadvantaged children, whose only other brush with nature might have been the beetles scuttling around the scullery floor of their home or the bugs that had almost inevitably infested their beds.

The almoners regularly organised day trips for the pregnant women and girls and new mothers being treated for venereal disease at the Royal Free Hostel, once they were safely through the infectious stage. Besides art galleries and cinemas, the zoo was a popular destination. The girls would spend time in the aquarium, sometimes with their babies, once they were a few months old, and they almost certainly visited one of the main attractions of the time: Winniepeg the bear, whose playful antics would become immortalised by Christopher Robin's father, A. A. Milne, when his Winnie the Pooh stories were published four years later.

Just after midday, the children were guided to the outdoor picnic area located near the monkey house. 'So, you work with Winnie?' one of the book club members said as she sat beside Alice at the end of a long wooden bench. A plump woman in late middle age wearing a purple coat with an elaborate brooch at the collar, she introduced herself as Cecelia and handed Alice a brown paper bag.

'Thank you,' Alice said, taking the bag and then helping a young girl sporting uneven pigtails and an extremely snotty nose to climb onto the bench. She turned back to Cecelia. 'And yes, I do.'

'You're quite the revolutionary I hear.'

Alice expressed surprise. 'How so?'

The woman took a bite from her sandwich then covered her mouth with her hand and spoke mid-chew. 'You take no nonsense from the powers that be. Basically, that means the men.'

The almoner frowned. 'Winnie told you that?'

Cecelia nodded. 'We love to hear about women living their lives on their own terms. It's too late for us, you see, but if you girls keep plugging away, maybe for you, things will be different.'

Alice raised her eyebrows and looked over at Winnie, who was holding court with some older children several feet away, on the opposite side of the table. They leaned towards her as they ate, interjecting eagerly and, every now and then, howling with laughter.

'Ah, look who it is,' Cecelia said a few minutes later, admiration in her tone. Several heads turned as the impressive figure of Alexander Hargreaves approached the table. Cecelia got to her feet. 'Children, this is Alexander Hargreaves,' she announced, when he drew near. 'He's the man we have to thank for today's trip.'

A loud cheer went up. Alexander smiled and dipped his head in a modest bow. When he looked up he made a sweeping gesture with his hand. 'My thanks to you, ladies, for your exceptional organisational skills.' Several of the women blushed. One or two rose and offered him their hand to kiss.

When eventually he took a seat opposite Alice she said: 'It must be wonderful to see the benefits of your fundraising efforts for yourself, Alexander. You must feel very proud.'

He gave a self-deprecating scoff. 'Oh goodness, no, not proud. Not when there's so much more to be done, but it's gratifying to see for oneself what can be achieved when we all work together. I do try to make an effort to come whenever –' The fundraiser was interrupted by a loud shout. A few feet away, a scuffle had broken out between a boy who had barely stopped scratching his head since leaving the settlement and a slightly older boy with an infected eye. Winnie got wheezily to her feet and separated the boys by pulling on their ears. 'Credit where it's due though,' Alexander said, as the typist made loud threats about banging their heads together. 'I think raising the funds is the easy part.'

Alice grinned. 'I should say so.'

There followed a lengthy conversation with Cecelia about the book club members' ambitious plans to raise enough money to take a group of children on a holiday to Eastbourne, and then, after Cecelia excused herself, Alexander asked Alice if she was prepared for the social work conference that was to take place next week.

'I have several cases I can summarise that might be of interest to the delegates,' Alice said with a grimace, 'but Miss Campbell has asked me to present them myself and it's not exactly my area of expertise.'

'I would be glad to help. I happen to have a bit of experience in that area.'

'Oh yes, of course, I forgot. Your after-dinner speeches.'

'Exactly. Several dinner guests nodded off during my last speech.' He smiled wryly. 'But I like to think that had more to do with the average age in the room being seventy-three than any lack of charisma on my part.'

Alexander invited Alice to join him for dinner that evening, when he promised to impart some of the benefit of his public-speaking experience. After a moment's hesitation, the almoner agreed.

Ciro's Restaurant and Jazz Club in Orange Street was an exclusive, white- and gold-fronted venue huddled at the rear of the National Gallery. Dressed in a tailored grey suit and a white shirt, with a silk cravat around his neck, Alexander was waiting outside when Alice arrived. 'I hardly recognised you with your hair down,' the philanthropist told her, smiling appreciatively. With a hand to the small of her back, he guided her into the impressive building that had once housed the Westminster public baths, and across the carpeted foyer.

A waiter led the way across floors of sparkling white marble and into a large dining area. Green and gold decor in the style of Louis XVI, white-linen-covered tables and mirrors spaced evenly between globed gas lamps on the walls, Ciro's was a place that exuded glamour and taste. There was a dance floor at the far end of the room, a few couples on their feet and dancing to the syncopated rhythms of the nearby band. It was a stage that had once been graced by Dan Kildare, the Jamaican-born pianist who, six months earlier, had strode into his estranged wife's pub and shot her and his sister-in-law dead.

Alexander and Alice were shown to a round table about fifteen feet or so from the dance floor. They were served with some drinks – Buck's Fizz was the new, popular choice in bars and jazz clubs across London – the thundering beat of the trap drums an energetic accompaniment to their conversation. Despite high unemployment and a large national debt, victory in the war and the end of daily trauma and worry had lifted the national mood. The enthusiastic embracing of jazz dance music reflected what turned out to be unfulfilled nationwide hopes for a bright new world. Around the country, restaurants were rearranging chairs and tables to accommodate the new craze for vigorous dance.

After ordering their meals, Alexander asked whether the

book club members had managed to get the children back to the settlement in one piece.

Alice took a sip of her drink and gave him a wry smile. 'The children were fine. As for the ladies … Well, let's just say that I think they shall sleep well tonight.'

Alexander smiled back. 'Bless them, the old dears. They're magnificent with the youngsters, especially Winnie. It gives her so much pleasure to see the children enjoying themselves.'

Alice nodded. 'I have never seen her looking so relaxed.'

There was a small pause. Alexander lowered his glass and settled his gaze on the almoner. 'You haven't quite hit it off with our Winnie yet, have you?'

Alice grimaced. 'That's the understatement of the year.' She tapped the stem of her glass thoughtfully. 'I don't dislike her. It's just – I don't know – she is so obstructive. Did you know that when it's just the two us working together, she turns off the lights when she leaves the basement, even though she knows I'm still down there? She does it every time without fail, then feigns ignorance as I stumble around crashing into things.'

Alexander grinned. 'Winnie takes time to warm to new people. She was like that with me for about two years after we first met. She doesn't find it easy to move with the times, bless her. I mean, she remains heavily suspicious of electricity, for heaven's sake.'

Alice pulled a face. 'I don't think it's *electric* she has a problem with.'

The tilt of Alexander's head suggested that he conceded the point. 'She does have her foibles. And perhaps she takes longer than most to warm to, but I've known her a long time. She has a good heart, Alice.' Alexander sipped his drink, lowered his glass to the table and then smoothed down his thin moustache. 'You do know, don't you, that Winnie's role is entirely voluntary?'

Alice stared at him in surprise.

'Have you never questioned why ours is the only almoners' department in London that enjoys administrative help? You know how tight the purse strings are.'

The almoner slowly shook her head. 'It just never occurred to me.'

'No, well, I suspect there is a lot you don't know about Winnie. And I suppose her funny ways are more easily tolerated if you understand what drives her.' Alice frowned. The fundraiser gave her an appraising look. 'It's not for me to share private information, but did you ever consider that, privileged as she may be in some ways, perhaps she has her own demons to wrestle with?'

'She lives in Artillery Mansions, and clearly doesn't need an income. It seems to me that she has little to complain about.'

Artillery Mansions was a grand block of stylish apartments located in Victoria Street, in the central London district of Westminster.

'Well, maybe if you tried talking to her.' He glanced away for a moment. When he looked back he said: 'You're so driven, Alice, and I admire that about you, but I sometimes think you're a little naive. Need doesn't always come dressed in rags, you know. Sometimes it's cloaked in lace and pearls.'

Alice kept her gaze on him as the waiter served their meal. Above them was a sliding roof that, on warm summer evenings, afforded diners a view of the London starlit sky. 'So, what do you make of Frank?' she asked a few minutes later, as Alexander twisted the claws from a lobster.

The philanthropist teased some pale orange meat from the legs using his fork and then focussed on the middle distance, considering as he chewed. 'I would say he's a man more suited to manual labours than anything of a cerebral nature,' he said with a wry smile. 'How he's made it in the business world I really cannot fathom, though buying and selling is not beyond the ability of the greatest of oafs, when it comes down to it. I suppose he's one of those half-wits you can rub along quite nicely with, as long as you're expecting neither sense nor intellect.'

Alice grinned. 'And Sidney?'

Alexander dabbed his mouth with his napkin. 'Coarseness in a person will always find a way to seep through, no matter what company they keep.'

Alice widened her eyes at that, but Alexander waved his napkin. 'I jest. The man has a good heart, I suppose.'

Alice went on to express her love for her role as almoner, her appreciation of the insight she gained into family life and the hope that through the course of each day, echoing the sentiments of St Thomas's Hospital almoner, Anne Cummins, she had done more good than harm.

'And yet still there are those not entirely convinced of the value of your work?'

'And there's the rub,' Alice said, proceeding between mouthfuls of steamed herring and potatoes to discuss the frustrations of her role; the ever increasing paperwork, the reluctance of some of the medical staff to take her seriously. 'Take Dr Harland, for example,' she said, lowering her cutlery to her plate.

'The chest chap?'

She nodded. 'If ever there was a more pig-headed man ...' She paused, looking at Alexander. He remained silent. Eventually, Alice said: 'I suppose you are going to tell me that I have him all wrong as well?'

The fundraiser raised his brow and dabbed his fingers on a napkin. Alice narrowed her eyes. 'What?'

'He's a man like any other as far as I can tell,' Alexander said, patting his mouth. 'A bit brutish in appearance I would say, but I hardly know him well enough to venture an opinion on his character.'

'Well, I do. And I find him obstructive, obtuse and, half the time, absent from his post.'

'I suspect a number of our doctors manipulate the system,' Alexander said, pulling the tail from the body of the lobster and slicing neat incisions into the underbelly.

'There is more to it than that,' Alice pressed. 'And part of my role is to ensure that the hospital is not defrauded, either by patients or staff.'

Alexander nodded. 'Indeed. Well, you almoners do an exceptional job, as far as I'm concerned.'

Alice gave him a half-smile. 'I think there are some

who would rather we vanished into thin air. But I'm going to get to the bottom of why that is, no matter how long it takes.'

The fundraiser opened his mouth to speak but then shook his head and picked away at the soft flesh of the lobster with his knife, peeling it away from the protective shell.

A severe frost settled over the capital on the evening of 13 January, and the pavements of Gray's Inn Road were icy as Alexander accompanied Alice home. It was almost 1 a.m. when he kissed her cheek outside the door leading to the nurses' home and then disappeared from view. It was as she turned to go inside that she was grabbed roughly by the arm. Alice swung around with widened eyes. The imposing form of Dr Harland was standing near the shadowy doorway, his dark, irregular features even more grizzled than usual. 'What do you think you're doing?' he demanded.

'I beg your pardon?!' Alice pulled out of his grip and stared at him with disdain.

The doctor leaned his face close to hers. 'I said, what the hell are you up to?'

Alice gaped at him. 'I hardly think that's any of your business, doctor,' she said scornfully, 'but since we're having this conversation, where is it you disappear to when you're supposed to be on duty?'

The doctor's expression altered, wariness replacing fury. He took a small step backwards. 'I have no idea what you're talking about.'

'Oh, I suspect that you do,' she said in a quiet tone. 'And if you think that sending me threatening notes is going to frighten me off, you are very, very wrong.'

'What are you talking about?'

Alice leaned towards him. 'Daisy Redbourne is ten days old today and no one but you, I and Elizabeth know anything about what happened, apart from her own mother. Her birth must be registered, or is there some reason you are hiding her existence?'

Dr Harland jabbed a forefinger at the air in front of her face. 'You need to watch yourself, Alice Hudson.'

The almoner stared after him as he stalked back to the main hospital building, an expression of shocked loathing on her face.

CHAPTER FOURTEEN

Can you not see the immense advantage to a hospital when
[an almoner] brings her expert knowledge to bear on the
patient? Watch her at work a minute. Here comes a young
girl of nineteen who has just seen the doctor. Incipient
phthisis [consumption]. The doctor has ordered a quart of
milk a day and fresh air in plenty. He might as well have
ordered champagne and oysters and a sea voyage. All are
impossible to a girl who is earning about five shillings a week
by working from dark to dark at stitching dress shirts or
evening blouses. Then the almoner gets to work ...

(E. W. Morris, Secretary of the London Hospital, 1910)

Alice usually manned the watching room in the outpatients
department at the beginning of the week, but three days later,
on Monday, 16 January, she requested permission to work her
way through the list of visits that had been neglected since the
turn of the year.

With Miss Campbell's agreement, she left the Royal Free at
just after 9.30 a.m. and travelled on the Great Western Railway
line, her boots touching the icy platform of Wembley Hill

station at a quarter to eleven. The exhibition gardens – a vast area that boasted football and cricket grounds, a large running track and a golf course, as well as a theatre, tea pagodas and bandstands – were located a short walk from the station. It was a place locals flocked to on cold winter days; parents sipping hot drinks while their children skated across the frozen lake. In summer, couples strolled arm in arm through the ornamental gardens, women twirling parasols above their carefully styled hair. In the process of being built, the Empire Stadium (later to be known as Wembley Stadium) was to host its first sporting event just over a year later, in April 1923.

By 11 a.m. Alice was running the gauntlet of leering labourers across the wasteland surrounding the park, where numerous building projects were in progress. Lifting her skirts and stepping over abandoned shovels and around upturned wheelbarrows, she ignored their smirks, stopping now and then to ask if any of them knew where Jimmy Rose worked.

It was close to midday by the time she spoke to someone who showed more than a faint glimmer of recognition at Jimmy's name. Standing a couple of inches shorter than Alice, with his balding head streaked with mud, the squat labourer slammed his shovel into the earth and rested his forearms on the handle. 'You mean James? About so tall,' he said, straightening up and raising one of his hands about a foot over his own head. 'Stocky Irish fella, crop of dark hair?'

'Sounds very much like him, yes. Do you work together?'

The labourer chuckled and put on an affected accent. 'You could say that, in a manner of speaking.' Another labourer, tall and thin, appeared at that moment and stood next to him. They exchanged looks, and then the short man spoke again. 'What does a nice-looking piece like you want with James?'

Alice stared both of them down and then said: 'I'd like to speak with his employer.'

'She'd like to speak with his employer,' the man parroted, nudging his co-worker with his elbow. They both looked at her, smirking, and then he added: 'He's away at the moment, love.'

'When is he due back?'

The tall labourer spoke for the first time. 'Depends who's asking.' They both grinned again, their amusement fading at the appearance of another man in wellington boots who was holding a set of plans in one hand and a cigarette in the other. 'This nice lady here's looking for James,' the short labourer said.

The man, whose demeanour suggested he was in charge of the other two, ran his eyes over Alice and then mumbled: 'Oh no, not another one!'

Alice folded her arms and directed her attention to him. 'I am not looking for James. I know exactly where he is. It is his employer I wish to speak to.'

'He *is* the boss, darlin',' the foreman said. 'Look, I suggest you come back in a week or so. He'll probably be back by then.' His eyes drifted down to the almoner's midriff. 'But don't go expecting any support for you or the little'un.'

'I beg your pardon?'

'Look, I'm assuming you've got yourself in a sticky situation, but you're not going to get much satisfaction from James. He's a man who prefers to take his pleasure and run, not that many of 'em let him get away with that.'

Alice's jaw dropped, but then she stilled. After a few moments she said: 'So you're telling me that Jimmy Rose is the foreman of this site?'

'Nope, he's not the foreman. I am. He's the owner. And if you're looking for maintenance, you'll have to join the back of the queue, but I can guarantee you now that you won't get a penny piece from him, darling, no matter how many kids you spawn.'

With the exuberant voices of the Salvation Army's marching band filling the air, the almoner spent the next couple of hours making house calls in the narrow alleys and crowded streets of Whitechapel. Her rapid footsteps and the briskness of her interactions suggested that she was furiously keen to wrap up the visits and get back to the Royal Free.

It was a quarter past three when she finally made it back to the hospital, and almost half past by the time she reached the chest ward. 'Ah, just the woman I need,' Sister Nell Smith said, looking up from the charts spread over the main reception desk.

'Give me a moment, Nell,' Alice said, bypassing the high desk and strolling at pace to the double doors leading to the male ward.

'Ah, here's a sight to brighten any man's day, so it is,' Jimmy said cheerfully from his bed. He stubbed out his cigar on an ashtray on his side table, rested his hands in his lap and bestowed her with a cheeky grin.

'Up,' Alice commanded, reaching behind him and grabbing the pillows that he had been leaning against.

'Wha–t?' Jimmy exclaimed, falling sideways. He propped himself up on one elbow and stared up at her agog. 'What did you do that for, darling?' The other patients in the ward abandoned their cigarettes, cups of water and books to their own side tables and stared at the unfolding scene, their eyes goggling with intrigue.

'I managed to locate your place of work at Wembley this morning,' Alice said, tossing the pillows she was holding to the foot of the bed. Jimmy paled. He shifted himself upright and leaned against the metal bedstead, regarding her sheepishly. 'And I had an interesting talk with some of the navvies there. I'm told that, besides your half-built restaurant, you own two houses, three cars and several pets.' She put her hands on her hips. 'What have you got to say for yourself?'

James glanced around the ward. A showman by nature, he gave the almoner another grin and said: 'Well, if you're going to be picky about it.'

There was a chorus of gasps and a couple of chuckles. One man in the far corner of the ward went into a coughing spasm. He banged his fist on his chest and fumbled in his bedside cabinet for his packet of cigarettes.

'Picky?!' Alice cried. 'You're using up valuable resources, Jimmy! Oh, I beg your pardon, I mean, *James*.' Another patient guffawed. Alice moved closer to the bed and lowered her voice. 'Why on earth would you do such a thing? When you have enough money to see any doctor you wish.'

'Well, that's just it, see. I wanted to see Dr Harland. Everyone for miles around knows he's one of the best. And the care you get in this place is far superior to anything you'd find privately, no matter how much money you have.'

Alice shook her head in apparent exasperation. Her eyes ran over the bed, and then she whisked several of the patient's blankets away. 'Come on,' she snapped coldly, piling the woollen bundle on top of the pillows. She leaned down and pulled his tatty old bag out from under the bed.

'Darlin', what are you doing now?!'

She plonked the bag on top of his bed next to the pile of pillows and blankets and then levelled her gaze on him. 'You surely don't think you're going to stay here, do you? After this?!'

Jimmy cupped his hands to his head. 'I'm clinging onto life with my bare fingernails here! Hovering between heaven and hell, so I am. You can't just throw me out in the middle of my treatment!' A couple of patients had abandoned their own beds to gain a better view. They shuffled barefoot towards Jimmy's bed in their night caps, grinning from ear to ear as the man coughed theatrically and gaped at the almoner.

'Oh, come now, Jimmy, you have the constitution of a baboon. How else would you have found the stamina to keep so many ladies entertained?'

Another series of guffaws broke out across the ward. Jimmy declined to respond. Instead, he stared open-mouthed as Alice opened the door to the cabinet beside his bed and began pulling out the clothes that were tucked away inside.

'Oh no, don't do that! Please! Look, tell you what. You're a smart woman, so you are. I knew that when I first laid eyes on you. Obvious, so it was. So how's about I make a deal with you?'

Alice stilled, his clothes dangling from her arms. She narrowed her eyes and gave him a sidelong glance. 'What sort of deal?'

James clamoured for the blankets and pulled them back over his bare hairy legs. He leaned back against the iron headboard, took a deep breath and released it slowly. 'I'm prepared to make a donation.'

'Yes?'

'I'll get the wife to dig out some bed linen and other bits and pieces. It's all good-quality stuff, and you can have it for nothing.'

Alice dropped the clothes on the bed and began stuffing them unceremoniously into the bag. Jimmy held out flattened hands and rose to his knees on the mattress. 'Alright, alright! Tell me what you want from me!'

The almoner paused in her packing and looked at him. 'We're hoping to open another mother and baby home in the near future, the capital outlay for which will be extensive. The Samaritan Fund is running low. *And* we have a long list of children who have never been to the coast.'

Jimmy dragged his hands down his face and let out a strangled little moan. A few drops of perspiration glistened on his forehead. Eventually he swallowed hard and asked in a small voice: 'So how much do you want?'

'I would say about five hundred would make a nice start.'

'Five hundred?!' Jimmy gaped at her. 'You mean five hundred pounds?! Honest to God, woman, I haven't got that sort of money going begging!'

Alice rammed the rest of the clothes into the bag and grabbed the handles. 'You'd better get some clothes on then, James, unless you're happy to roam the streets of Holborn in your underwear.'

Jimmy sank down onto his haunches, his shoulders sagging. 'Alright, alright, you win! Five hundred it is. Now, for the love of God, woman, will you leave me be?!'

Alice gave him a satisfied nod. 'Look at it this way,' she said, smiling demurely. 'You'll sleep more soundly in your bed tonight, knowing what a good deed it is you have done.'

A slow clap from a patient in a nearby bed gained traction as Alice crossed the ward. By the time she'd reached the nurses' station at the end of the ward, where a student nurse sat with her jaw dropped open, loud applause and hoots of laughter had broken out across the ward.

The almoner grinned as she passed through the double doors at the end of the ward, but quickly grew serious as Sister Nell Smith ran down the corridor towards her, a wheeled trolley being pushed along by two concerned-looking nurses behind her. 'Nell,' the almoner said, but the nurse jogged past her, stopping when she reached the open doorway of a large side suite. 'Risk of respiratory arrest,' Nell called out briskly, gesturing for the nurses to move past her into the room. 'Ten-year-old boy with severe breathing difficulties,' she continued urgently. 'His mother brought him in after finding him collapsed at home.'

Alice spun around and caught up with Nell in the doorway. 'I know the family,' she said. 'This is Billy Simpkins. I saw him on a home visit a couple of weeks ago.'

The nurse didn't answer, but beckoned Alice to join her in the room, where two young medical students and the nurses had surrounded the trolley. Billy was conscious and sitting upright on the unforgiving mattress, his shoulders up around his ears as he gasped for air. One of the students leaned close to the patient, trying to fix an oxygen mask over his mouth.

Alice stood at the foot of the trolley and watched as Billy fought away, his eyes bulging. 'Keep it on, love, it will do you good,' Nell said sternly, bustling over and elbowing a space for herself at the head of the trolley. She raised the mask to the boy's nose but his panicked arms flailed outwards, almost knocking her sideways.

Moments later, Tilda arrived in the doorway, her younger son in her arms. 'Oh, my poor boy!' she cried, rushing into the room and gulping back a sob. Billy's eyes widened, his distressed mother exacerbating his condition so severely that his lips gained a bluish tinge.

'Doctor will be with us any minute now,' Nell said, her voice tense. The air of urgency in the room sharpened.

At that moment Dr Harland appeared. The medical team parted reverentially to make room for him at the head of the bed. 'I'm the doctor here,' he said, running a calm eye over the distraught child. 'There's nothing to worry about. You're at the Royal Free and we're going to take good care of you.'

Billy gaped at him, hands clawing at the air. 'Help him!' Tilda screamed. 'Do something!' Her baby's face turned puce, his eyes widening in alarm. He began to bellow.

'Get her out of here,' the doctor snapped quietly. As one of the nurses guided the hysterical woman away, Dr Harland dismissed two of the staff gathered around the bed and directed a request for some ephedrine towards one of the medical students. After checking that the boy's airway was clear, he took the syringe that was handed to him wordlessly and injected it into the top of the boy's thigh. Within seconds the drug took effect, the boy calming enough for a nurse to administer some oxygen. His thin body sagged back against the trolley, although he was still blue around the lips and struggling to breathe.

'I want a chest X-ray taken as soon as he's stable,' Dr Harland said as he pressed his stethoscope to the boy's chest. 'And would someone please fetch some more pillows to prop him up.' He then asked the remaining nurse to find out whether the child had been exposed to any specific irritants. She blushed hotly and left the room.

'Now, young man, there's no need to take such drastic action just because you'd like to spend the afternoon somewhere warm,' the doctor said smoothly, either oblivious or entirely disinterested in the adulation from the staff around him. He eased the child forward and ran the stethoscope across the top of his back. The boy lifted his head. 'Don't look at me like that,' Dr Harland continued above the loud whistles emanating from the boy's chest. 'There has been a run of you lot lately and I'm not happy about it.'

Billy made no response but his eyes became alert with interest, his rapid breaths slowing with the doctor's every word. 'You look like a man with a discerning palate to me,' the doctor continued. 'Am I right?' The boy gave a weak nod then closed his eyes, the effort of trying to draw breath draining him. With his attention focussed on the child, whose teeth were chattering beneath the mask, the doctor addressed one of the students: 'A cup of strong coffee, if you please.'

The boy opened his eyes, his brows creasing in puzzlement. 'It's for you, young man, not me. It will help loosen your airways.' Billy's head lolled against the trolley as the doctor shone a light in his eyes and ran practised fingers along his clavicles then upwards, around his neck and the back of his head.

Dr Harland gave a quiet commentary during the examination, his voice low and calm. The remaining medical students listened intently and scribbled notes on their pads as he spoke. After several minutes, once the bluish tinge to the boy's lips had been replaced with a healthy pink colour, the doctor grabbed a chart from the wall. He scrawled some notes, and then looked up, his gaze flicking to Alice for the first time. 'Doctor,' she said stiffly. He dipped his head in reply, told Billy he would pop in to see him later, then left the room.

'That's it, my love, you get that down you,' Nell Smith clucked, as the boy sipped at a cup of steaming coffee a few minutes later. Painfully undernourished, his ribs bulged prominently beneath the skin of his pigeon chest, the skin on his arms wrinkled and pale. Poor nourishment meant that many of the Royal Free's patients were at risk of losing their lives to ordinary childhood diseases like whooping cough, scarlet fever and croup. Measles, for example, had taken the lives of more children in the past century than any other illness, largely because its victims were weak before the illness had even struck.

Parents regularly dragged ailing children from the dank basements in which they lived, through the doors of the hospital, hoping that doctors might offer a magic cure. Once under their radar, the almoners did what they could not only to improve the day-to-day lives of the underprivileged children, but also to bolster their chances of survival, should another illness strike.

Billy grinned between mouthfuls, apparently chuffed to have been offered such a sophisticated brew. As he sipped, Nell turned to Alice. 'You can say what you like about that man,' she said quietly, 'but he's fabulous when it comes to emergencies, especially with the children. He really is a marvel.'

Perhaps in appreciation, or at least in recognition of his skill, Alice pursed her lips and said: 'So it would appear.'

CHAPTER FIFTEEN

The first question is not 'Is this person deserving?' but
'Can we in this instance effect an improvement or cure?'
There must be a quality of sternness in the kindness that
is to stamp out vice [but] many lives made hopeless by
pressure of circumstances and by association with vice,
would be made saved [by a] fresh start.

(C. S. Loch, *How to Help Cases of Distress*, 1895)

Alice's footsteps echoed on the floorboards of the hospital chapel a few minutes later, muffling the faint rustle as her long skirt swept against the pews. Gaslight flickered through the arched windows above her, lifting the colours from the stained glass and directing them to the board of honours on the other side of the space, where the names of all those associated with the Royal Free who had sacrificed their lives in the Great War were displayed in letters of black and gold.

The stillness of the chapel, its rituals and muted light, offered patients and their relatives a temporary reprieve from the struggles that were waiting to engulf them in the outside world. Generations of Londoners had sought solace in the silence that echoed off the stone walls, delaying the moment when they had to step back into their everyday lives.

Tilda was sitting in the front pew, the nurse who had escorted her out of the examination room holding her in a half-restraining, half-comforting hug. Walter, her baby son, was crawling around in the space between pew and pulpit. All three of them looked up when Alice approached, and then Tilda sprang to her feet. 'He's going to be alright,' the almoner said in a hushed voice. The woman's shoulders sagged with relief. Walter looked between his mother and the newcomer in mild puzzlement, then ventured over on hands and knees to examine the dust collecting at the base of the font.

'Can I see him?'

Alice took a long breath and placed gentle hands on the woman's upper arms. 'He's stable,' she said, her breath fogging the cool air. 'But let us allow the nurses some time to do what they must.'

Tilda nodded. She and Alice thanked the nurse and, as the chapel door fell shut behind her, the almoner motioned for Tilda to sit next to her on the pew. They sat in silence for a moment, and then Alice angled herself sideways. 'You do realise, Tilda, that high emotion and anxiety are bound to exacerbate your son's condition?'

The woman stiffened and turned away. 'I know how tempting it can be to gloss over the truth, but the longer you stay silent, the more dangerous your situation becomes.'

Tilda burst into sudden tears. Walter stopped trying to catch the dust motes and looked up, his bottom lip wobbling. Alice handed Tilda a handkerchief and then picked the baby up. She positioned him so that he was facing the stained-glass windows, angled away from his mother, and bobbed him up and down on her knees. His mother dabbed at her cheeks. 'It's my fault he's so ill!' she gasped between sobs. 'You don't have to tell me. I know it's all my fault!'

Walter whimpered. The almoner patted his back and turned to Tilda. 'Your fault? Quite how exactly is any of this your fault?'

Tilda took a tremulous intake of breath. 'I've tried to be a good wife, a good mother,' she whispered, 'but I'm afraid I've just messed it all up. Everything.'

Alice looked at her. 'Things don't always work out as we would hope,' she countered, 'but it seems to me that you have been trying your best and, given the circumstances, been rather too harsh on yourself in the process.'

Tilda shook her head and lifted Walter onto her own lap, his back resting against her swollen stomach. She lowered her forehead to the nape of his neck and cried softly. Alice folded her hands in her lap and waited. When Tilda turned her tear-streaked face towards her again the almoner asked: 'What contribution is your husband making towards this ambition of a happy home?'

Tilda's eyes flicked away. She stroked the hair back from Walter's forehead, stared into the middle distance and sniffed. 'Because if my assessment of the situation is anywhere near accurate,' Alice continued, 'his contribution is entirely negative.'

A few moments passed, and then Tilda turned to face her again. She took a deep, shaky breath. 'I can't seem to make out my head from my tail these days,' she admitted quietly, a single tear rolling down her cheek. 'I used to be able to soothe his anger, but now, well, it's not so easy when you're carrying babies, is it? I mean, look at me.' She looked down at herself and then up again. 'He's lost interest, and who can blame him?'

Alice's nostrils flared. 'I'm afraid I have never held with such old-fashioned views, Tilda. A wife is not a pet or a slave. We are moving towards an era where women will be valued as people with equal worth to men. There will be blood and tears along the way, and it may be decades before we get there, but each of us must make our own efforts to bring that day closer. You bore your husband two wonderful children and you have another on the way. He should be thanking his stars for it and cherishing you all.'

Tilda raised an eyebrow and looked at Alice askance as if wondering whether she'd heard her right. There was another silence, and then the almoner said: 'We can fix Billy's body, but what of his mind? Returning him to the same environment will only arouse the same symptoms.' Her gaze sharpened on the expectant mother and then she added: 'And what if, on the next occasion, he doesn't make it here in time?'

Tilda eyed Alice over the top of Walter's head, tears rolling down her cheeks. 'What choice I got?' she demanded. 'Every woman needs the protection of a man, especially them what's in my condition.'

Alice scoffed, staring pointedly at the bruises beneath Tilda's eyes. The woman flushed. She lowered her son to the floor and hung her head over her bump, the hanky she was holding flitting from one trembling hand to the other. The silence expanded. Alice eventually placed a gloved hand on top of hers. 'Allow me to help you, Tilda.'

As well as their efforts to support lone parents, the almoners did their best to help women who were suffering domestic abuse. By shining a light on new pathways opening up to them, new possibilities that were never before imagined, they helped to release the powerless from the prison of abusive marriages.

The woman looked up. 'Help me? How would you do that? You mean by sending me and the kids off to the workhouse?'

Alice shook her head. 'I am not talking about the workhouse. I may need some time, but before Billy is discharged, I hope to have found a place for you. In the meantime, you must stay here, at the hospital, where you'll be safe.'

Tilda stared at her considering, then burst into a fresh wave of tears. After a moment Alice spoke again. 'You will mourn your marriage, I understand that, just as you have had to grieve for the love you hoped to have, but I have seen lots of women build new lives in place of the old. You must believe that you can too, for the sake of your children, if not for yourself.'

Tilda bunched her hanky up into a ball and dabbed her eyes and agreed that, yes, she did believe. The almoner let another few moments pass and then said gently: 'Your parents are probably still downstairs, if you would like to see them?'

Tilda looked up in surprise. 'They're here, at the hospital? Why?'

Alice pressed her lips together. 'It is not for me to say. But I know they would love to see you.'

'I can't.'

'Why not?'

Tilda threw her hands up in the air and stared at Alice. 'Why do you think I haven't seen them for months?' She balled her tongue up into the inside of her cheek so that the partially healed gash at the side of her lip bulged outwards. 'I can't let them see me like this! It would turn them right over.'

Alice levelled her gaze. 'Not if they know you don't have to live that way anymore.'

Perhaps it was the prospect of an existence free from fear, or simply the act of unburdening herself, but the floodgates opened then, Tilda disclosing the grim details of late-night beatings, with Billy getting caught in the crossfire as he sought to protect her. She paused now and again, glancing at Alice as if to gauge her reaction.

The almoner expressed no surprise. She listened silently, giving an impression of unfazed calm, offering only the encouragement of a nod, or an 'Um' when the gap between disclosures stretched out for too long. 'I did think of running to my mum and dad loads of times, but it wouldn't have been fair,' Tilda said, after a particularly long silence. 'They got hardly no space as it is, and besides,' she added bitterly, 'Rich threatened to burn their place down if I ever breathed a word to them.'

When it was clear that she had nothing else to add, Alice squeezed her hand. 'You have been so very brave, Tilda. Now, how about we go and see your son?' Tilda gave the almoner a tearful nod and then leaned over awkwardly, picking up her toddler. The scent of fresh flowers in the air mingled with incense and ancient oak as they walked side by side down the aisle, adding to the renewed sense of calm.

It was almost 6 p.m. when Alice approached Ted and Hetty in the outpatients department. They looked up in surprise, startled at her announcement that she had some special news. Tears sprang to Hetty's eyes when Alice told her the details. 'Oh my Lord, what a terrible thing!' she said, shaking her head. As she followed Alice into the chest ward, her husband looked equally choked beside her.

Alice guided the pair into the side room where Billy and his mother were waiting, and then stood by the door, waiting in silence as the couple gathered their sobbing daughter into their arms. Billy, whose cheeks had gained a healthy pink glow, beamed at them from his bed, his own eyes filled with tears.

When the three of them pulled apart, Ted cupped his daughter's bruised face in his hands. His own eyes grew shiny as he touched the pad of his thumb gently over each of her injuries, shaking his head in regret. 'It's alright, Dad, it's over now,' Tilda said softly, taking his hands and grasping them in her own.

Often, the almoners came into contact with patients when they were going through the lowest points in their lives. Vulnerable and bewildered, many opened up about their pasts, admitting to family secrets that had long since been buried.

Hetty stretched her arm out to Alice. 'Thank you,' she mouthed quietly. 'Thank you so much.'

★ ★ ★

Alice and Sister Nell Smith spent the next half an hour raiding wards and store cupboards until they had sourced all the equipment they needed to transform Billy's side room into a temporary home for the small family. They placed a cot at the end of Billy's bed and a mattress on the floor beside it, leaving a narrow path between the two so that the nurses could move freely around.

Dr Harland's mouth fell open when he came in on the hour to review his patient and found the room full of people. 'What's going on here?' he snapped, his gaze falling accusingly on Alice.

'Supper,' the almoner answered simply, as Nell opened the door with her hip and bustled in with a tray of tea, bread and dripping, and cold cuts of meat. Billy and his mother and grandparents stared at the bounty as if they'd never seen such wonder in their lives.

'This is a hospital, Miss Hudson, not a Lyons' tea shop!' the doctor roared.

'The good physician treats the disease; the great physician treats the patient who has the disease. Isn't that what Sir William Osler used to say, doctor?' Alice said coolly in reply, the tilt of her chin giving the impression that she was prepared to brook no further argument. After a moment she turned to help Nell as the nurse bustled around, handing out cups and saucers and plates. The doctor followed her with his eyes as she moved across the room, then conceded with a small nod; one that perhaps had more to do with lack of sleep than any leaning towards magnanimity.

CHAPTER SIXTEEN

The almoner may in the course of his work have occasion to
deal with cases of lunatic persons, or he may have to make
arrangements for cases of pauper lunatics and cases of
lunatics wandering at large.

(C. S. Loch, *How to Help Cases
of Distress*, 1895)

The first Friday afternoon in February found Alice back at
Banstead Mental Hospital.

Thirteen miles south of the centre of London, Banstead was
a town well known for its fresh air, as well as its horse racing.
Ironically, considering that it was the destination of choice for
depositing horse manure by rail from the streets of London,
physicians regularly sent their ailing patients to convalesce in
what Sir Robert Hunter, Honorary Solicitor to the Commons
Preservation Society, described as 'perhaps the most bracing
[neighbourhood] to be found within a short distance of the
city ... to roam and gallop over such commons is the breath of
life to those who have emerged from the smoke and noise of
London, while to those who never set eyes on a blade of grass

from one year's end to another they still serve as a reservoir of pure air'.

The population of the small parish of Banstead had doubled in 1877, when the mental hospital, then known as London County Lunatic Asylum, first opened. Thought to be an ideal place to smuggle away 'mad' relatives, the hospital was built on land known locally as 'The Hundred Acres', where a windmill and the accompanying miller's houses had once stood.

A set-apart world designed with self-sufficiency in mind, the hospital had its own heating and water supply as well as day rooms, dormitories, attendants' rooms, stores, bathrooms and a wing of specially designed padded cells. There was a bakery in the grounds as well as a chapel, laundry, sports ground and kitchen garden. Tucked away beneath overhanging trees stood the hospital cemetery, and since the average stay for patients was thirty years, many of them ended up interred there. The hospital accommodated 2,500 patients at its height, but was closed in 1986 and converted for use as a prison.

A light wind played at the hood of Alice's cape as she followed the stone track from Belmont Railway Station. The tracks had been laid to ease the path of horse-drawn carts carrying coal and other supplies from the station to the hospital. Sheep grazed nearby on the open heath, rabbits emerging from the hedgerows and, at the sound of footsteps, burrowing beneath the gorse.

The weather since the beginning of the month had been unsettled but unseasonably mild and the trees overhanging the gates of the hospital were already budding with pale green leaves, the air over the Downs fresh with the promise of rain.

It was almost 2 p.m. when Alice signed in at the gatekeeper's lodge. The porter, a man in his mid-thirties whose lips failed to stretch far enough over his teeth to meet, followed her to the gate after asking her business, as if reluctant to let go of the opportunity for conversation.

The nurse seated at the reception of Block A showed no such interest on Alice's approach, and no sign of recognition either, even though she had been the one to accompany the almoner to the day room on her last visit. In response to the nurse's blank expression, Alice reminded her of her name and occupation and then repeated Charlotte's full name.

'Yes, I know who you are,' the nurse said, dropping her pen to her desk and giving the almoner her full attention for the first time. 'You came last month.' Alice nodded and pulled her handbag higher onto her caped shoulder, as if readying herself to pass through the locked wooden gate leading to the wards. There was a pause, and then the nurse said: 'You upset her too, as I remember. Anyway, I'm afraid I can't let you in. Miss Redbourne had a visitor two days ago and she's limited to one a week. Doctor's orders.'

Alice's brows drew together. 'A visit? From whom?'

The nurse pulled her chin in and flicked through the paper-work in front of her. She squinted down through her thick-lensed glasses, then looked up. 'A gentleman, I believe.'

'Her father?'

There was another fruitless rooting through the papers and then she said: 'I don't believe so, not from what I recall. I was dealing with another patient at the time but I remember reading the update on the log.'

'And what was her demeanour following the visit?'

'Agitated, I believe. But she's picked up since.'

'Exactly when was this visit?'

The nurse looked sideways and pursed her lips. 'I was off-duty yesterday, so it must have been the day before, on the first.'

When pressurised to provide a description of the visitor, the nurse sighed and got to her feet. 'If it's imperative, come and ask her yourself.' There was a significant amount of muttering and grumbling as the nurse escorted Alice into Block A, the dim passageways lined with hot water pipes resembling the bowels of a ship. They passed the ward and the day room, and then the almoner was motioned into a large dining hall, where several patients were moving around and carrying chairs to and fro.

A nurse stood against the far wall directing operations, and two male patients passed back and forth as they moved heavy-looking wooden tables and lined them up at the edges of the room. Dinner had been cleared away, and the evening supper would be served on trays. Meals were plain during the 1920s, but an improvement on those served to the hospital's earliest patients – meat and potato pie was a staple for dinner in Banstead Hospital at the end of the nineteenth century, with gruel and bread and milk alternated at breakfast and tea. Patients were also entitled to three pints of ale; a balm to help them survive the rigours of each day.

'She's coping well,' the nurse said briskly, as she followed Alice into the hall. 'So don't go upsetting her like last time. I don't want her losing her wits and tearing the place up again.'

Alice nodded her agreement and then looked around. 'What's going on in here?'

The nurse explained that the patients were helping to make preparations for the weekend; the latest films available were shown on a large projector screen each Friday evening, and then on Saturdays came the highlight of the week: a dinner and dance attended by patients and staff.

'What did you expect?' the nurse said, chuckling in response to Alice's look of surprise. 'A lot of moaning and screaming and rattling of chains? Times have changed, you know.'

'We're going to watch a Charlie Chaplin later,' Charlotte told Alice a few minutes later, her voice bubbling with excitement. She was wearing a clean grey dress, her hair neatly brushed into a long plait, which hung over her left shoulder. 'I slept through most of last week's film, I was so tired, but I feel much better today.' They were standing together near the stage, where patients sometimes performed their own plays, the costumes they wore tailored by fellow inmates.

Alice smiled. 'That's wonderful, Charlotte.' Her expression grew thoughtful as she removed her cape and gloves and set them aside on the stage. She straightened and then settled her gaze on the teenager. 'But I'm wondering why you have not yet asked me about Daisy.' The almoner had called in on Elizabeth on the afternoon of the 2nd to check on the infant;

when she had leaned over to coo at her, she had been rewarded with a beaming smile. With Daisy over a month old, the almoner had made several attempts to persuade Dr Harland that her birth should be registered as a matter of urgency, all to no avail.

The girl's expression faltered. 'Oh, y–yes, how is she?'

'She is very well.' Alice's gaze sharpened. 'But then, perhaps you had already heard?'

The girl's eyes skittered to the stage. When she looked back, she shook her head. Alice continued to look at her hard. 'I'm told that you had a visitor on Wednesday. A gentleman ...' Charlotte nodded, her cheeks turning crimson. 'I don't mean to pry, but would you care to tell me who it was?'

Charlotte began fiddling with the collar of her dress. She appeared disgruntled. 'It was a friend, that's all.'

'Daisy's father?' The teenager shook her head. Alice considered her for another moment then glanced away. Across the room, a middle-aged woman with long thin grey hair tied up in a ponytail and a girl around Charlotte's age were carrying a large bucket of coal between them. They lugged it breathlessly over to a wide fireplace and then brushed their blackened hands over their clothes. The almoner took a slow breath in and settled her gaze on Charlotte again. She asked: 'Have you had any previous association with Dr Harland?'

'Who?'

'I believe you know who I mean. Elizabeth's brother ... the doctor who helped to deliver Daisy.'

'No,' came the quick reply.

Alice narrowed her eyes. 'Are you quite certain about that?'

'Why would I lie?' Charlotte snapped. There was a note of hysteria in her tone. One of the nurses supervising the two women as they heaped shovels of coal into the hearth glanced over and frowned.

'Listen, Charlotte,' the almoner said, leaning in. 'Doctors are obliged to follow a strict code of conduct. They have a duty towards the welfare of each and every one of their patients, so if there has been the slightest impropriety –'

'Stop it,' Charlotte cut in, her fingers running over themselves in a frantic motion. She backed away and wrung her hands together. 'Please, stop going on and getting at me.' Her eyes filled with tears and there was a panicked expression on her face.

Alice held out a placating hand. 'Don't get upset,' she said quietly. 'I'm not suggesting that you are being deliberately deceitful. It is just that, sometimes, when we are frightened, it is difficult to know who we can trust, is it not?'

'I don't know what else you want me to say!' Charlotte cried, raising trembling hands to her hair. A few tendrils escaped her plait and hung over her widening eyes. 'I don't know why you have to ask me all these questions!'

The nurse at the fireplace finally abandoned her post and began walking towards them. 'I'm sorry, Charlotte. I didn't mean to upset you,' Alice said. The girl eyed Alice from beneath her long fringe and gave a small nod. 'I'm working on a placement for you,' the almoner continued as the nurse slipped a protective arm around Charlotte's shoulder and gave the almoner a cold look. Alice gathered up her cape and gloves. 'I will visit with some more news soon.'

By mid-afternoon the temperature had dropped, the mildness of the day lost in a whirl of cold winds and loose leaves. Alice tightened her cape and folded her arms around its dark wool as she crossed the driveway towards the gates, which now stood open, a dark-coloured Bentley on its way into the grounds.

Several other cars were lined up at the gatekeeper's lodge. A portly gentleman with a head of thinning grey hair leaned out of the window of the first car as Alice approached. He spoke briefly to the porter then drove slowly on, following the Bentley as it rolled towards the main hospital building.

Alice leaned into the wind and frowned at the misted-up windows of the next vehicle. When she reached the gates she stood aside as the porter waved the car in, then followed its path with her eyes. She turned at the sound of a loud command, then edged past the next car as the porter held out a flattened hand to signal that the next driver should wait.

After signing herself out in the visitors' book, the almoner asked if she could take a moment to examine the register of recent guests to the hospital. The porter blinked. 'I'm afraid I can't allow that,' he said, puffing out his chest. 'It's against policy. All manner of things start to go wrong if you don't stick to hospital policy.'

'Gosh, yes, so I should imagine,' Alice said with a demure smile. 'It is such a responsible job you have, isn't it?'

The man eyed her warily, perhaps puzzled at her sudden

friendliness, but very quickly submitted to having his ego stroked. 'Well, you're right there, Miss. I mean, without a meticulously maintained log, them inside aren't to know who's in and who isn't. If there's a fire, or an evacuation of some sort ...' He stopped mid-sentence and took quick, loping strides out of the lodge to wave the waiting cars through. 'No, without a responsible guard at the gate,' he continued when he returned, 'the security of the whole place falls apart. Then there are the privacy issues. You can't just go letting anyone rifle through the records now, can you? You're venturing into dangerous territory if you go down that road.'

'Absolutely, I see. But, I mean,' she glanced up at him through her thick lashes and gave him another glowing smile, 'do I look dangerous to you?' A few beads of sweat appeared on the porter's forehead. A flush crept up his neck. 'I just need to check back a couple of days,' Alice continued sweetly. 'I promise I won't trouble you for long.'

'A lady like you couldn't possibly trouble me,' he said, treating her to a wide smile of prominent yellow teeth. 'Now, tell you what. I'm just going to see these next few cars through the gates. What you do while my back is turned is up to you.'

Alice gave him another coquettish smile. As soon as he left the lodge, she began flicking rapidly through the thick parchment in the register, running a forefinger down the lines of black ink. 'Do you recall this fellow?' she asked when the porter returned, a couple of minutes later. She pointed to a name written in capital letters midway down one of the pages – 'CYRIL GARDNER'.

The porter shook his head. 'I don't take too much notice of most visitors. Now, if it was a lady like you, that'd be a different matter.'

The almoner ignored the compliment and pressed on: 'Old? Young? Middle-aged? Tall? Portly? Surely you must remember something about him.' The porter shook his head. Alice sighed. 'Well, in that case,' she said briskly, 'I shall let you get on.'

His face fell. 'Oh, don't do that,' he said, moving closer. 'Stop here for a while. I get a tea break soon.'

The almoner made brisk apologies and moved to the door. Outside there was a swishing sound as another faceless driver rolled his car over the tracks. Alice stopped at the threshold of the lodge and turned back to the porter. 'Is there a meeting of some sort going on this afternoon?'

The porter walked to the door, peered over her head at the line of cars, then motioned the drivers through with a flick of his hand. 'Meeting? No, that's more visitors. Regulars.'

'Visitors? Yet you are waving them through without asking them to sign in?'

He nodded. 'That's because they're not going into the hospital building. They're going to pick the patients up at the door.'

Alice frowned. 'They are picking relatives up?'

The porter bellowed a laugh, a spray of spittle hitting the air. The bunch of keys at his belt rattled. 'No, love. Not relatives. At least, not in most cases.'

Alice frowned. 'Who then?'

Another car pulled up. Alice leaned forward and peered through the windscreen as the porter waved the vehicle through. She straightened. 'They're all lone men,' she said flatly, turning to examine the porter's face.

'Yep. Friday afternoon, isn't it? It's when the gentlemen knock off early, so's they can spend an hour or two unaccounted for.'

The almoner looked at him and then shook her head. 'I'm afraid I must be misconstruing what you are telling me.'

He grinned. 'No, I don't think you are, Miss. Pop here for a bit of female company, don't they? Before heading home to the wife for the weekend.'

Alice turned slowly back towards the cars. A thin man in a dark suit was glaring at them out of the window of his car, his gloved hands tapping impatiently on the steering wheel. 'Where do they take them?'

The porter shrugged. 'Out for a drive, I would guess. But then, there's plenty of woods to go to if they fancy a stroll, eh? Although it might be a bit nippy this time of year for what they have in mind. Then again, I suppose an hour in the comfort of a Bentley isn't too arduous a task, eh? Not when the alternative is being stuck inside those walls over there.' He dipped his head towards the hospital then waved his hand, motioning the next driver through the gates.

Alice shook her head as if trying to absorb the information. 'So what you are saying is that these men befriend a particular patient and then take her out once a week?'

'Not a specific patient, no. I think they take whoever's available at the time. There's only a certain number of patients that get let out. Most of 'em have to stay locked up, or they're chaperoned as they wander the grounds. The men like to mix it up a bit, so I've heard. They like a bit of variety, you know.'

The almoner's face clouded with fury. 'Who sanctions these outings? Do the doctors know about this?'

'I'd be surprised if they didn't.'

'It's disgraceful.'

The porter shrugged. 'Dirty old dogs, I grant you. But they're not doing anything plenty of others don't. The men get to unwind before the weekend and the girls get a chance to see all the glory that Banstead has to offer. Everyone's happy, eh?' He gave her another toothy grin. Alice turned on her heel and stormed away, her cape billowing out behind her.

The line of blackbirds perched along the top of the gates took flight as the engine of the next car revved up, then followed the others up the drive.

When Alice descended the stairs to the basement an hour later, her face was drained of colour. Winnie eyed her over the top of her spectacles. 'Are you alright, dear? she said. 'You look quite faint.' It was 5 p.m. and the typist was the only member of staff still on duty in the office.

'Fine,' the almoner said. She nibbled her thumbs and paced the floor. After a minute or so she sank down into the chair opposite Winnie's desk. There was a long pause and then she fixed the typist with an intense look: 'Can I talk to you, Winnie?'

Suddenly energised, Winnie's knees cracked as she sprang to her feet and bustled over to the boiler. A few minutes later, she lowered a steaming cup of tea on the desk in front of Alice and, with a loud huff and a wince, sat back in her seat. Alice rubbed her hand over her forehead, heaved a sigh and began to speak.

The typist nodded along with her every word, the creases on her forehead deepening as Alice described the cavalier attitude of the drivers and the amused reaction of the porter in response to her shock. When the almoner fell silent, Winnie said: 'Well I never did! Still it's the way of the world, my dear.'

'Well, it shouldn't be,' Alice raged. 'It's wrong!'

Winnie took a tired breath in. 'It's been that way since time immemorial.'

'So what you are saying is that we should just avert our eyes, shrug our shoulders and pretend nothing is going on?!'

The typist took a sip of her tea and smiled sagely over the top of her cup. 'I didn't say that. There are things that can be done. I have an idea, as it happens. Are you free next Friday?'

Alice gave a slow nod of intrigue, but then she grimaced. 'Oh no! I'm not free. We have the conference.' She cupped her cheeks with her hands and looked at the typist. 'It's such bad timing for me to be away. I have a million things to do.' She picked up her cup and then put it down again. 'Winnie, what exactly was it you had in mind?'

CHAPTER SEVENTEEN

Statistics show that every year the birth rate from the worst
end of our community is increasing in proportion to the birth
rate at the better end, and it was in order to try to right that
grave social danger that I embarked upon this work to
counteract the steady evil which has been growing for a
good many years of the reduction of the birth rate on the
part of the thrifty, wise, well-contented, and the generally
sound members of our community, and the reckless breeding
from the semi-feeble minded, the careless, who are
proportionately increasing in our community because of the
slowing of the birth rate at the other end of the scale.

(Marie Stopes, quoted in *The Trial of Marie Stopes*,
edited by M. Box, 1967)

The weekend conference organised by the almoners took place
at High Leigh on Friday, 10 February 1922.

The sprawling Victorian manor house was once owned by
Robert Barclay, a member of the famous banking dynasty, and
had been transformed into a conference centre after his death
in 1921. Surrounded by forty acres of Hertfordshire countryside,

it was an idyllic setting, one regularly hired out to missionaries and those involved in charitable relief. Its close proximity to the metropolis made it a convenient choice for the almoners from the London hospitals.

Alice had embarked on the twenty-mile journey up to Hoddesdon by rail earlier that morning, accompanied by colleagues Frank, Alexander and Bess Campbell. After depositing their trunks in their respective rooms, the small party filed into one of the large oak-panelled function rooms, arriving in their seats at just before a quarter to nine.

After an introduction from a representative from the Charity Organisation Society, Bess Campbell glided onto the stage in a crimson gown and a lace stole. She spoke about the importance of sharing good practices with colleagues and, unlike the St Thomas's almoner, Miss Cummins, whose shyness caused her to mumble and falter when making public speeches, Bess used her hands animatedly as she spoke, capturing everyone's attention with no hint of nerves.

Among the audience were delegates from a number of charitable organisations as well as representatives from the clergy and government departments concerned with housing and education. The futility of working in isolation was becoming clear to all involved in social work, and Bess added her voice to those stressing that improved communication was the way forward if reformers were to stand any hope of improving outcomes for the destitute.

As her speech came to an end, Alice rolled her shoulders and took several long, slow breaths. Her eyes locked with

Alexander's when she took her place at the podium, and the fundraiser gave her a small nod of encouragement. Perhaps to put herself at ease, she opened by joking with the audience that when trying to decide on a career at the end of the Great War, she had drawn up an alphabetical list of the possibilities open to her and settled on the first one she came to after 'actress'.

Miss Campbell smiled and nodded as Alice spoke about some of the cases she had dealt with during her first year in post: the young child she had taken under her wing whose parents had delivered her to the hospital for treatment and then failed to return; the patient who had fallen into a deep depression after a leg amputation, who was now working cheerfully in the hospital kitchens.

The almoner told delegates about her efforts to encourage prostitutes into more respectable lines of work and the lengths she and her colleagues went to in helping those addicted to drugs and alcohol. 'The joy of my own work comes, not from meeting people when they are at their lowest ebb,' she said, beginning to get into her stride, 'but from offering a sanctuary away from what, for so many of our patients, is a hostile, frightening world. Witnessing their transformation as they begin the long climb towards self-respect and independence is such a privilege,' she added, lifting her gaze from the podium for the first time, 'and it chills me to think of what would become of them if the safety net of our department were to be removed.'

She went on to describe how she had grown wise in recent months to the games people play, citing Jimmy's case as an example in point. There was widespread mirth among the audience as she recounted her final visit to Jimmy on the ward, and when the almoner descended the stairs to the right of the stage, at just after half past ten, she looked like a woman who'd just received a pardon at the foot of the gallows.

Sporadic, whispered conversations broke out across the floor as Alice took her seat, falling into a revering silence as Alexander Hargreaves, smartly dressed in a white shirt, colourful cravat and dark, waist-coated suit complete with a flower in the buttonhole, took to the stage. The philanthropist cleared his throat and surveyed his audience, then linked his hands behind his back. 'I wonder how many of us,' he enquired with melodious confidence, rolling back and forth on his heels, 'can claim to be true social reformers, rather than mere thoughtful observers.'

His eyes roved over those gathered in the manner of a priest delivering a sermon, and then he paused to allow his enquiry to sink in. After a few moments he began a slow walk across the stage, his hands still linked behind his back. He spoke about the stark inequalities on view in London day after day, the traders who blindly rode the trains into work while homeless children froze to death in the railway arches beneath them. 'The time has come,' he said stirringly, 'for each and every one of us to transform ourselves into people of action, and to stop wasting our time espousing useless, empty words.' He stopped pacing and turned to face his audience, whose zeal was beginning to mirror his own in intensity. 'Let us reject those who dismiss the poverty of the masses as inevitable,' he intoned, his arm outstretched towards them, his palm turned upwards to the ceiling. He made a claw with his hand and then clamped his long fingers into a fist. 'Let us work together to bring an end to the misery of destitution. The success of our joint efforts, my friends, need know no bounds.'

He dipped his head modestly as the audience erupted into spontaneous applause.

The fundraiser was stopped by a number of delegates as the audience spilled from the foyer into the grounds later that afternoon, each of them keen to make the acquaintance of the most impressive speaker of the day. Skilled in steering any interaction towards furthering his cause, he managed to convert three vague enquiries into his work into hard donations before he and Alice had finished their stroll through the formal gardens.

'Impressive,' Alice said as they sat side by side on a stone bench. She tilted her head towards the sun and closed her eyes momentarily. The skies over England on the tenth day of the month were bright and clear, with seven to eight hours of sunshine being reported in the south.

Alexander cradled his hands in his lap and looked at her. 'What is?'

She opened her eyes and turned to him. 'The way you get people to bend to your will. It is quite something.'

Alexander pursed his lips and smiled. 'I suppose I can be rather inspired, when I'm passionate about something. And I do usually end up getting what I want.' His eyes lingered on her and then he said: 'But I'm nowhere near where I need to be yet.' As they explored the woodlands, he told Alice about his drive to raise enough funds to build a new convalescence home in Eastbourne as well as increasing provision for inpatient care at the Royal Free.

By dusk the temperatures had cooled significantly, the wind gaining in strength and driving all but the heartiest delegates back into the house. After a formal dinner, Alice retired to the drawing room, where a log fire was raging. Alexander joined her half an hour later, at almost 9 p.m., after extracting himself from a heated conversation about the recently established Free State in Ireland. 'You appear to have carved yourself a rather decent hideout over here, Miss Hudson.'

The almoner lowered the novel she was reading to her lap and grinned up at him. 'Haven't I just? But please, feel free to join me.'

Alexander sat himself in one of the high-backed armchairs opposite her. 'I shan't mind if you object to my inflicting my company on you again. I'm afraid I have rather dominated you this weekend.'

The almoner shook her head. 'Not at all. Some men are not equipped to share a conversation with a woman unless it involves either a threat or an innuendo. It's nice to be taken seriously for a change.'

Alexander interlinked his fingers and cradled his knee within the arch, lifting it into the air without taking his eyes from hers. 'Can I be so bold as to ask how a woman as handsome as yourself has managed to escape matrimony for so long?'

The almoner's cheeks coloured. 'I am married to my work,' she said quickly, and then added: 'And I suppose I have never met a man who interests me enough to sacrifice it. I think that is good enough reason to remain single. After all, a woman should be able to function quite sufficiently without a man propping her up, should she not?'

'Quite. Ab-so-lute-ly. Well, it pays to be discerning. But you must have had plenty that have expressed an interest?'

'I generally have little time to ponder on it.' She dropped her eyes to her lap, where her gloved hands were resting on her book.

Alexander cleared his throat. 'Listen, I'm not one to take an interest in rumours, but there has been talk' – Alice looked up sharply – 'of associations and the like …'

'I prefer to mind my own affairs than to pay attention to idle gossip,' Alice interrupted, picking at a grey woollen bobble on her skirt.

Alexander tilted his head. 'So a certain medical man has expressed no formal interest in you?'

She looked up, eyes wide, the two bright red spots colouring her cheeks darkening: 'If you're talking about Dr Harland, I think I mentioned before that he has done nothing but obstruct my every effort since I arrived in the post. I have no idea why, though I suspect it may have something to do with the fact that I am on to him.'

'You're referring to his practising privately?'

Alice nodded. 'He has every right to run a private practice, but not on the Royal Free's time. Anyway, that is not the half of it, believe me. He –' She stopped abruptly and then clapped her hands down on her book. 'Never mind.'

Alexander stroked the sleeve of his shirt and kept his eyes on her. 'Perhaps you should consider alerting the British Medical Association, if you're serious about your concerns.'

The almoner pursed her lips. 'It may come to that,' she said, without quite meeting his gaze. She shook her head.

'What is it?'

Her eyes fell to the book on her lap. 'I don't know what else I can say except … It is complicated.'

Alexander gave her a considering look. 'I'd be careful, Alice. Maintain a healthy distance from the man, if at all possible.'

The almoner looked up sharply. 'I have several patients under his care. A certain degree of interaction is unavoidable.'

'Well, if that's the case, what is it that they say? If you're supping with the devil, use a long spoon.'

The almoner stared at him for a long moment and then said: 'Why do you say that? I thought you knew little of him?'

Alexander raised a brow and rubbed his thumb slowly over his fingers. 'Let's just say that I don't much care for the man. I've come to realise that he lacks the social etiquette you might expect from someone in his position.'

'What do you mean?'

There was a small pause and then Alexander said: 'Well, when I spoke to him a few days ago he was extremely abrupt. Of course, that could be something to do with the fact that I was demonstrating outside that new clinic in north London at the time, just as he was leaving.'

Alice frowned. 'Marie Stopes' clinic? The family-planning centre?'

Alexander nodded. 'I have grave concerns about the abominable processes going on in that place as it is,' he said, his mouth twisted in distaste. 'But what piques me most is Stopes' insistence on inflicting her evil onto the poor. It is an idea that I find particularly objectionable.'

'The clinic's advice is proving extremely popular for some of our patients. We've had some of them in tears because they haven't managed to be seen. The queues have been known to reach a mile long on occasion.'

Alexander snorted. 'They are pawns, with absolutely no idea that they are complicit in engineering their own downfall.' The fundraiser leaned forward in his chair. 'Stopes actually believes that the perfection of the human race can be achieved by the use of those vile contraptions she doles out. She thinks that if only mankind could rid itself of those lacking in moral or intellectual fibre, we could move onwards to a golden age. But who are any of us to judge who should be sterilised and who should not? It is outrageous.'

Alice tilted her head. 'There are plenty of intellectuals who subscribe to the idea of eugenics. They see it as the only way to reverse mankind's regression to the savagery of distant ancestors. Even one of the Royal Free's own gynaecologists holds the view that better specimens could be produced, though she fears those most in need of contraception would be too stupid to use it.'

Alexander sagged back in his chair and stared at her. 'Don't tell me you share an enthusiasm for some of these views?'

'Of course not. I absolutely resent the promotion of the idea that somehow the world would be a better place if only the

213

poor were wiped from it. I'm simply saying that I believe there is some good in what they are trying to achieve. Some of our patients are so overburdened. I saw a mother recently who had given birth to ten children, and only two had survived. The poor woman had lost all of her teeth and was half-starved, and yet she was pregnant again, expecting her eleventh. Were it not for the Samaritan Fund covering the cost of dentures, I do believe she would have withered away with the infant inside her. I can see the sense in relieving someone like that from the relentless cycle they're stuck in.'

Alexander pulled a face. 'Nature has a way of resolving these things without having to resort to un-Godly methods.'

There was a pause, and then the almoner said: 'What was the doctor doing there? At the clinic? Was he working?'

After making it clear that he was disinclined to stoop so low as to gossip, Alexander told Alice that he had heard rumours that Dr Harland was a keen believer in eugenics himself. 'I felt morally bound to share my objections with him. I told him in no uncertain terms that I found his engagement with the clinic thoroughly distasteful, only to receive a steam of vitriol for my pains.'

'Well, a man with such radical views does not belong at the Royal Free!' Alice cried.

Alexander nodded. 'I told him he would do well to hold his tongue, and that was it – he went off like a rocket. Such a dis-agreeable fellow. It was quite the spectacle.'

The almoner huffed out some air. 'The poor are blamed for everything that is wrong with this country as it is. Well, the poor and the refugees! The very least they deserve is someone sympathetic to look after them when they are ill. I mean, if the doctor believes in eliminating people just because they're destitute, what other dreadful practices might he be involved in?'

Alexander raised an immaculately groomed eyebrow. 'Well, quite.'

CHAPTER EIGHTEEN

'The habit of begging naturally leads to the exaggeration of facts; often true and pitiable, which become the beggar's stock-in-trade. The habit of responding to begging letters leads to the encouragement of lying. The fault is with both beggar and giver ... the donor gives as a quittance a contribution; which is probably spent ... turned to evil uses. The one lacks charity and gives money; the other learns the lesson of begging ... [Donors should] support only useful and well-regulated charitable institutions ... Many so called charities exist by begging of strangers ... One worthy of mention is the Volunteer Fire Brigades, which appear[ed] in the dress of firemen [but were] quite useless for extinguishing fires.

(C. S. Loch, *How to Help Cases of Distress*, 1895)

The conference concluded at 3 p.m. on Sunday, 12 February with a rousing speech from Alexander Hargreaves. The philanthropist then bade farewell to his colleagues and set off for the Glasgow Royal Infirmary, where he was to meet with a society of Scottish fundraisers. Alice, Bess Campbell and Frank took a

West Anglia line train back to London and disembarked at Liverpool Street Station at a quarter to five, plumes of steam billowing around their ankles.

The Royal Free Hospital must have been a welcoming sight in the dusk, the light from its many windows bestowing the pavements of Gray's Inn Road with a silver glow. Like the medical staff resting in their rooms along the dark passageway of the nurses' home, Alice sank into bed exhausted that evening, and woke to a misty dawn.

The faint click of Winnie's typewriter keys was a familiar sound to the almoners as they descended the stairs to the basement. The typist got to her feet with a groan when Alice came into the office the following Monday. 'Welcome back, dear,' she said, dumping a thick pile of post unceremoniously into the almoner's outstretched hands.

Alice sighed, perhaps in anticipation of the unpleasant task before her. Begging letters were regularly received by the almoners. Sifting through the post each morning and identifying those deserving of further investigation was a duty that usually fell to a junior almoner like Alice.

A number of sighs could be heard above the whistle of the boiler as Alice scanned the letters and then dropped several into the waste paper bin. When she was almost two-thirds through the pile, however, she stilled, one of the letters still gripped in her hand. She ran her eyes over the type several times, and then sprang to her feet.

Without a word she left the basement and hurried to the chest clinic, almost colliding with Jimmy when she reached the top of the stairs on the first floor. On sight of her, Jimmy dropped the luggage he was holding and pulled her into a bear hug, lifting her feet from the ground.

'Jimmy!' she said with a laugh, straightening her hat and smoothing her clothes when he'd released her.

He grinned. 'You're a tough woman, Miss, but you brought out my better nature, so you did. I feel so light on my feet with all the goodness in my heart, I think I could probably float home. All I need to decide now is which woman to bestow myself on first.'

Alice rolled her eyes and shook her head at him. 'You are incorrigible, Jimmy Rose.'

Head nurse Nell Smith was in the process of shifting a pile of files from her high reception desk to the floor when Alice walked into the department, her thin arms quivering with the effort. 'If you've finally turned up to claim that cup of tea, your timing's dreadful,' the nurse huffed. 'I have six bed baths and a chest drain to organise, and two of my nurses have just come down with diarrhoea.'

Alice grimaced. 'No, I would like to see Dr Harland, if he is here?'

At that moment, Dr Harland emerged from his office. 'Miss Hudson, a word.'

If Alice had intended to conceal any dislike she might have harboured towards him after the revelations from Alexander, she most certainly failed. At the sound of his voice, her expression hardened. She gave Nell Smith a look before turning and walking towards him, her gaze fixed somewhere to the right of where he stood.

'I spoke to my colleague this morning, the one treating that patient of yours,' the doctor said brusquely as she came to a stop in front of him. The emphasis on the pronoun was heavy with the suggestion that her presence in the hospital was of continuing inconvenience to him. 'He's come to the unfortunate conclusion that nothing more can be done for her, and since you're so heavily involved with the family, we thought it best that you should be the one to break the news.'

Alice's features crumpled. She had been to visit Hetty at home after her recent mastectomy, and, though in considerable discomfort, she had appeared to be making good progress. The news that her daughter and grandchildren had been boarded out in a cottage home in Harrow through the Waifs and Strays Society had cheered her, especially when Alice told her that the Samaritan Fund had covered the cost of purchasing a wringing machine, so that Tilda could provide for herself by taking in laundry, when she finally came to moving into a place of her own. 'But –' the almoner began.

'The cancer has spread,' Peter Harland cut in sharply. 'Nothing more can be done.'

'I see,' Alice said, nibbling on her lower lip. 'I shall go and see the Woods this afternoon.' The almoner glanced over her shoulder towards reception, where Nell had abandoned all pretence of tidying the files and was watching the pair with undisguised intrigue. When Alice turned back she dipped her head towards the closed door of the doctor's office and said under her breath: 'May I have a word with you? In private.'

The doctor closed his eyes briefly then looked up at the ceiling, nostrils flaring. 'My colleague is a highly skilled physician, Miss Hudson. If he says there's nothing more to be done, it means that he's tried everything he can.'

'It's not about Mrs Woods,' Alice said through gritted teeth, her eyes flicking to Nell and quickly back again. She gave him a meaningful look. 'It's another matter.'

The doctor's expression clouded over. 'I don't have time to –'

'If we could just step inside your office,' Alice interrupted. The doctor shook his head. 'I really need to speak to you privately,' the almoner hissed, and then added: 'about Charlotte.' She tried to sidestep him but he shifted his weight and folded his arms.

'I'm not having you in there.'

Alice glared at him. 'Why ever not?!'

'Because it's the only space in the entire hospital that's free from your woman-ism and I intend to keep it that way.'

She stared at him in disbelief. 'As you wish,' she said scornfully, with another quick glance towards Nell. The nurse had turned away and was in the process of delivering a severe dressing down to a young, tearful nurse whose apron had come adrift. 'I have just received written confirmation of a placement for Charlotte, one where her baby will also be welcome, and so it is imperative for us to register the birth as a matter of urgency. Daisy is six weeks old today.' She paused and withdrew the letter she'd just received from the pocket of her skirt. With no sign of any change in the doctor's expression, Alice continued: 'It is excellent news, is it not?'

Dr Harland looked at her. 'I don't believe the young woman is in any fit state to live freely in the community, Miss Hudson. Now, if that's all?' He made a move to retreat back into his office, but Alice went after him.

'No, that is not all at all.' When he turned back she asked: 'How would you have any idea of the state Charlotte is in?'

The doctor sighed. 'I'm basing my assumption on her condition when we last saw her. The girl can't be allowed to wander at large, for heaven's sake. She needs specialist help.'

'I believe with some support she is perfectly capable of living in the community. If you would come with me to Banstead and see her for yourself, unless of course ... you have already done so.'

The doctor glared at her. 'Why is it you're so determined to pull me into other areas of expertise?! First, gynaecology, now psychiatry! I'm in no position to override the opinions of the doctors at Banstead Asylum –'

'It is not an asylum!' Alice cut in again. 'It is a hospital! And come on, you must hold some sway?'

He shook his head. 'None whatsoever. And anyway,' he mumbled, glancing away, 'the infant is progressing satisfactorily where she is. It's best for everyone if we stick to the status quo.'

Alice's jaw dropped in disbelief. 'You can't possibly mean that?! You want to leave Charlotte's child with your sister? Permanently?!'

'She's better off where she is. Being dragged around the slums of London by an unstable youth isn't going to improve her life chances, is it?'

'You cannot do that! Elizabeth is nearing middle age already; I cannot imagine her dealing with the rigours of a toddler, let alone a teenager.'

'My sister is in perfectly good health as it happens.'

'But what about when Daisy is of an age to play? She won't be allowed to move in that museum of a house, just in case she breaks something, or gets a mark on the precious furniture. And I can hardly imagine Elizabeth kneeling on the floor to play – the woman dresses in full-length gowns and pearls to take tea alone. It is a most unsuitable placement for a child long term; most unsuitable.'

The doctor gave her a sardonic smile. 'I'll be sure to pass onto my sister your good thoughts and best wishes.'

The almoner stared at him. 'I press on you most ardently to reconsider. How can it be fair for the poor girl to mourn a part of herself that still lives?'

'This is not any of your concern. The girl has warmth, shelter and food, and so does her child. Leave things as they are, for pity's sake!'

Alice continued to stare at him, and then her eyes narrowed. 'Why would a man with convictions such as yours be so keen for a low-born child to reside within his own family?'

The doctor's shoulders tensed. Alice continued to stare at him, and then she began to nod slowly. 'So it was you, wasn't it?'

'What madness are you talking about now?'

'The note. I suspected as much, but now I know. You sent it. You were trying to frighten me off.'

'You have finally taken leave of your senses, woman,' he said, turning away.

'It won't work, doctor!' Alice called after him. 'The harder you push, the deeper I will delve.'

CHAPTER NINETEEN

It can be truly said that [an almoner] is as necessary to the real efficiency of the hospital as the supply of good drugs.

(The Almoners' Council Report, 1910–11)

Almoners like Alice spent much of their time among people who lived in the most difficult of circumstances. 'My world is naturally centred in small streets; the huge tenements and the sordid houses,' the St Thomas's Hospital almoner, Cherry Morris, was to report in 1936. 'I wish I could take you to one of our centres … an old public house at the corner of two streets, one inhabited mainly by very low class people (near Waterloo station) and the other a street of small cottages that ought not to exist in civilised society. There is a large London County Council school near, and the noise of the children, barrel organs [and] street brawls lasting into the night is appalling … a district odour of fried fish pervades.'

In 1895, C. S. Loch suggested to almoners that applications for relief could be categorised into three distinct classes: 'thrifty and careful men' to whom relief should always be given; 'men of different grades of respectability, with a decent home' whom,

Loch suggested, should be judged on a case-by-case basis; and, finally, 'the idle, loafing class, or those brought low by drink or vice', for whom relief would only 'maintain them in their evil habits'.

Attitudes had begun to soften with the arrival of the new century, but the almoners still clung to the fundamental principle that every man was ultimately responsible for his own welfare, and that charity should only be given to those willing to stand on their own feet at the earliest opportunity.

Ted and Hetty Woods' lodgings lay close to the Royal Victoria Dock, the decrepit three-storey building sandwiched between a coal merchant's and an abandoned soap factory. It was close to two o'clock when Alice went through the scarred outer door, the distant toot of a ship's horn a reminder of the goods and trade passing over the waters of the Thames.

There was mould on the walls of the Woods' apartment block, and an overpowering stench of ammonia in the air, overlaid with a faint sooty tang. Two doors led off the hall to the right, the staircase on the left leading to the first floor.

Alice stepped over a small pile of rubble that had been neatly swept to one side and knocked on the wooden door at the end of the hall. Ted answered, his eyes cloudy. After a moment they cleared and he gave her a bright smile of recognition. 'It's Miss Alice, love,' he said over his shoulder, then shuffled back and gestured the almoner in.

The room was small and damp, the air dusty with soot and smoke. There was rush matting on the floor and a table and two chairs against the far wall. There were several broken panes in the window above the table, the holes plugged up with balls of newspaper. Hetty was sitting in the middle of a worn sofa on the left-hand side of the room, her feet resting on a brick that had likely been warmed in the nearby hearth. There was a bed covered with a lumpy mattress and threadbare sheet against the opposite wall. A battered but freshly polished chest of drawers stood next to it, a small pile of neatly folded clothes on top.

Hetty tried to get up when Alice came in. She shuffled to the edge of the sofa, her pale face creasing with the effort. The almoner waved her back. 'Don't get up on my account, Hetty,' she said, removing her cape and crossing the small space.

Hetty leaned back with a chesty wheeze and patted the cushion next to her. 'Can I get you a drink, Miss Alice?' Ted asked as the almoner sat beside his wife. The stench of rotting skin no longer hung over Hetty, but there was a faint clinical smell in the air muffled with rose water.

'Oh no, Ted, thank you. I have come with news, as a matter of fact,' she added, in response to their curious glances.

'Is it Tilda?' Hetty asked, smiling. 'We went to see her the other day. Beautiful that place is, absolutely beautiful. She's doing ever so well. We don't know how to thank you, duck.'

'That's wonderful to hear.' Alice said warmly, then her gaze dropped to her lap. When she looked up again, she rolled her lips in on themselves and reached for Hetty's hand. She glanced at Ted before she spoke, who seemed to have sensed the gravity of the impending conversation. Forehead crumpled, he shuffled forwards and sat silently on his wife's other side. 'I don't have any further news about Tilda, Hetty,' Alice said, 'but I do have some news from your doctor.'

A shadow passed across Hetty's face. She glanced briefly at her husband then took a deep breath and focussed her eyes back on Alice. 'Bad then, is it, duck?' she asked, though there remained a hopeful glint in her eyes.

There was a short pause, and then Alice said softly: 'Yes. I am afraid so, yes.'

'But there's still stuff they can do, I expect, Miss,' Ted offered. 'Those doctors work wonders these days, don't they? Marvellous they were with Hetty when she was in for her operation. Absolutely marvellous, weren't they, love?'

Hetty nodded, her lower lip beginning to tremble. 'They were, duck, absolutely marvellous.'

Perhaps moved by the hope in their voices, Alice began to answer but then faltered. She cleared her throat, and then said: 'We can manage your pain, Hetty, but nothing more can be done to treat the disease. I'm very sorry.'

The couple stared at her in silence. After a few seconds Hetty's right hand found Ted's left, and then she closed her eyes. Her husband reached around with his free hand and touched her cheek with the pad of an arthritic thumb. A moment later, they leaned into one another, foreheads touching. Alice stood up and crossed the room; a deliberate kindness. After a few minutes, when they'd pulled apart, she returned. 'There is plenty we can do to make things a bit easier for you both,' she said, adopting a business-like tone. She knelt on the rush matting in front of them and produced a notepad from her bag.

'Firstly, I shall apply for a crisis loan on your behalf. That way we can improve things around here and make them a bit more comfortable for you.'

Hetty pulled a hanky from her sleeve, patted her face with it and gave Alice a grateful look, but Ted shook his head. 'We'll not rely on charity, Miss Alice. I know you mean well, but we'll manage on our own the same as we always have, thanks very much.'

Like many of their neighbours, Ted and Hetty's finances were delicately balanced. It was a time when the majority of wage earners lived hand-to-mouth, so that even a short period of ill health could have a huge impact on family life, perhaps even tipping them over the edge into destitution.

The almoners had no reluctance in helping a couple like Ted and Hetty, who had worked hard throughout their lives. The only barrier to help came, perhaps, from their own sense of pride.

Alice looked between them and then settled her gaze on Ted. 'It is not charity so much as one group of people helping another. Would you not do the same for your neighbours? For your friends?' Hetty turned to her husband, but Ted kept his eyes fixed stubbornly ahead at a point above Alice's shoulder, his expression set. The almoner reached for his knobbly hand and grasped it. 'The way I see it, it is your turn now. Let us wrap our arms around you in your time of need, Mr Woods.'

Hetty squeezed his other hand. When he finally turned to her, she gave him a beseeching look. His shoulders sagged. 'Alright, Miss,' he said with a conceding nod. 'If it'll help make Hetty more comfortable, we'll accept.'

Alice nodded briskly and scribbled something in her note-book. It wasn't unusual for the almoners to make enquiries in the community in search of a neighbour who might, for a few shillings, act as a temporary home help. When Alice looked back at the couple she asked: 'Would you like me to tell Tilda the news?'

'Not yet, duck,' Hetty said quickly. 'She's just sorting herself out. Let her make the most of a little bit of happiness first. We'll give her as long as we can.'

It was almost five by the clock on the wall of the basement when Alice arrived back in the office. After only the briefest of glances in the almoner's direction, Winnie hurried over to the boiler and rustled up two cups of strong, sweet tea. She listened in silence as Alice relayed the afternoon's events, then took the almoner by surprise with a disclosure of her own: the loss of her son just a few months into the war. 'I know my melancholy humours can be burdensome, dear, but it's difficult to force cheer sometimes when the memory of it is still so raw.'

'And you shouldn't have to, Winnie,' Alice said with feeling. 'You shouldn't have to.' She grasped Winnie's hand. 'I'm so sorry. For the way I've been and – I shouldn't be burdening you with all of this.'

'Oh no, please don't apologise,' Winnie said, clamping her other hand over Alice's own. 'When I hear about someone else's struggles, suddenly there's a reason for hope, a purpose to the day. It takes me out of myself, if you know what I mean?'

Alice looked at her and nodded.

The typist smiled sadly, but her expression changed suddenly at the sound of a creak on the stairs on the other side of the door. There was a pause, and then she leaned close to Alice and said: 'I must speak with you about another matter.'

'What is it?'

Winnie's eyes skittered to the door. She waited, head cocked, and then turned her attention back to Alice. 'It's Frank.' She took a breath. 'Something's not right. Sometimes –' She stopped abruptly at the sound of a loud clatter, the metal clamp of Alexander's mouse trap slamming down on the small body of a rodent.

Alice winced, her shoulders tensing. When she looked back at Winnie, the typist was staring at her intently. 'Sometimes I wonder whether he's a man to be trusted, Alice.'

'Frank? Why would you say that?'

Winnie leaned forward conspiratorially. 'Well, you know Eileen Cook from the book club?' Alice shook her head. 'Yes, you do. She helped out last week at the zoo. White hair. Pencilled-in eyebrows sharp enough to kill?'

Alice shook her head again. Winnie flapped her hand. 'No matter. Anyway, her husband knows several board members on the COS, and one of them told him, in confidence, mind, that Frank was offered a position on the board on the strength of his experience as a man of business, and yet it's becoming obvious to all of them that he hasn't a clue about business, or their work.'

Alice's lips twisted, as if unconvinced. 'And I didn't like to say anything about it before now,' Winnie continued, 'but a week or so ago, I caught him rummaging through your desk.'

The almoner's gaze sharpened. 'Frank was looking through my things?'

Winnie nodded. 'I asked if there was anything I could help him with and he glossed over it with one of his silly jokes. Make of it what you will, but, personally, I'm not sure I trust the man. As I said, dear, there's something not quite right.'

CHAPTER TWENTY

Patients admitted for care, treatment and isolation included upper class domestics and members of the women's services who were well aware they had fallen short of their own standards, [as well as] young girls ... highly painted and verminous ... almost totally ignorant of discipline, morals and the amenities of civilized life.

(The Royal Free Annual Report of 1921–22)

Alice spent the rest of the week working on tasks passed to her by the Head Almoner, Bess Campbell. On Tuesday, 14 February she trawled the red-light haunts of Whitechapel searching for two working girls who had failed to turn up for their follow-up appointments at the VD clinic.

The Great War had left many young people with the conviction that life was short, and when opportunities to make a living presented themselves they were seized upon whenever possible. Fearing that reckless abandon, friskiness and licentious behaviour was reaching epidemic proportions, the Committee on Unmarried Mothers chaired by the Archbishop of York in 1915 appointed 'a skilled lady investigator', likely an almoner, with hopes of establishing whether the situation was quite as wild and loose as feared.

The investigator, along with a league of 'women's patrols', travelled around the country and questioned locals on their intimate habits; no doubt one of the more awkward tasks she had carried out in the course of her career. After gathering information from sixty-two towns, she concluded that the rumours were unfounded. It's difficult to know whether her interviewees were really that chaste, or simply wary of confiding what they got up to on a Saturday night to a stranger, but her findings flew in the face of statistics published in a report by the Royal Commission on Venereal Diseases in 1916, which stated that 10 per cent of the male population had syphilis and many more suffered with gonorrhoea.

'In the female venereal disease department, though many patients still slip away before discharge,' observed the *British Medical Journal* in 1923, 'the almoner carries on educative activities, consoles and sympathises with innocently infected married women when they realise the truth as to the cause of their sufferings, and finds homes or occupations for some of the girls ... The girls who have been especially difficult to deal with have nearly all been found to be mentally defective.'

The almoners and officers from the Salvation Army were often the ones who stepped in to pick up the pieces when the girls came a cropper after plying their trade on London streets.

The girls protested loudly when Alice located them. Alice managed to persuade them to accompany her back to the Royal Free VD department with the mixture of humour and firmness that had confirmed her appointment as almoner a year earlier.

The next two days were swallowed up with the almoners' publicity campaign to encourage more educated women to join their ranks. Alice travelled up to Leeds to speak to prospective applicants, while almoners from St Thomas's Hospital reached out to locals in Liverpool, Newcastle and Glasgow.

Leeds General Infirmary had only recently become the first hospital to provide training for almoners outside of London. Authorised by the Institute of Almoners in 1919, the facility opened up opportunities for candidates who had previously been unable to put themselves forward because they couldn't stretch to the expense that a visit to London would incur.

It wasn't until the early part of the following week, on Tuesday, 21 February, that Alice managed to find time in her schedule to visit the chest clinic again. The clock on the wall above reception displayed the time as 4 p.m., and with the nurses in their daily handover meeting, the almoner walked straight to Dr Harland's office and rapped firmly on the door. There was no answer from within, so after another token tap she let herself in.

The room was small, the desk positioned in front of the window taking up almost the entire width of the space. Shelves ran the length of the wall on the left-hand side of the room. Thick textbooks, some in Latin, filled the shelves from eye level and below, the ones above lined with glass jars and vials of differing sizes, each sealed with a stopper of cork.

Alice closed the door behind her and moved towards the shelves. Chin tilted upwards, her gaze ran over the various liniments and potions, stopping every now and then to examine the elaborate black script on each label. A number of the jars contained pickled organs, the body parts having been removed for examination during post-mortem examinations.

About halfway along the row, Alice stopped dead, her eyes widening. The jar directly above her was filled with formaldehyde, a cream-coloured mass suspended in the pale amber liquid. Alice reached up, gave the jar a quarter turn and then whipped her hands away in shock. A small, perfectly formed foetus was floating weightlessly inside the container, the tiny fingers of one hand and lifeless rosebud lips pressed up against the glass. Alice stared in silence for half a minute then slowly raised a hand again. As her fingertips made contact with the glass, the door swung open behind her.

She spun around, the colour draining from her cheeks. Dr Harland stood in the doorway, his face clouding with anger. 'What are you doing in my office?!'

The almoner opened her mouth but quickly closed it again. After a pause she said: 'There's no need to overreact. As I said before, I need to have a private word with you.'

'And I told you, this is a woman-free zone! There's nothing for you in here.'

Recovering, Alice pulled on the cuffs of her blouse and squared her shoulders. 'Someone is blackmailing me and I intend to find out why. I also intend to find out exactly what your connection is to Charlotte Redbourne, and why you are refusing to do your legal duty to register her daughter's birth.'

The doctor walked into the room and slammed the door behind him. 'There's always some drama with you, isn't there?' he said, moving slowly towards her. 'There always has to be something.'

Alice glared at him then snatched a note from her pocket and waved it in front of his face. 'Look!' she snapped. 'It says "I KNOW WHAT YOU DID".'

He stopped a couple of feet away from her. 'So what has that got to do with me?'

'It's obvious! It means what *we* did. The concealment of Daisy's birth. What else would it be?'

The doctor gave her a look of contempt. 'I have absolutely no idea, but with the way you carry on, it could be any number of things.'

'I beg your pardon?'

'Look, is there a single person in this place you haven't upset? I mean, come on, I'm imagining all manner of catastrophes. You've likely infuriated enough people to fill the beds in these wards three times over since your appointment, Miss Hudson. Now, if you'll get back to what you're supposed to be doing, I need you to –'

'I will not leave this office until you agree to tell me the truth.'

Dr Harland cupped his hand over his forehead. 'For pity's sake, woman, will you let it drop?! We have critically ill patients that need our care, and one in particular that you'll –'

Alice moved towards him. 'Why are you so keen to have me abandon my investigation?'

The doctor gave an abrupt, humourless laugh. 'Would you listen to yourself?!' he said, striding back to the door and wrenching it open. Alice followed him into the corridor, and he spun around to face her. 'Can you not get it into your head that you're a clerk?! Nothing more. All of this asking around and questioning people is ridiculous! Dangerous even!'

'Oh, dangerous is it? Is that a threat, doctor?'

'For pity's sake!' The doctor jabbed at the air menacingly. 'You're getting yourself involved in things that are way outside the remit of your job and you know it. Now, for the love of God, woman, will you please keep yourself out of it?'

'So what would you have me do? Stay in my office writing prettily on little pieces of paper and then filing them away? That is all you think a woman is good for, is it not?' The almoner paused for a beat and then gave him a cold assessing look. 'How do you know that I have been asking around any-way?' she said slowly.

'What?'

'I said, how could you possibly know that I have been ques-tioning people? Have you been following me again?'

The doctor threw his hands up in the air and then rubbed angrily at his forehead. After a moment his hands dropped to his sides. 'Alright,' he said, beckoning at the air with his fingers. 'Let's hear it. What exactly is it I'm supposed to have done?'

'You are an active promoter of eugenics for a start,' Alice said, as he folded his arms. 'That makes you an almighty hypocrite.

You claim allegiance to an organisation that prides itself on helping the most vulnerable in society, and yet you believe that anyone less than perfect should be obliterated from all existence!'

He narrowed his eyes. 'Who told you that?'

'Never mind who told me. You should not be practising here if you –'

'Even if that were true,' he cut in, 'who are you to judge a man for his political ideas? If a belief in eugenics were to bar a man from practising medicine, you'd have to expel most of the doctors here!' He unfolded his arms and beckoned at the air again. 'So, come on then, what else do you have on me?'

Alice faltered for a moment, but then she levelled her gaze again. 'I know that there's an association between you and Charlotte Redbourne. And possibly even Molly Rainham as well.'

The doctor, who had been blowing out some air, stopped. Alice stared at him. 'Well?'

He rolled his eyes, but a pulse throbbed in his temple. 'Will you just leave be what doesn't concern you?!'

'But Charlotte's welfare does concern me and, somehow or other, I'm going to find out what your involvement was.'

The doctor let out a loud groan 'There you go again! You just can't help yourself, can you?' He leaned closer and said through gritted teeth: 'Stop meddling in other people's lives!'

'Will you please stop shouting at me?! You are one of the most ungentlemanly men I have ever had the misfortune to meet, and with the people I come across day to day in the community, that is really saying something!'

He gave her a long look. 'A gentleman is only a gentleman if a lady remembers to be a lady.' Alice glared back at him, her cheeks growing increasingly puce. 'And while you're working yourself up into a frenzy, perhaps I should take advantage of the moment of blessed silence to relay some news. Hetty Woods has just been admitted to the ward with pneumonia.'

'What?'

'Just what I say. While you've been gallivanting around playing Mrs Hercule Poirot, an elderly woman has fallen critically ill. I thought perhaps, if you have the time between your investigations that is, you might be good enough to relay the news to her daughter.'

Alice arranged for a telegram to be sent to the cottage in Harrow, and Tilda arrived at the hospital less than two hours after receiving the news. It was just before half past six. 'Is she on the gate?' she asked, as soon as she arrived at the almoners' office. She was still wearing her white apron, her housekeeping cap poking out of the pocket of her coat.

Alice steered her towards the stairs. 'Yes, I'm afraid so. Come, I'll walk you up to the ward.'

'On the gate' was a term that lingered on well into the twentieth century, its origin from the days when the names of all critically ill patients were displayed on the gates of the porter's lodge, to ensure that relatives were permitted a quick entry to the hospital, even outside of visiting hours. Casualty staff were also often referred to as 'the gate team'.

Sister Nell Smith got to her feet as soon as they appeared at the chest department reception. 'She's in a side room, my dear,' the nurse said gently, guiding the heavily pregnant woman across the corridor with a hand on her arm.

Tilda stopped outside the door to the room and turned tearfully to Alice. 'Will you come in with me, Miss Hudson?'

'Yes, yes, of course.' Alice slipped her arm around the trembling woman's shoulders and walked with her into the room. Nell followed close behind. Ted rose from a deep chair beside the bed as soon as he saw them, and held his arms out to Tilda. She ran to him and the pair fell into a tearful embrace. When they pulled apart, Ted swapped places with his daughter so that she could take the chair he had just vacated.

'Don't leave me, Mum,' Tilda sobbed miserably, taking hold of her unconscious mother's hand. She looked up at her father, tears streaming down her face. 'She can't go, Dad. There's so much I need to say! I need to tell her how very grateful I am to have her as my mum. I need to tell her how much I love her. I want to say sorry for the last few months. I never meant to –'

'She's not gone yet, pet,' Nell said, moving closer. 'You can tell her all you want to say. There's still time.'

As Tilda leaned close to her mother's grey face and murmured in choked sobs, Sister Smith returned to Alice's side. 'She told me when they brought her in that she's been seeing people standing at the foot of her bed over the last few days,' she told the almoner in hushed tones, 'so I think she knew what to expect.'

Having nursed soldiers through their final hours, Alice nodded sombrely. Deathbed visitations, the common and unexplained phenomenon of patients who were close to death reporting strikingly similar stories of people standing at the end of their bed, sometimes beckoning, sometimes watching silently, are reasoned away by modern medicine as a series of small strokes, or delusions as the result of strong pain-relieving medication. Known among nursing circles as the gathering of spirits, those caring for the dying were well used to hearing about the welcoming committees of long-dead relatives, who made an appearance in their final days to take their loved ones 'home'.

'We're here, Hetty,' Ted said gently, taking up a position on the opposite side of the bed. He gripped his wife's lifeless hand in his own. 'We're not leaving you, love.' Tilda looked over at him then rested her head in the crook of her mother's arm and sobbed.

It was then that Hetty, who had lapsed into a coma an hour earlier, made a croaky sound and opened her eyes. Tilda's head shot up. 'Mum?!' she cried, smiling through a round of fresh tears. Seemingly oblivious to her daughter, Hetty, in a moment of terminal lucidity, stared over Tilda's shoulder at a spot across the room. Perhaps tapping into the mysteriousness that's only present outside of the range of the fully conscious, her face lit up in a radiant smile.

'Someone has come for her,' Nell said to Alice out of the corner of her mouth. She leaned close to the almoner. 'It won't be long now.'

The unseeing haze over Hetty's eyes seemed to clear at the nurse's words. She blinked several times, and then her gaze settled on her daughter. 'Tilda,' she said, her voice bubbly from the liquid on her chest, but full of affection. There was a look of utter peace in her expression as she stroked her daughter's face. 'My Tilda.'

'Mum!' Tilda managed to gasp, tears rolling down her cheeks. She planted gentle kisses on her mother's forehead then cupped her face in her hands, grasping hold of the last opportunity to say goodbye. 'I'm so sorry, Mum. I love you so much.'

Ted watched quietly from the other side of the bed as his wife wiped away their daughter's tears, his own eyes red and glassy. After a few moments Hetty turned her head on the pillow and smiled through cracked lips. She lifted her hand to stroke Ted's damp face, then glanced around the room. 'Oh, hello, duck,' she said breathlessly, when she saw Alice. 'It's – so – good of you to come.'

Alice moved forward and patted Hetty's arm. 'Hello, dear Hetty,' she smiled, her own eyes moist. 'They are taking good care of you, I hope?'

Hetty nodded and gave her a listless smile. She closed her eyes then blinked, opening them again with effort.

Dr Harland entered the room at that moment. Ted immediately got to his feet and dipped his head respectfully. Alice and Nell took a step back, the almoner's expression hardening. Tilda scraped her chair away from the bed. 'Are you comfortable, Mrs Woods?' the doctor asked gently as he listened to the woman's chest.

'Yes, lovely – thank you, doctor,' she wheezed falteringly.

'How's the pain?'

'Oh, not too bad, thank you,' she whispered, her eyelids fluttering to a close again.

He touched her shoulder. 'I want to know the second it isn't, do you hear?' he said quietly. 'I'll stay close by.' She gave him a grateful nod, her eyes still closed. The doctor turned towards the door without a glance in Alice's direction, but Nell stopped him halfway across the space with a hand on his arm.

'You should get some rest,' she hissed. 'Your shift ended hours ago.'

'I don't need reminding of my working hours, thank you, Sister,' he snapped. Nell rolled her eyes and shook her head at him, but she gave him an affectionate pat on the back before he left. Alice gave the nurse a questioning glance.

'He'll not leave his patient,' she explained in a whisper. 'He might be a miserable sod, but there's a heart buried in there somewhere.'

Across the room, Hetty heaved a shuddering breath. Tilda turned, hair wild and dishevelled, and gave Nell a panicked, questioning glance. The nurse moved briskly to the bed, wrapped a cuff around Hetty's upper arm and measured her blood pressure. 'I'm afraid it's dropping quite rapidly,' she said softly, folding the sphygmomanometer back in its long silver box.

She and Alice backed into the shadows of the small room, waiting in silence as Tilda and Ted patted Hetty's hands and stroked the hair back from her face. As her mother's breathing slowed and the colour drained from her skin, Tilda climbed awkwardly onto the bed and lay as close to Hetty as her swollen belly would allow, nestling her face into Hetty's shoulder and clasping her arm.

'She's gone,' Sister Smith said, a few minutes later. She touched a gentle hand onto Tilda's shoulder and looked at Ted, whose bottom lip was trembling. 'I'm very sorry.'

It was just before 8 p.m. when Alice stepped into the corridor. A few feet away from the side room, she sank back against the wall and closed her eyes. She jerked upright a couple of seconds later at a noise across the corridor, pushing herself upright at the appearance of Dr Harland. 'She's gone,' she said evenly, though her features were drawn tight.

He gave a small nod.

'I've told the family they can stay with her as long as they wish. I'm going to fetch some money from the office so that they can take a. taxi home when they are ready. I don't want them wandering the streets bereft.'

The doctor took a long slow breath in. 'It's not for you to say who stays and who leaves, Miss Hudson,' he said, moving past her. 'If the room is needed, they will be moved into the corridor.'

She stared after him. 'You cannot hear a woman to make decisions without deference to a man, can you?' she called after him.

He stopped and half-turned, shaking his head. 'It's been a long day, Miss Hudson,' he said wearily. 'I'm going home.'

'You just don't care, do you? Your sister was right. You don't have a care for anyone.'

He strode towards her then, his chin set in a hard line. 'Can you not just stick to what you're supposed to be doing, instead of trying to take over wherever you go? You're a menace, woman!'

'How dare you!' the almoner said, her eyes burning. 'I seriously fear there is something wrong with you!'

His fists clenched at his side. 'I don't have the time right now to listen to any more of your melodramatic witterings or accusations! Just get out of my department.'

He spun around and strode off along the corridor but Alice hurried ahead of him and whirled around, blocking his way. 'You're not normal!' she shouted, the pins coming loose from her hair so that it fell down around her face. 'You have the empathy of a lizard!'

'And you have the devil's own temper!' he said in return, glowering. 'Now, please, get out of my way.'

She looked at him, then shook her head. 'I refuse to be a part of this any longer,' she hissed, but then her voice caught. She swallowed hard, tears welling in her eyes and spilling over onto her cheeks.

Dr Harland stared at her in alarm. He looked to and fro, then lifted a hand to rub the back of his neck. There was a pause, and then Alice patted her gloved hands to her cheeks and made a move to step around him. At that moment the doctor flung his arm out and seized her by the wrist. She looked up at him scornfully and tried to free herself, but within seconds she allowed herself to be pulled against him. His arms enclosed around her and then he lowered his chin to the top of her head.

'I'm alright,' she said, after a minute or so. She released herself with a hand to his chest, then stepped away, her cheeks damp and flushed.

'Get some sleep, Miss Hudson,' he said quietly.

Alice held his gaze for a moment, her eyes wary, then turned and walked hurriedly away.

CHAPTER TWENTY-ONE

Co-operation between the doctor and the social worker
is absolutely necessary if their common ideals – the raising
of the standard of public health and the extermination
of disease – are to be realised.

(Surgeon at the Annual Meeting of the
British Hospitals' Association, 1913)

The almoner passed under the flickering lamps of the main
reception area of the hospital a few minutes later, her staccato
steps echoing around the empty space. Lit only by the amber
light from the street lamps on ground level, the stairs leading to
the basement were shadowed and dim. Outside the heavy oak
door to the almoners' office, Alice stilled, head cocked to the
side, her hand resting on the handle. Half a second later she
burst into the room. The office lay empty, but the door to the
medical records store stood open, a light glimmering faintly
from inside.

Alice crossed the room and paused at the door. After a
moment she felt her way along the dark passage with a flattened hand on the domed wall, the only sound an occasional

plink as drops of moisture fell from the domed ceiling onto the cold stone floor below. A dark shadow loomed on the wall at the far end of the first aisle. Alice rounded the corner, then reared back in surprise. 'What are you doing here?' she demanded, when the figure turned to face her.

Frank tucked the file he was holding under one arm and took a long drag on his pipe. 'I might ask the same of you, Alice.'

'I have been with a patient,' she said, wrapping her cape around herself and folding her arms over the top. 'I came down to get some money for the relatives to ease their way home.'

Frank slipped the file onto a nearby shelf and gave her a half-smile. 'That's thoughtful of you, but you won't find any money in here.'

'Obviously not,' she said coldly. 'But I noticed the light.' Frank removed the pipe from his mouth and nodded, still regarding her with mild amusement. 'And what about you? What are you doing here?'

Claiming that he was under pressure to complete his report to the Charity Organisation Society, Frank told the almoner that he was putting in some extra hours, to try and get ahead of himself.

Alice swiftly refuted the claim and then added. 'You have no business being down here after hours anyway.'

Frank held his pipe between his teeth and struck a match on the wall. Cupping his hand around the flame, he relit the tobacco and took another long drag. He moved towards her and said: 'I understand why the good doctor gets so frustrated with you now. You really are a bulldog, aren't you?'

'The doctor?' Alice gave her head a small shake and blinked. 'You mean Dr Harland? The two of you have been discussing me?'

Frank's half-smile faded. He set his chin and gave her a steady look. 'Let's just say I know a thing or two about the pair of you.'

'Oh?'

He nodded. 'Enough to lose both of you your jobs, at the very least. Perhaps even more than that.'

Alice took a step backwards. 'I'm not scared, Frank,' she said, with a brief glance over her shoulder.

He gave a low, croaky chuckle. 'And nor should you be, my dear. At least,' he added, blowing out a lungful of smoke, 'not of me.'

Alice frowned. 'What is that supposed to mean?'

Frank withdrew his pocket watch and glanced at it, then cupped it in his hand and squeezed it. 'Listen, Alice, all you need to know is that there's a stink around here that needs airing, and that's exactly what I'm here to do.'

She ventured towards him again. 'What stink?'

'The details are not for the ears of a gentlewoman.'

'I am hardly faint-hearted, Frank. You should know that by now.'

'Look,' he said, slipping his watch back into the pocket of his waistcoat and taking the pipe from his mouth. He waved the stem at her. 'There's no need for you to involve yourself in any of this. Go back to your room, speak of this to no one, and I'll make sure I keep a lid on things my end.' He gave her a wink and tapped the side of his nose then turned away as if to conclude their conversation.

The almoner scoffed a laugh and spoke to his back. 'Why does every man in this hospital think he can tell me what to do? You're not the boss, Frank.' She stepped towards him, stopping when she was about a foot away. 'As far as I'm concerned, you are here to conduct an audit and to report back to the COS on the value of the almoners' work. That should not necessitate examining the private records of any of our patients.'

Frank turned back to her and sighed. 'You have no idea what you're getting yourself into, Alice.'

Her gaze sharpened. 'You may be right, but I think I'm getting close, Frank. And it's making certain people very nervous.'

There was a pause. He gave her a steady, considering look. 'So, what do you intend to do now?'

The almoner took another tiny step back. 'I'm going to call a meeting in the morning,' she said, her voice shaking slightly. 'I'm going to tell everyone about our conversation and see what they make of it.'

'If you do that, my dear, I'll make it known that you concealed the birth of a child and falsified your reports. You'll lose your job and so will your doctor.'

Alice stiffened. 'How do you know about that?'

Frank shrugged.

A beat passed, and then Alice said: 'He most certainly is not *my* doctor. And I wanted no part of any of this in the first place. It is time the truth came out.'

The almoner turned to leave, but Frank grasped her shoulders and spun her around. 'I can't let you do that, Alice.'

She tried to pull away, but his grip on her arm tightened. He pulled her back against him, clamping a hand over her mouth when she tried to shout out. 'Listen to me,' he whispered urgently in her ear. 'I will tell you why I'm here, but only if you agree to keep it to yourself. Do you hear me?'

Alice thrashed and struggled, but after a few seconds she gave in with a small nod of her head. Frank released her slowly then grabbed her upper arms and turned her around to face him. 'I'm a detective with the Metropolitan Police,' he said quietly, lowering his arms. 'I've been working undercover for a number of weeks on an investigation which is close to reaching its conclusion. It's vital that my cover is not compromised.'

Alice stared at him agog. 'How am I to believe that?'

Frank withdrew a warrant card from his jacket pocket and held it out to her. She stared at it for a few seconds then demanded: 'What investigation?'

He slipped the card back into his pocket. 'I'm afraid I can't tell you that.'

'Is it regarding an assault on a young girl?'

Frank looked at her with increased interest. 'Why would you ask that?'

Alice shared her suspicions about Dr Harland, revealing her conviction that there was a connection between him and Charlotte. She also told him about the times when Dr Harland went missing from duty and her concerns about some of the male visitors to Banstead Mental Hospital.

Frank chewed the end of his pipe and listened in thoughtful silence. Eventually he said: 'There's no law against one person choosing to accompany another on a drive.'

Alice stared at him, eyes blazing. 'But these are vulnerable patients we're talking about. Surely they lack the capacity to make that choice?'

Frank shook his head. 'Perhaps.'

'It's morally reprehensible, at least?'

The detective pursed his lips. 'Arguably.'

'And what about Dr Harland's connection to Charlotte? She received a visit from someone, a male by the name of Cyril Gardner. I believe that he and the doctor are one and the same. I suspect that he paid her a visit using a false name to silence her, in case she intended to reveal that he is the father of her child. If that is the case, not only has he abused his position of trust, but –'

Frank gave a low chuckle. 'You really are in the wrong job, Alice. If only the force would admit females as detectives, I'd take you on as my protégée.'

'So I am correct, then?'

'Not exactly. But I admire your tenacity. It's a quality that some in the force lack, and it's not something you can teach.' Alice continued to stare at him. 'It was me,' Frank explained eventually. 'I am Cyril Gardner.'

The almoner shook her head slowly. 'I don't understand.'

Frank admitted that it was he who had gone to visit Charlotte at the beginning of February, using Cyril Gardner as his cover name. In the course of his investigations, he said, he had questioned Elizabeth and met Charlotte's daughter, Daisy.

'How did you find out, about the baby?'

Frank grinned. 'I am a detective, my dear.'

'I still don't understand,' Alice said, looking up at him. 'Why would you have reason to question Elizabeth?'

Frank levelled his gaze. 'Alice, all I'm asking is that you give me your trust for a few more days. Go about your business as usual, and let no one suspect anything out of the ordinary. Will you please do that? It's of the utmost importance that the people closest to you have no idea of my true identity.'

Alice stared at Frank for a long moment, and then gave him a reluctant nod.

CHAPTER TWENTY-TWO

Inquests have been held on the bodies of several women in and out of Islington who died from the after effects of abortion. It is said that women come from all parts of London, and even from long distances in the country, to place themselves under the care of Islington abortionists ... such practices under the very noses of the police would be impossible if they did their duty.

(*Islington Gazette*, Monday, 24 June 1889)

Early the next day, on the morning of Wednesday, 22 February 1922, Alice left her room in the nurses' quarters of the Helena Building and made her way over to the main hospital. It was a little before 6 a.m., an hour from sunrise, and the air was sharp with cold.

As it had been last evening, the outpatients department lay silent but for the clatter of mop and bucket as the hospital's domestic staff, then known as 'scrubbers', prepared the space for the onslaught of a new day.

The stillness peculiar to early mornings met Alice as she opened the double doors and stepped into the chest department. Sister Nell Smith, working the night shift, was usually to be found at reception, but on this particular day she was absent from her desk, perhaps busy calming a distressed patient, or instructing the ward's scrubbers on the importance of cleanliness and hygiene. Like the almoners, the matrons employed by the Royal Free enjoyed a reputation for stoic fortitude, with an extraordinary ability to remain calm, whatever difficult circumstances were thrown at them.

Alice, who had signed two shillings over to a shaky Ted Woods and his daughter last night to cover the cost of a taxi fare home, waited for a moment at reception, then turned at a clicking sound as the main door to the department opened behind her.

A wheeled trolley clattered through the double doors, Sidney Mullins propelling it along from behind. The mortician's ruddy face brightened when he saw Alice. 'Morning, pet. Is Sister around?'

'Not at the moment, Sidney. Are you here for –'

'Woods,' he said, checking his notes on the trolley in front of him.

'Over there,' the almoner said, inclining her head towards the side room on the other side of the corridor.

Sidney gave her a grim nod. He emerged from the room a couple of minutes later, a shrunken, white-sheeted form stretched out on the trolley. Several sensationalist newspaper headlines about people being buried alive had led some members of the public to make living wills asking to be decapitated on their apparent death, or stabbed through the heart with a stiletto.

Some families clung to their dead loved ones at home, releasing the bodies for burial only once maggots had taken such a hold of the flesh that they dropped onto the floor. With most unspoilt for choice when it came to living space, such precaution often meant sharing their parlour with a decaying corpse. As a conscientious mortician, Sidney would have been alert to any signs of a patient emerging from deep coma in his mortuary.

Alice stepped aside and lowered her head as Sidney passed by. Several medical students and nursing staff had begun to arrive for their early morning shift. Three nurses who were standing in a circle fell silent at Sidney's appearance. They flattened themselves against the wall and dipped their heads respectfully as he passed, but two male medical students further along the corridor continued their animated conversation, one of them cackling loudly.

Sidney grabbed his notepad from the head of the trolley and knocked their hats from their heads. 'Show some respect, lads,' he barked. Stunned into silence, they grabbed their hats from the floor and then stood to attention, shame-faced, with their hands clasped behind their backs.

When Sidney disappeared from view, Alice crossed the corridor and went into the empty side room. The steel-framed bed where Hetty had slept stood empty, the sheets that had been stripped from the mattress in a pile on the floor and the oxygen mask back on its hook on the wall.

Alice rested her hand on the bare mattress then turned and headed back to reception. At the empty desk, the almoner scribbled a note to Sidney Mullins asking him to furnish her with details of the undertaker who was to deal with the body of Mrs Woods, since it was her intention to make an application for some material assistance towards the cost of burial.

About ten feet away from Nell's reception desk, on the left-hand side of the corridor, the door to Dr Harland's office stood ajar. Alice pocketed the note and walked past the office towards the stairs, then stopped and took a few steps back. She tapped on the door of the doctor's office and waited. When there was no answer, she stepped inside.

Half a minute later, Alice flew from the office and over to the stairs, a small card clutched in her gloved hand.

At half past eight that morning, Alice arrived at Fenchurch Street and hammered repeatedly on Elizabeth Harland's front door. After a delay of several minutes, the older woman appeared, her jaw dropping at the sight of the almoner. 'It is not a convenient moment,' the older woman said briskly, before attempting to close the door.

Alice stepped forward and slipped her booted foot into the gap. 'It is important, Elizabeth. This cannot wait.'

Elizabeth hesitated for a moment then stepped aside. Alice followed her through to the back parlour and remained standing, despite the woman's invitation to sit. The room had been restored to its former neatness, the only evidence of an infant an empty glass feeding bottle standing on one of the highly polished mahogany shelves. 'Well?' Elizabeth said with impatience. 'What is so urgent?'

Alice proceeded to ask where Daisy was, her face creased with concern.

'She's sleeping,' replied the woman curtly, before adding: 'She has colic. She woke several times during the night.'

'I should like to see her,' Alice said, beginning to pace in a slow circle around the room.

'Then you shall have to return at a mutually agreed time,' Elizabeth snapped, moving towards the door with a sweeping gesture.

'I really must insist on seeing the child. I cannot leave until I have checked that she is safe,' the almoner said with biting finality. It was then that the door to the parlour opened and Dr Peter Harland stepped into the room, the baby, wrapped in a white blanket, sleeping in his arms. Alice stared at him, eyes wide. 'So, it was you,' she said scornfully. 'I knew it.'

'What?' he demanded as he took a step towards her. 'What is it that you think you know?'

'I found this on your desk,' Alice said quietly. She produced a card from the pocket of her cape and held it out to Elizabeth, though her gaze remained on the doctor.

His face stiffened with anger. 'So, it's a birthday card from my sister. What were you doing ransacking my office? Rooting through my personal property?' Several feet away from him, Elizabeth reddened and sucked in her lips.

'Why did you do it, Elizabeth?' Alice asked, ignoring the doctor and turning to settle her gaze on his sister.

The older woman hesitated, then began to stammer. 'I

have not, I mean, I have absolutely no idea what it is you think – I …'

'My instinct was whispering something to me from that very first night, Elizabeth,' the almoner cut in, waving the card in the space between them. 'I dismissed it because Charlotte was my priority at the time, but I should have known that you were not to be trusted. The handwriting –' she said in explanation, turning to Peter Harland. 'It matches the writing on the threatening note that was sent to me. And now I'm left wondering whether the two of you are even related in the way you claim.'

The doctor stared at her with his jaw hanging slack, but when the almoner turned back to Elizabeth, the older woman dropped her gaze and looked away.

'You are lovers, as well as siblings, are you not?' Alice ventured, her gaze remaining on Elizabeth. 'You should know that I have come across several cases such as yours in the last year; more than you might ever imagine, I should think.' She paused, glancing over at the horrified doctor and then back to Elizabeth. 'Fear of producing a monster prevented you from having a child between you, didn't it?' Alice continued. 'So you used a young girl to produce an infant that was at least related to one of you.'

Dr Harland gave a harsh laugh and moved further into the room. 'At first I thought you were quite a sensible woman, albeit highly strung,' he said, the baby beginning to wail in his arms, 'but it's clear now that you're not just a firebrand. You are genuinely, certifiably unhinged!'

Elizabeth strode over and took the waking infant from him. 'She's perfectly sane, Peter,' she said evenly, cuddling the baby to her chest. 'I did send the note.'

The doctor blinked between them, pained confusion evident on his face. Eventually he let out a moan. 'Why in God's name would you do that?!'

'I thought it would scare her off. I just wanted to make her go away!'

The doctor cradled his head in his hands and staggered past them, dropping heavily onto a chaise longue. Elizabeth rounded on him. 'I'm sorry, Peter, but I did warn you. I told you I can't give her up, not now. You can't ask it of me.'

Alice stared at her. 'Are you expecting me to believe that he knew nothing of this note?'

Elizabeth turned to face her. 'He did not.'

'But the two of you are lovers, are you not? And Daisy is his child?'

Peter Harland groaned loudly. Elizabeth shrieked a laugh. 'For heaven's sake, I spent half my life raising him. He most certainly is not my lover!'

Alice shook her head. 'I don't understand.'

Elizabeth heaved a heavy sigh and sank down into an armchair. 'We lost our parents in the blizzard of '91,' she said, staring down at the baby resting in the crook of her arm. 'I was sixteen but Peter was just a young boy. We muddled along together as best we could. I tried my best to be a mother to him, but I'm afraid that left no room for finding a relationship of my own.'

Behind her, Peter rubbed his broad hands over his eyes and then dragged them down his face.

'Oh, stop with the guilt, will you?' Elizabeth said, shifting around in her chair. 'I don't regret it for a single second. I'm so proud of what you've managed to achieve, given the cards you were dealt, Peter. Prouder than you'll ever know. But you must see that I'm owed this. It's my turn now.'

There was a pause. Alice stared at him, then turned back to his sister. 'But Daisy is not yours, Elizabeth,' she said, her tone softening. 'She was never meant to be yours.'

Elizabeth sprang to her feet. 'You were the ones who turned up at my door,' she spat out, eyeing Alice resentfully. 'I never asked for any of this. You brought the girl here and let her bleed out all over my rug.'

'She already has a mother,' Alice said evenly.

'Oh, but what life can she give her?' Elizabeth demanded, her voice rising. 'And what life would she have for herself? Do you think any man will be interested in her when they find out that she has a child in tow? I can attest to the fact that they'll run for the hills at the first sign of a dependant, let alone a bastard one.'

'For God's sake, Lizzie,' Peter Harland barked. 'I told you not to let yourself get carried away with this.'

'Oh yes, that's easy enough for you to say! You're not the one who's carried a hole around inside you all these years, Peter.' There was a pause. Elizabeth appeared to make efforts to gather herself before continuing. 'Can't you see this is better for all of us? Without a scar on her reputation, the girl will be able to find work, perhaps even gain the chance of a good marriage.'

'But Charlotte will not be whole until her child is returned to her.' Alice's voice was firm, but her features had softened. Elizabeth looked down at the baby, a tear rolling down her cheek. 'You must satisfy yourself with being her aunt, not her mother.'

Peter Harland let out a loud scoff. Elizabeth looked up sharply. 'Where on earth would you get such an idea?'

Alice eyed the doctor with a level gaze. 'Do you think I had not guessed?'

Elizabeth swivelled on her heel towards her brother, who held up despairing hands, and then turned back to Alice. The baby began to moan in her arms. She got to her feet and said: 'What are you talking about?'

Alice kept her gaze on Peter Harland. 'Do you think I missed the look that passed between you and Charlotte on that first night? I couldn't quite grasp hold of it at the time, but something has been niggling at me ever since. And then I came to realise – you and she were in a relationship. You are the child's father.'

Dr Harland gave a bitter laugh and dropped his head back into his hands. 'There is no point in denying it,' Alice persisted, looking down at him. 'It is not a coincidence that you brought us here, to Elizabeth's door. Believe me, I know exactly what sort of man you are.'

'I don't think you have the faintest idea what sort of man he is,' Elizabeth interjected bitterly, beginning to bob from one

262

foot to the other to soothe the fretting infant. 'And how on earth would he ever have been able to get near the girl, with all that hissing and scratching going on?'

'Well, *someone* got close to her, Elizabeth. And you said it yourself the first day I met you. Your brother is dour, cold and completely lacking in any sense of empathy.'

'Now you listen to me,' Elizabeth said, dipping her head fiercely towards the almoner. 'I may not be reticent in high-lighting my brother's frailties, but I love the bones of him. You'd be hard-pressed to find a man finer than him.'

'So it is honourable to pursue an agenda of ridding society of its most vulnerable, is it? And it is fine to use one's privileged position to take advantage of young girls?'

Elizabeth blinked. 'I'm not following any of this.'

'Were you aware that your brother frequents the Marie Stopes clinic with the intention of promoting a superior race?'

'It's not politics that takes him there! You may find the idea inconceivable, but my brother and I have strong social con-sciences. He works a few shifts at the clinic now and again, that's all. He's trying to help society's most vulnerable, for pity's sake!'

'I don't believe that either of you can claim the high moral ground for proposing that some women shouldn't have babies simply because they are poor!'

Elizabeth stared at her. The doctor took a long slow breath and got to his feet. 'What I'm trying to do, what all of the doctors who work at the clinic are trying to do, is to relieve some of the strain on the most wretched of women, so that they can begin to take control of their lives. What is so wrong with that?'

Alice's gaze flicked between Elizabeth and the doctor. 'What is your connection to Charlotte? It wasn't just that look. I know from her reaction when I mentioned you. She was —' She stopped, scrambling for the right word, '— frightened.'

The doctor sighed. He ran his fingers through his hair, took a few paces back and forth, and then turned to face her. 'I met Charlotte only once before the night she gave birth. It was a year or so earlier. She was brought into the hospital in a panic and was referred to me with breathing difficulties —'

Alice nodded. 'As I suspected. Something you categorically denied when I asked you directly.'

'Will you let me finish?' he said, glaring at her. She gave him a small, tight nod. He took a breath and then continued. 'Once stabilised, she confided in me that she was several months into an unwanted pregnancy and had sought the help of an abortionist, one of those butchers across town. He'd gone about his business with a metal catheter but Charlotte had fainted and then fled in a panic. On examination I found that she was still pregnant, though bleeding heavily and —' The doctor stopped, flicking his tongue over his lips.

'Peter, you are not obliged to share any of this with her.'

He looked at his sister. 'She won't stop, Elizabeth, not until she has the truth. It must be done.' He turned back to Alice. 'I have lodgings close to the hospital. It's convenient for times when I'm on-call or working late. I took Charlotte there as soon as I could and finished what had been started.'

CHAPTER TWENTY-TWO

There was a loud intake of breath from the almoner. 'So you broke the law.'

Dr Harland took a step towards Alice. 'Do you have any idea what it's like to face a dilemma like that? What would you have had me do? Refer her to one of those herbalists you see advertising in the local paper, so that they could get to work on her with one of their lead potions? Or should I have sent her home, where she might have been so desperate that she got to work on herself with her mother's meat skewer? Because that's what would have happened.'

'You should have reported the case to your superiors and sought advice.'

'The girl was beside herself. It was an urgent situation and I had to make a rapid clinical judgement.'

The almoner turned to leave. Peter Harland caught her arm. 'What are you going to do? If you report me, I'll be made a scapegoat. I could be imprisoned. Is that what you want?'

Alice made a noise of exasperation in her throat. 'Oh, I don't know!'

There was a long silence, each of them avoiding each other's gaze. A few feet away, Elizabeth lifted the baby onto her shoulder and rocked back and forth, patting her gently on the back. When the infant had quietened, she glanced across the room and asked: 'Where on earth did you get the idea that my brother is in favour of eugenics?'

CHAPTER TWENTY-THREE

The almoner's function is neither to preach a moral, nor to
act as a machine to turn out ready made plans for the future.
The almoner can only help in so far as she is able to establish
her position as a friend and advisor who is prepared to
assist when the need arises, and realises that her chief task
is to foster in the girl herself that courage and
determination without which her life cannot be rebuilt,
for those who have suffered disillusionment the
future makes very hard demands.

(*The Hospital Almoner: A Brief Study of*
Hospital Social Science in Great Britain, 1910)

On the Friday of that week, Alice made the same journey to
Banstead Mental Hospital as she had three weeks earlier – the
two o'clock train taking her from Victoria to Belmont Railway
Station, where she disembarked and travelled the rest of the
way on foot.

It was almost forty-five years since the first patient had been
transported by omnibus to the hospital. Johanna Farell, a
woman who believed that she was possessed by the devil, was

266

escorted by two wardens through the gates of the newly built asylum on 27 March 1877. While apparently being 'clean in her habits', after less than two years in placement, Johanna 'did not seem to have any intelligence left'.

The first male patient, Mr John Scanlon, arrived the next day. Mr Scanlon had allegedly made two murderous attempts on the life of a detective; one using a loaded pistol while under the influence of chloroform, the other by sneaking arsenic into the detective's glass of ale while he sat in a public house. Not only did Scanlon exhibit a 'general wild state of manners and language' but also stood accused of 'exposing his person' in Shepherd's Bush.

Mr Scanlon suffered continued delusions until he met what was described in the records as a 'rather sudden death' on 11 March 1886. He was buried in the grounds of the hospital shortly afterwards, just short of nine years after his committal.

Patients from all walks of life passed through the doors of Banstead Mental Hospital through the decades that followed, some for the crime of being gay, others for having a child out of wedlock. Commentators noted a startling rise in the number of people falling victim to mental illness around the turn of the century. Industrialisation was considered by some to be the cause; its effect on the public disorientating, particularly at a time when God seemed to be withdrawing from their lives.

At just after 3.30 p.m., the hospital came into distant view. It was Alice's third visit since Charlotte had been admitted in early January, only this time she wasn't alone. Keeping in step beside her was the almoners' office typist, Winnie Bertram. She trudged along breathlessly, handbag looped over her arm, her face red with effort. Behind them, marching purposefully through the woods, pasture and open fields of Banstead, came thirty-five wellington-clad members of the Women of Westminster Book Club.

It was two hours from sunset but there was no sign of the temperature dropping. Warm air from the Azores had brought record highs to the country that day, some areas reaching 55 degrees Fahrenheit. The high walls surrounding the grounds of the hospital, austere through the chill, overcast days of winter, perhaps appeared less so against a cloudless blue sky.

The buck-toothed porter's face lit up when he caught sight of Alice through the window of the gatekeeper's lodge. When he emerged, however, and took in the army of grey-haired comrades surrounding her, his jaw dropped in surprise. Alice stepped forward and spoke quietly in his ear. He frowned, then his disappointed expression was replaced by a toothy grin. A few minutes later, he waved the almoner through the tall wrought-iron gates and watched as she led the women over the stone tracks, and into the grounds.

A dark Bentley rolled over the tracks about ten minutes later, quickly followed by several other top-end vehicles. As the cavalcade neared, the Women of Westminster Book Club members stepped out of the shadows. Linking hands, they formed a line across the entrance to the hospital.

The driver of the first car, a middle-aged man with black hair smoothed back from his forehead and a pencil-thin moustache, stuck his head out of the window and stared at the women in astonishment. Winnie, who was nearest, strode over and leaned down to speak to him. His eyes widened further. Moments later, with a loud crunch of gears, he threw the car into reverse and turned in a tight circle. Winnie straightened with a look of satisfaction as he sped away, then hoisted her handbag high onto her shoulder and dusted her hands.

One of her fellow readers stepped forward as she returned to the line – a tall woman dressed in a tweed jacket and matching long skirt. As she made her way over to the next car, several other women marched forward, one to each of the remaining cars in the line.

Within a minute, all of the cars, about twenty in total, began performing panicky three-point turns over the grass, each of the drivers desperate to make their escape. As they drove away, in haphazard lines three or four wide, the women clapped and cheered.

At the gate, the buck-toothed porter stood outside the entrance to his lodge, watching the unfolding spectacle with amazement.

The women had a spring in their step as they left the grounds that afternoon. Walking in pairs, they made their way along an unlit road that led to Banstead village, where they intended to reward themselves with a celebratory drink in the local pub, the Woolpack.

Alice and Winnie, remaining behind, passed through the main entrance to the hospital, and signed themselves in at reception. The two women entered the main dining hall of Block A soon afterwards, through one of the doors nearest the stage.

Charlotte was stacking wooden chairs up against the far wall when Winnie and the almoner entered. Dressed in a long shift with a woollen shawl draped over her shoulders, she was chatting to a fellow patient as she worked, often throwing her head back in laughter. She smiled warmly when she caught sight of Alice, and came straight over to speak to her.

'Charlotte, this is Winnie,' the almoner said, touching the typist's arm. 'She works with me. I hope you do not mind my bringing her along.'

Winnie gave her a motherly smile. The teenager acknowledged her with a small smile then turned to Alice. 'I've been given a leading role in the show tomorrow night,' she told the almoner, her eyes bright. 'And Doctor says I'm making good progress.'

'That's wonderful, Charlotte. I'm so pleased to hear it.'

Charlotte hitched her shoulders up and clasped her hands in front of her. 'I'm hoping it won't be too long now, before I can get out of this place. I can't wait to see Daisy.'

Alice appeared to weigh her words carefully before answering: 'We shall have to get you settled somewhere first.'

Charlotte frowned, her features stiffening. 'She's alright though?'

Alice reassured her that she had paid a visit to Elizabeth and the infant a few days earlier and then added: 'She is thriving.'

The teenager expressed relief and went on to ask how long it would be before a reunion with her daughter could take place. There was a pause, and then Alice said: 'I am working on it, Charlotte. I have identified somewhere for you to stay. You are to join the staff of a beautiful country house. As soon as we have a release date for you, we can make arrangements to take you up there.'

Immediately ill at ease, Charlotte insisted that she could not possibly consider a placement away from home. 'I told you before, I can't go nowhere else. I've got to get home.'

'You cannot go home, Charlotte. It is not possible.'

The girl appeared distressed. She clasped her hair and began to pant. 'I have to! I have to go back! You need to speak to me mum and dad again, please!'

'I have, my love. Your mother will not hear of it. And even if I somehow managed to get her to agree to allowing you back, there is no way she would be willing to accept Daisy. And with your mother so fixed in her ideas, your father will most certainly not entertain the idea either.'

'I know! I didn't mean Daisy as well. I'd go back and just visit Daisy as much as I could, and they'd never need to know nothing about her.'

The almoner shook her head, but then her eyes narrowed. 'I don't understand. I thought you desperately wanted to be with Daisy?'

Charlotte burst into tears. 'I do! But I can't just leave!'

The almoner glanced at Winnie and then back again. 'Why not, Charlotte?'

A wizened-looking middle-aged woman with thinning grey hair passed behind Alice and beckoned another patient over. The pair of them pulled a chest out from the hollow space beneath the stage and began taking out colourful costumes and frilly scarves. Alice eyed Winnie then led the trembling teenager to a quiet corner of the hall. She cleared her throat. 'Charlotte, I have been speaking to Dr Harland.' She paused. The girl clutched her hands in front of her. The almoner reached out and placed her hands over Charlotte's. 'I know about the –' There was a pause, and then she added: '– the operation.'

Charlotte flushed and cast her gaze downward. She responded in a small voice: 'I was scared. I didn't know what else to do.'

Alice tilted her head. 'It went horribly wrong?'

Charlotte raised her gaze to meet the almoner's. Her eyes filled with tears. 'It was terrible. I was so panicked I thought I was going to die. I crawled to the Royal Free, and someone carried me in.'

'And what happened there?'

'I was in such a state. I could hardly breathe, but the doctor, he –'

'Dr Harland?'

Charlotte nodded. 'He calmed me down and told me to meet him somewhere and – and –' she said falteringly, 'then he made it all go away.'

Alice pressed her lips together and patted her hand. 'It's not an easy thing to admit to.' There was a pause, and then the almoner ventured: 'So you had never met the doctor before that day?'

Charlotte shook her head.

'He is not the older man we spoke of before? Daisy's father?'

The teenager looked at Alice with wide eyes. 'No. He was kind to me. That's the reason I sent Molly to him.'

Alice dropped her hands down to her sides and stared at her. 'Molly?' she repeated. 'Molly Rainham?' Charlotte nodded. 'You sent Molly to see Dr Harland?'

On further questioning, the teenager admitted that she and Molly had been friends for a year or so before the young mother's death. Molly had become anxious, according to Charlotte, after discovering that she had fallen pregnant.

'It was not her husband's child?'

'Course it was. He came home on leave. But Molly said that he would have a fit of the vapours if he found out she was expecting again, 'cos they couldn't afford another mouth to feed. That's when I told her about Dr Harland helping me,' Charlotte said tearfully. 'And she went to see him.'

Alice shot Winnie a look and then levelled her gaze, her eyes shining with intensity. 'And he took her to his lodgings?'

Charlotte shook her head. 'No, no, that's the thing. He refused to help her. He sent her away.'

Winnie came closer at that moment, stopping when she was a couple of feet away. The almoner gave her a sidelong glance, then turned back to Charlotte: 'And so Molly consulted with someone else?'

'I dunno. I never saw her again after that. Next thing I heard, she'd been found dead.' Charlotte's lip wobbled. 'And the poor baby too.'

Alice gave a grave nod. At length she asked: 'Can you tell me why you are so desperate to return home, Charlotte? It seems to me that you were not at all happy there.' The teenager bit her lip and folded her arms tight against her chest. 'Are you concerned about your brothers and sisters? Or perhaps your mother's drinking?'

Charlotte let out a high-pitched, humourless laugh that drew attention from one of the nurses. She put a hand to her mouth and then shook her head and looked at the almoner. 'Mum's not like that, honest. You just don't know what she's really like.'

Alice took a step closer. 'Tell me, then. Tell me what she's like. Because as far as I can tell, there's enough income going into your house to –' Alice stopped. Her eyes widened, and then she began to nod. 'Of course,' she said suddenly. She shook her head. 'I cannot believe it hadn't occurred to me before.'

Charlotte flushed. Winnie stared, her expression blank. Alice touched the teenager's arm. 'Your father, he is reliant?'

The teenager looked away, but then gave a slow nod and began to cry again. Winnie rushed forward and put her arm around her. At some length, Charlotte admitted that her father was a heavy cocaine user. 'That's why Mum has to work so hard,' she said, her voice trembling. 'Most of our money goes on the powder, and she has to do all sorts to make enough to buy food.'

CHAPTER TWENTY-THREE

'Why did your mother not confide in me?'

The teenager drew her forefingers across the rims of her eyes, sniffed and then said: 'She was terrified someone would come and take the little ones away. She made me swear not to tell no one. You won't do nothing awful, will you? Please say you won't take them away!'

Alice held up a hand. 'We're not monsters, Charlotte. Your parents will be offered advice and support, nothing more.'

Charlotte seemed unsure. Winnie gave her a reassuring pat on her shoulder, and she appeared to relax. Eventually she said: 'I tried my best to help. That's why I went to the studio. And that's how I ended up meeting Molly.'

Alice nodded, though her expression was blank. 'The studio?'

'I saw the adverts, see,' Charlotte said, looking from the almoner to Winnie and back again. 'I thought that if I had me photograph taken I had a better chance of being an actress. I knew if I could do that, my mum wouldn't have to work so hard and everything wouldn't be such a struggle.'

Alice lifted her eyebrows. 'Having photographs taken is an expensive business.'

Charlotte shook her head. 'Oh no, it didn't cost me nothing. I put in for it after seeing the adverts. I got paid for having them done.'

Alice looked at her. 'Advertisements? For what? What sort of photographs are we talking about here?'

Charlotte flushed and looked down at the floor. 'It weren't what I thought it would be! It was an advert asking for models.

275

I thought it was a way to get me started on the stage. I f-felt awkward when I was told to undress. I didn't like doing it, but I'd already promised the money to Mum and she was so relieved. She stands and irons all them clothes till I think she might faint on the spot. I couldn't let her down, not when she was so desperate.'

Alice glanced at Winnie, who pressed her lips together and gave a weary sigh. After a long moment of silence the almoner returned her attention to Charlotte and said: 'Molly wanted to be an actress too?'

Charlotte shook her head again. 'No, no, she was there to get some tickets to sell.'

'Tickets?' The almoner's brow furrowed. 'I'm afraid you have lost me, Charlotte. Please start at the beginning and tell me everything.' After careful questioning and lots of reassurance, Alice managed to elicit the details. Charlotte had first met Molly in the reception area of a photographic studio in Hampstead. They had chatted together while waiting to be seen and, despite their age difference, a friendship had blossomed between them.

'She was so kind to me. Nicer than anyone I'd ever met before; like the big sister I'd always wished I could have.'

Alice gave her a sad smile and then asked: 'Did Molly divulge what she wanted the photographs for?'

'She didn't want photographs – I told you, she weren't there for that. She told me she wanted to help raise some money for the hospital. She said someone there had been good to her after her baby was born and that she wanted to do something nice in return. She came to the studio to collect the tickets so she could sell them and help the sick children on the wards. There was another advert, see, asking for help with fundraising for the hospital.'

The colour drained from Alice's cheeks, but Charlotte appeared not to notice. She continued to gush about Molly's generosity, her efforts to help others and her gentle nature. 'She was good in that way. I never heard her say a bad thing about no one, but, oh my, when I told her about me posing in the nude and dancing for Mr Hargreaves, you should have heard her. She went absolutely stark, staring mad! I never went back to the studio after that.'

Winnie and Alice exchanged glances, and then the almoner sprang to her feet.

CHAPTER TWENTY-FOUR

If any person over the age of sixteen years who has care of
any child under the age of sixteen years, wilfully assaults,
ill-treats, neglects, abandons, or exposes such child, or
causes or procures such child to be exposed in a manner
likely to cause such child unnecessary suffering, or injury
to health (including mental derangement), that person
shall be guilty of a misdemeanour.

(C. S. Loch, *How to Help Cases of Distress*, 1895)

Alice and Winnie returned to the Royal Free to find a police
constable guarding the door of their basement office, hands
clasped behind his back, the strap of his helmet pulled tightly
against his chin. Another one of his blue-tunic colleagues was
standing just inside the room, next to Frank, helmet under his
arm. The officer at the door lifted a hand to bar their entrance,
but Frank turned and motioned them in with a wave of his
pipe.

Alice sidestepped the detective with lowered eyes and moved
towards Bess Campbell, who was sitting, quietly composed,
behind her desk. Winnie, her double chin wobbling with

intrigue, followed the almoner across the office with a breath-less wheeze.

When the new arrivals stopped at Bess's desk, Frank turned back to face Alexander Hargreaves, who was seated behind his own. 'So, as I was saying, Sir, I'd like you to step outside for a moment, if you would.'

Alexander gave Bess Campbell a puzzled glance then looked up at Frank. 'And as I told *you*, Frank, I have far too much to do. Go and fetch that silly man from the mortuary if you want to play one of your childish games.'

Frank lifted an eyebrow. 'So be it,' he said, turning around and gesturing one of the constables over with a small nod of his head.

The constable donned his domed helmet and stepped forward. Standing to attention with his chin tilted upwards, he cleared his throat and said: 'Alexander Hargreaves, I am arresting you on suspicion of the indecent assault of several women, including a fifteen-year-old girl, Charlotte Redbourne.' The constable proceeded to read the fundraiser his rights.

When the officer had fallen silent and stepped back to his post at the door, Alexander snickered softly and shook his head. 'Good heavens, man,' he said, addressing Frank. He rose from his chair and stepped elegantly around his desk, perching on the edge and linking his hands on top of his lap. He surveyed the detective with a sneering smile. 'Is there no level to which you will not stoop for a moment's entertainment?'

Frank took a drag on his pipe and then cupped the polished bowl in the palm of his hand. 'As I informed you a moment ago, Sir, I am a detective with the Metropolitan Police's Criminal Investigation Department. I can assure you, this is not a joke.'

A frisson passed over the room. Winnie turned from Frank to Alice and Bess Campbell and then back again, her jaw gaping. Alexander stood up, placed his hands at his slim hips and eyed Frank contemptuously. 'And I told you, I'm not one to fall for such a ridiculous stunt, whatever lengths you may have gone to.'

Frank grinned and flashed his warrant card in front of him. 'Oh, how readily you accepted me as a bumbling fool, Alex. It's what we'd been banking on all along.'

Alexander's expression faltered for a moment, but then he looked down his nose at the detective. 'I am to believe that you have been entrusted with investigating cases of impropriety? And yet you have not more than a couple of brain cells to rub together.'

Frank dipped his head. 'If you say so. But imbecile or not, I am still bestowed with powers of arrest.'

There was a pause and then Alexander drawled: 'I have no knowledge of the incidents to which you refer.' His tone was unconcerned.

'Well, we'll go to the Yard and see what we can do about establishing your innocence there.'

Alexander grasped the lapels of his jacket in the manner of a barrister addressing a jury. 'My only misconduct has been the neglect I have shown other areas of my life in deference to the generosity with which I have managed the appeals of this and many other hospitals,' he intoned, his chest puffed out. 'I have worked tirelessly through the years to ensure that each establishment is furnished with the very latest equipment necessary to keep them at the forefront of medical excellence. Do you have any idea what sort of position half the voluntary hospitals in this city would be in were it not for my contributions over the years?'

Frank delivered a slow clap. 'Another of your speeches delivered with aplomb, Alex, but I'm afraid, this time, it just won't wash. Your goose is now well and truly cooked, and in my opinion, you should consider yourself lucky that you've managed to evade the law for as long as you have.'

There was a pause and then Alexander said in a silky tone: 'Need I point out the precariousness of your position, Frank? Accusing someone like me of such debauchery is a hazardous business. Careers have been ruined for far less.'

'Not debauchery, Sir,' the detective returned crisply. 'These are cases of indecent assault.' Frank proceeded to summarise the facts of the case and confirmed that during the course of his investigation he had managed to track down a number of women and girls who were willing to testify that they had been persuaded to perform lewd dances in a state of undress.

'Damn your impudence! Those malicious, sordid rumours have been circulating for years. No one but an oaf would pay them any heed!' Beginning to lose his composure, Alexander stroked a hand over his oiled hair and looked appealingly at Bess Campbell. A moment later, his hand fell to his side. 'You knew about this?' he said scathingly.

Winnie goggled down at her boss, her jaw hanging down to her chest. The Head Almoner gave a small nod. 'I agreed to Frank's appointment, but only with the intention of clearing the name of someone I thought to be most honourable. I can honestly say, Alexander, that I have never been so thoroughly disappointed in anyone in all my life.'

The fundraiser's mouth dropped open. His cheeks flushed red with anger, but he recovered quickly. 'No matter,' he said, brushing at the lapel of his jacket with elegant fingers. 'These are preposterous allegations,' he said, his eyes on Frank. 'And I refuse to be spoken to in such a way by some half-wit who barely knows his left from his right.'

'All of us are subject to the law, Alex,' Frank said. 'However lofty our manner.'

Alexander's mouth hardened into a tight slant. 'A word to the wise,' he said quietly, his face close to Frank's. 'Those who dabble in the affairs of someone in my position may find a whole house of cards tumbling down around their ears. You do realise, don't you, that I am a magistrate, as well as a major fundraiser and philanthropist?'

Frank dipped his head. 'I do indeed. And in my humble opinion, concealing your foul deeds in a cloak of righteousness compounds your crimes and makes you a hypocrite as well as a pervert.'

Alexander's mouth opened and closed several times. When he'd recovered he said: 'I shall be lodging a complaint with your superior first thing in the morning. I know him well, as it happens.'

'By all means, Sir. I'll make arrangements for someone to bring a notepad and pen to your cell.'

The fundraiser's face turned puce. 'This is absolutely ludicrous! I may have taken some photographs of a few hussies here and there, but I never laid a finger on a single one of them. They were right little pieces anyway! Filthy strumpets entirely lacking in morals, and not one of them was what you would call truly bedworthy. They were of no more value to me than common whores.'

Peter Harland stepped forward out of the shadows at that moment, his uneven mouth clamped in a tight line. Alice and Winnie exchanged glances. Frank held out a warning hand towards the doctor without turning around. Alexander stared at him. 'You?' he said scornfully. 'What has this to do with you?'

The doctor declined to answer. Frank turned and gave the constable by the door a small nod. He stepped forward, but Alexander backed away. 'Ask any of my colleagues,' he said in a rush. 'They will vouch for my integrity and my good name.' He turned expectantly, first one way and then the other. The air crackled with an uncomfortable silence. 'Winnie?' he said eventually, his eyes settling on her. The typist turned her head away. Humiliation brought another angry flush to Alexander's cheeks. His eyes flicked to her left. 'Alice?'

The almoner stared at him coldly.

'This is utterly ridiculous!' Alexander complained, stamping his foot. 'We are talking about a few upstarts who want nothing more than fame and notoriety. No doubt one of them thinks that coming out with these loathsome accusations is the way to achieve it. And there I was, offering them an opportunity to better themselves from a genuine sense of charity.'

'You mean, you used your power, influence and prestige to draw desperate people into your lair,' Alice said, 'knowing only too well that they would be too frightened of the possible repercussions to report you.'

'None of them complained, and neither did their parents.'

'No, they didn't. They turned a blind eye to your actions, focussing instead on the financial benefits of association with someone like you, but the fact that these women and girls had no one to safeguard them makes your actions even more deplorable, not less.'

Alexander pulled a hanky from the pocket of his waistcoat and dabbed his brow. 'Those girls were no different to any other woman I have ever met.' He ran his eyes pointedly over Alice. 'You all use your womanly wiles to get what you want, then complain when a chap tries to capitalise on it. You all say one thing and mean another, when it comes down to it, and don't try to pretend that you're any different, Miss Hudson.'

Peter Harland lunged between Frank and the constable. Grabbing Alexander by the throat, he spun him around and slammed him against the wall. The fundraiser gave a little whimper, his eyes wide with fear.

The police constable's hand hovered over his truncheon, his eyes flicking between his boss and the scuffle going on in front of him. Frank picked at an invisible thread on the collar of his shirt. 'Frank!' Alice shrieked.

The detective pulled his pocket watch from his waistcoat and studied it. After several beats he looked up, gave the throttling a contemplative glance, then threw his colleague another small nod.

The constable moved forward and slapped a firm hand on the doctor's shoulder. 'I'll take it from here, thank you, Sir.'

When Peter Harland backed away, the police officer turned Alexander around and pulled his hands behind his back. After securing him with a pair of handcuffs, he led him out of the room, the fundraiser making offended, whimpering protests as he was manoeuvred up the dim staircase. 'Get your filthy hands off me, you damned viper! I will have your jobs, all of you!'

Alice hurried to the door and called up the stairs after him: 'You are going to pay for Daisy Redbourne's upkeep, Alexander, I will make sure of that!'

When Alexander's wails had faded away, silence lowered itself over the basement. After a few moments, Alice turned to Frank and looked at him keenly. 'What brought you here, Frank? How did you know what was going on?'

The detective sat on the edge of Alexander's desk. 'A number of disturbing rumours had alerted our attention over the years, but there was no solid evidence of any impropriety, and no one in the community willing to talk to us. It was only when we received a tip-off from a hospital employee that we felt we had something firm to move forward with. Any accusation must be treated with caution of course, and though the rumours were stacking up, there wasn't much else to go on. So, with someone in Hargreaves' position ... Well, the only way to bring someone like that down was with an investigation on the inside.'

The almoner stared. 'And who was this employee?'

Frank lifted his brows. 'I'm afraid I can't reveal my source.'

There was a soft rustle across the room. 'It was me,' Dr Harland said softly from the shadows.

Alice's eyes widened in surprise. 'You? I don't understand.'

The doctor explained that he had witnessed Molly arguing with Alexander on the street after she had visited to ask for his help in terminating her pregnancy. When Molly was found dead a few days later, he called police to report his suspicion that Alexander may have somehow been involved in her death.

'Molly found out what had been going on at the studio,' Alice said flatly. 'Charlotte told us.'

Frank nodded: 'We suspect that she threatened to expose him.'

Alice frowned at him. 'But Molly died as the result of a botched operation?'

Frank nodded again. 'There was no foul play involved. At least, not from Alexander. He is a dandy and a pathetic excuse for a man, but he is not, I suspect, a murderer.'

Alice turned back to the doctor. 'You knew about this scheme? And about Charlotte posing for him?'

'Not at first. But after seeing the way she reacted on the night of Daisy's birth, when you suggested bringing her to the Royal Free, I started to wonder whether he might be the reason she was so resistant.'

Alice gave another slow nod. 'So that's why you insisted on taking her to Banstead?'

Dr Harland nodded. 'I thought it was the safest option. Alexander is a weak and cowardly individual, but I had no way of knowing that at the time. That's why I wanted Daisy to remain with Elizabeth. I had no idea how great the risk to her might be.'

'And you kept all of this to yourself.' Alice started pacing in front of Bess Campbell's desk. 'You let me socialise with the man. I went out to dinner with him! And yet you saw no reason to warn me!'

'For all I knew, you were an accessory before the fact.'

Alice stopped mid-pace and rounded on him, her jaw dropping open. 'You thought I was complicit?! In something as foul as this?!'

He shrugged. 'Not at first, but when I saw the two of you socialising together, I thought perhaps ...' Alice's cheeks flushed with fury. 'Oh, for pity's sake! You were never in any danger.'

'How could you possibly know that?'

There was a small pause and then he said: 'Because I would never let that happen.'

Alice turned and paced some more, then stopped and turned. 'So I was right. You were following me?'

The doctor gave a small nod. 'Frank couldn't watch Alexander around the clock. I had to be certain.'

Alice's brow furrowed. 'So, all those times you were absent from the ward ...'

'I wanted to make sure he didn't hurt anyone else.'

'But how did you keep tabs on us from up on the chest ward?'

The doctor pressed his lips together. Across the room, Winnie began fumbling with the contents of her handbag. Alice glanced at her. The older woman stilled, then looked up sheepishly. 'Oh yes, alright. It was me, dear.'

'Winnie?! You were spying on me?! Why did everyone know about this except me?'

The older woman's face slackened. 'I didn't know, not about Alexander.'

Dr Harland stepped forward. 'I asked Winnie to help me to protect a patient. She knew how disturbed you were about Molly's death. I told her that you were compromising the health of another patient because you were desperate to help her.'

Alice stared at Winnie. 'So all those times I thought you were being awkward ...'

'It was him,' Winnie said, pointing to Dr Harland with her chin wobbling. 'He led me to believe that you were unstable. I had no idea about any of this. This is an entirely different kettle of fish.'

Alice looked at the doctor. Their eyes fixed. After a long moment, Bess Campbell cleared her throat. Everyone looked at her, and then Frank walked over to fetch his hat from the stand in the corner of the room. He tipped it towards his colleagues. 'Well, thank you, all. It's been an experience.'

Bess Campbell, Winnie and Dr Harland said their goodbyes. A noisy conversation struck up between them. The detective

gave Alice a meaningful look and she followed him to the door.
'Frank?'

'Alice,' he said, reaching for the almoner's gloved hand and
lifting it to his mouth. 'It's been a pleasure getting to know you.'

The almoner clasped his hand and shook it. 'It has certainly
been interesting, Frank,' she said with a grin. 'But I have to say,
I'm rather looking forward to things getting back to normal. As
normal as it gets around here anyway.'

Frank laughed, but then his expression turned serious. 'I
wanted to ask you about what you said earlier, to Alexander,' he
said, above the murmur of conversation across the room. 'Do
you have any evidence that he's responsible for Charlotte Redbourne's predicament?'

Alice stared at him. 'Well, no, not exactly. I made the assumption after she told us about the photographs.'

'But she didn't name him specifically?'

'She implied it.' The almoner frowned. After a moment she
shook her head and said: 'Actually, I suppose she didn't specifically, no. She was in a distressed state so we did not linger over
the details. It was I who made the assumption.'

Frank nodded. 'Don't worry. We'll piece the whole unfortunate picture together in the fullness of time. But in my
experience, these things generally follow the same pattern, and
after taking statements from several women, I would say that
molestation is not Alexander's modus operandi.'

Alice looked over at Winnie and then back to the detective,
her expression creased. 'But, Frank, if Alexander is not responsible, who is?'

CHAPTER TWENTY-FIVE

[The almoner] was freshly interested in [their] plight, in what
they had just been through and what was still before [them]
... It does [anyone] good to become aware, if only for a
moment, that someone, especially a stranger, is really
delighted with the chance to help [them]. They knew that she
really cared about them, that she had a stake in their
fortunes, [and] that what hurt them hurt her.

(A letter from the American physician Dr Cabot on the dedication
of the almoners of St Thomas's Hospital, 1918)

The next morning, Saturday, 25 February 1922, the leftover
tasks that might usually have absorbed the beginning of Alice's
weekend were firmly swept aside. Huddled in her long cape,
cloche hat and ever present gloves, the almoner set out early for
Banstead Hospital, arriving at the gatekeeper's lodge just after
10 a.m.

'Back again, Miss?' The toothy porter gave her an enthusiastic smile and followed her to the gate. 'Those dirty old dogs got
a fright yesterday, didn't they? I don't suppose they'll show their
faces again.'

Alice smiled. 'If they do, I want to know about it. You can reach me at the Royal Free.'

'Oh, I'll give you a nudge, don't you worry about that,' he called through the gates after she had passed through.

Southern England had been battered by a series of thunderstorms overnight. The softened grass gave way under Alice's boots as she made her way to the main hospital. A plump nurse with swollen ankles escorted her to the day room, where Charlotte was sitting quietly, reading a book. The teenager looked up when Alice walked in and, after a flicker of surprise, gave her a tentative smile. 'We've been keeping her hands busy with lots of painting and needlework,' the nurse told Alice, as if Charlotte was out of earshot. 'We find quilting works wonders for patients, especially those with a temper.'

The almoner suggested a stroll in the courtyard. Charlotte nodded. The nurse limped off to fetch the teenager's hat and coat, fussed over the fastenings so that she was buttoned up to the neck, then unlocked the doors leading to the garden. She sank heavily into one of the armchairs and watched them through the glass, her bloated feet raised on a stool.

Outside, Charlotte slipped her arm through Alice's as they strolled around the old walled garden. It was a tranquil place and they might have been anywhere, were it not for the smoke billowing from the industrial-sized chimneys behind them, and the occasional, high-pitched wheedling cry of a patient. It was a bright, cold morning, the newly washed cobbles beneath their feet glistening in the winter sun.

They walked to a wooden bench at the far end of the garden

and sat side by side. Charlotte nodded along silently as Alice updated her on Alexander's arrest. She grinned when the almoner described the fundraiser's reaction to events, but when Alice kept a studied gaze on her face, her smile disappeared. 'What will happen now, about Dad's habit?' she asked quickly. As an almoner, it was a ruse Alice would have been familiar with; an attempt to delay the more painful but inevitable conversation that lay ahead.

In a patient tone Alice said: 'As I told you before, he will be offered support. We have hostels for people who have become slaves to their vice. I will see to it that he gets help, I promise you.'

Charlotte nodded silently. Alice reached for her hand. 'Charlotte, Alexander is not the father of your child, is he?'

The teenager snatched her hand away. She dropped her gaze to her lap, shoulders tense.

'You must see that this avoidance cannot continue forever,' Alice continued. She reached out and touched the teenager's chin, gently steering her gaze upwards. When their eyes met she said: 'Now is the time for you to summon all of your courage and tell me the truth.'

The teenager angled her face away, her gaze skittering over the lawn. When she eventually turned back to face the almoner she whispered under her breath: 'I'm afraid.'

'I know. But trust me when I say that we will not let anything happen to you, Charlotte. This I can promise you.'

The teenager took a deep breath and swallowed hard. Above her, the clouds moved quickly across the sky. 'I can't,' she said eventually.

Alice's gaze sharpened. She touched Charlotte on the shoulder and said: 'If we are to keep your brothers and sisters safe, it is vital that you share what you know with us.'

Charlotte sprang to her feet and began pacing back and forth across the cobbles. Alice rose, apologised for pressing her, then emphasised the importance of safeguarding the welfare of the younger children. The teenager stopped at that and spun around. 'Why is it me that has to tell the secret, when I never wanted it forced on me in the first place? It's shameful. It's humiliating, and I just wish to heaven that it would all go away!'

Alice levelled her gaze. 'In my experience, the only way to make terrible secrets lose their power is by exposing them to the air, Charlotte. The longer they stay hidden, the more they fester and grow.'

'All right!' Charlotte blurted out with an angry sob. 'I will tell you, though I pray to God you'll not think me wicked like me mum does.' She took a few gasping breaths, tears rolling down her cheeks, then blew out slowly, settling her gaze on Alice. 'It was my dad. He hurt me, and I don't want him doing to the younger ones the things he did to me!' She covered her face with her hands and wept.

The almoner was at her side in seconds then, patting her on the back and sweeping her long hair behind her ears. After drawing her back towards the bench, she sat by her side and put her arm around her back. The teenager dropped her head onto Alice's shoulder, allowing herself to be consoled. After several minutes, when she had quietened, the almoner kneeled in front of her and clasped both of her hands.

'You have been very brave, Charlotte. We can now see to it that your brothers and sisters are safe.'

Charlotte began to pant again, her chest heaving rapidly up and down. 'But how are you gonna do that? By taking them away and sticking them in the workhouse?! That's not safe, that's worse. I've heard about them places. And it'll break my poor mum's heart. Oh, she'll hate me! I never should of said nothing!'

'Please, let's not get carried away with panicky ideas. I have no intention of seeing any of them in the workhouse.'

'But you mean to take them away?'

'That depends.'

'On what?'

Alice fixed her with a steady look. 'Did your mother have any idea what you were suffering?'

Charlotte shook her head, tears rolling down her cheeks. 'I tried telling her once, but I couldn't find the words. She was so dead set on keeping ourselves to ourselves in case someone found out about Dad's habit, I weren't sure she'd cope with hearing that as well.'

The almoner squeezed her hands. 'Well, then, if you're telling the truth, it is likely that the children can remain where they are.'

Charlotte nodded, her shoulders sagging with relief. Some moments passed. Eventually, when the teenager had dried her eyes, Alice sat beside her again and said: 'I'm sorry you didn't feel able to confide in me, Charlotte.'

The girl's eyes widened. 'Dad said I must never tell!' she cried. 'He said it would break Mum and she'd end up in the

Bedlam. And Mr Hargreaves said no one would ever believe me if I ever said anything about the things he was doing. He said no one would ever let me onto the stage if I tried to spread rumours about important people.'

Alice shook her head. 'I'm so sorry. They were terrible secrets to have to keep to yourself. Was there no one else you felt able to confide in?'

'I told Mum about Mr Hargreaves,' she said in a voice thick with tears. 'But she said he was an important man and I was to keep him happy. She did her best to help, even saved up and bought me a silk chemise for the photos. She said that's how all actresses get their jobs. I suppose it'll never happen now.'

There was a pause and then Alice got to her feet. 'Come now, Charlotte,' she said, reaching out her hands. 'A new life awaits you. There are big changes ahead for girls like you. Absolutely anything is possible.'

CHAPTER TWENTY-SIX

A devoted soul ... can store up power ... from delight
in a snowstorm or in sunshine after rain ... waiting for
its chance to be passed on in some way.

(American physician Richard C. Cabot on the
dedication of London hospital almoners, 1918)

A month after Charlotte's disclosure and Alexander Hargreaves'
arrest, Alice travelled by tube to London Bridge station and
from there made the short walk to The City of London and
Tower Hamlets Cemetery. It was Monday, 27 March 1922 and
the sky was granite grey, the air sharp with a northerly wind.

Cold air currents from Ireland had brought icy showers of
hail and sleet to the capital over the last few days, but the worst
was not over; the most severe weather of the whole winter was
still to come, with Londoners set to confront a raging blizzard
just a few days later, on the 31st.

Alice tucked her gloved hands inside her cape as she walked,
head bent against the wind, into one of the high-gated
entrances. She wove her way between the frosted headstones,
most of which had fallen into disrepair, and the unmarked,

weed-covered shared plots. She stopped when she reached the final resting place of Hetty Woods, who had been buried in the presence of her family, a small number of neighbours and Alice herself, four weeks earlier.

A large number of those buried in the cemetery had been too poor to cover the cost of their own plot, and so were lowered into shared public graves, where they would rest for eternity alongside several unrelated others. Alice had seen to it that the cost of Hetty's plot was covered by the hospital Samaritan Fund, along with a small granite headstone carved with her name.

It wasn't unusual for the almoners to pay their respects to patients who had outlived all those they knew, or perhaps those whose relatives were lying low to avoid footing the bill. By sending the lonely off with some reverence and dignity, they hoped to redress the balance of their withered lives.

Crouching down, the almoner laid a small bunch of daffodils on the mound of freshly dug earth.

From Bow, Alice travelled west to Harrow, where she spent an enjoyable hour with Tilda and her family. Ted, who had been invited to stay with his daughter by the owners of the large cottage on the proviso that he took on the responsibility for maintaining the gardens and the owner's newly purchased motor car, greeted Alice with a smile, his newborn granddaughter, Clara, cradled in his arms.

★ ★ ★

Before journeying back to the Royal Free, the almoner stopped off at Dock Street. It was her second visit in four weeks, having accompanied police officers soon after Charlotte's disclosure, who were charged with apprehending her father – legislation passed in 1908 meant that sexual abuse by a family member was an official matter, and no longer one to be dealt with solely by the Church. Mrs Redbourne had fainted in shock, according to the report Alice later filed with Bess Campbell, the woman hysterically beating her husband with a poker as police officers led him away.

Humbled by his arrest and her exposure as a woman with several different income streams, Mrs Redbourne quietly admitted Alice into the house on this latest occasion, her head bowed. She scurried off to the kitchen as Alice checked the skin of the younger children to make sure that their scabies infection had cleared up, returning with a hot but greasy cup of tea.

'I can see no trace of the infection now,' Alice said after taking a tiny sip of the drink. An awkward air prevailed in the living room, alleviated to a degree when Alice knelt on the floor and played with four-year-old Jack, who appeared to have calmed since the removal of his father.

Half an hour later, when Alice pulled on her hat and gloves and walked to the door, Mrs Redbourne followed her and asked: 'Will I – I mean, is there any chance of Charlotte coming home anytime soon?' Without her mask of brusque resentment in place, the woman appeared smaller, more vulnerable.

The almoner turned at the end of the hall. Adopting a non-committal tone, she said: 'I am not without sympathy for your situation, Mrs Redbourne, but I believe it is in Charlotte's best interests to reside elsewhere, at least for now.'

Fierceness returned to the woman's stance. Colour flooded her cheeks. 'How was I to know what was going on? I mean, I knew about the Tokyo, course I did. That bastard took every spare penny we had and stuck it up his nose, but I could go along with that. Least it kept him more cheerful and out from under my feet. But she's my girl. If I'd of had any idea about …' Her hands clenched into fists. She folded them beneath her bosom, her lips tight with fury. 'Surely you realise that? I can't be blamed for something I didn't even know about, can I?!'

Alice's expression softened. She patted the woman on the arm, and suddenly her expression crumpled. Her lips puckered and her eyes filled with tears. 'I didn't want her ways corrupting the others, see. I thought it was wayward behaviour, and that has a way of rubbing off. I never would of chucked her out if I'd known the truth. But she never said nothing to let me know any different. Why didn't she say nothing?!'

'It's often the way, I'm afraid. Fear of breaking up the family. Shame. It's a toxic mix.'

Mrs Redbourne nodded. 'Well, now I know what it was all about, my heart wants out of my chest, it's so broken.'

Alice gave her a sad, sympathetic smile. 'Both you and Charlotte have a lot to come to terms with. A reunion is something that we should aim towards, perhaps when Charlotte is sufficiently recovered.'

CHAPTER TWENTY-SEVEN

As the years pass I realise increasingly how many things there
are that I cannot do, persons I cannot help ... But there are a
few things I can do. I can take off my hat to ... Lady Almoners
... when I see a beautiful piece of work. The almoner is an
artist in human relations. We must learn from you here.

(American physician Richard Cabot on the work of the
St Thomas's Hospital almoners, 1918)

On what would prove to be the warmest day of the following
month, with 67 degrees Fahrenheit being observed on the
temperature dial of Kew Observatory, Alice signed herself in
for the last time at the gatekeeper's lodge of Banstead Mental
Hospital.

It was 10 a.m. on Friday, 14 April 1922, and although the last
fortnight had been unseasonably cold, the heathland surrounding the hospital was alive with signs of spring. Around the
perimeter of the grounds, the faded browns and greys of winter
were giving way to vibrant shades of green. The song of the
sparrows nesting in the alcove of the clock tower looming over
the main entrance to the hospital and beneath the pediment

displaying the four scimitars of the Middlesex county shield was perhaps more noticeable on that day. The fruit trees on the farmland tended by the patients beyond the main hospital building were beginning to blossom, and newborn lambs grazed over the open heath.

By the time Alice reached the main entrance, Charlotte had been escorted onto the cobbled driveway. At the almoner's appearance, the starched nurse standing at the teenager's side gave her a brief hug, then disappeared inside.

Without preamble, Charlotte said: 'The detective says Dad's gone?'

The almoner nodded. 'He's being dealt with.' Charlotte winced, but Alice patted her arm. 'There is nothing for you to regret, Charlotte. You have been very brave.'

The girl blinked in the sunlight, regarding Alice with hesitation. 'And Mum?'

'I have spoken to her. She was horrified by the revelation.'

Tears filled Charlotte's eyes. 'She's angry with me?'

Alice gripped her upper arms. 'Not at all. She wants to see you, but I have suggested we give it some time.'

'Does she know about Daisy?'

The almoner dropped her arms and pressed her lips together. 'I didn't say anything. It's for you to decide if and when to tell her. But, come, let's discuss this another time. We have things we must do.' As Alice guided Charlotte away, the teenager took one last look over her shoulder. Behind her, a heavy bolt rattled noisily into its latch.

★ ★ ★

Alice and Charlotte arrived at Fenchurch Street at midday on the morning of the 14th. As they neared Elizabeth's house, Charlotte slowed her step and gave Alice an anxious glance. As the almoner had done almost fifteen weeks earlier, she slipped her arm through Charlotte's and guided her gently up the steps.

Dr Harland opened the door and gave the pair a rare smile. Charlotte returned an approximation of a smile, her mouth trembling. She clutched Alice's hand tightly and followed her into the hall, but at the sound of a small mewing cry she broke free and ran towards it in a rush.

Elizabeth was standing at the far end of the living room by the window. Charlotte hesitated in the doorway, her eyes fixed on the baby wrapped in a shawl in the older woman's arms. Elizabeth gave her a twitchy smile and moved towards her. 'We've been waiting for you,' she said, her voice husky and strained.

'She's so beautiful!' Charlotte cried when Elizabeth reached her. She leaned forward and looked down at the baby, tears running freely down her cheeks.

The baby stared sleepily up at the new arrival with puzzled eyes. Charlotte put her hand over her mouth, gave a half-laugh, half-cry, and then reached out her arms. Carefully, after a moment of hesitation, Elizabeth handed the baby over.

Faced with the prospect of losing Daisy entirely, the older woman had agreed that Charlotte should take over the two rooms on the top floor of her extensive property. No charge would be made for board and lodging, Elizabeth assured Alice, as long as her high standards of cleanliness and hygiene were maintained, and all housekeeping duties were diligently taken care of.

Charlotte stared in mute wonder at her daughter's face, Elizabeth watching on with a stoic, somewhat watery smile. The teenager planted a kiss on the baby's forehead, pulled back with a look of adoration on her face, then stroked her cheek and kissed her all over again. Alice and Dr Harland watched the reunion from the doorway.

They left the house just after half past twelve, Alice closing the door quietly behind her. Falling into step beside Peter Harland, she could perhaps be content that in the course of her first year working the district, she had, in the words of the St Thomas's almoner, Anne Cummins, most certainly done more good than harm.

REFERENCES

Charlotte's case: 'A.B. was referred to hospital at fifteen years old by a Rescue Society after being sexually assaulted by her own father'. Her baby, when born, was boarded out 'in a delightful home in the country' and arrangements were made for the girl to visit as soon as she was well (London Metropolitan Archive (LMA) reference H1/ST/A59/C/1).

'Charlotte will go to Banstead Asylum voluntarily': the Mental Treatment Act of 1931 allowed for voluntary boarders within mental hospitals, although some hospitals, such as the Maudsley in London, were already admitting self-referring patients (*The Hospital Almoner: A Brief Study of Hospital Social Science in Great Britain*).

Hetty's case: '[The almoner] helps cancer patients to whom the hospital can no longer be of benefit' (LMA reference H1/ST/J2/1); 'Two patients who are suffering from advanced cancer have been visited and cheered in their homes, and have been reconciled to going to one of the Homes for the Dying. Other similar cases are at present being visited' (Memorandum by Almoner respecting the Work of her Department during 1904, LMA reference H71/RF/R/01/001).

The *St Thomas's Hospital Annual Almoner's Report* of 1924 was to highlight the case of an almoner who suspected that heartbreak over a long estrangement with her son was the root cause of one of her patient's many illnesses. The almoner went to great efforts to reunite the pair and the patient, who made a full recovery, later said of the almoners: 'Not only do they heal sore bodies, but also heal sore hearts' (LMA reference H1/ST/A59/C/1).

Jimmy's case: 'M.N. an uneasy looking gentleman who stated that he was a lorry driver but on enquiry was found to possess a fleet of lorries, his own car and a very excellent house' (LMA reference H1/ST/A59/C/1).

Also rejected for treatment was a young man 'who stated that he was out of work' but on investigation was found to be 'the son of a master tailor, employing, even in the slack season, nine men and four or five girls' and living in an 'exceedingly comfortable' home.

Another young patient's father was 'an East End merchant in a large way of business, who considered that "as the hospital has thousands of pounds, he might as well have some of them"'.

And then there was 'A.P. suffering from bronchitis, stated that his doctor had urged him to come to the hospital ... He owned a coffee house, his takings averaging £12 a week. He told the almoner "that he had paid a consultant's fee of 4 guineas on one occasion, and was therefore 'entitled' to hospital treatment for the rest of his life!"' (*British Medical*

Journal (Supplement), 5 February 1910, from a speech by Mrs E. W. Morris at a meeting of the Kensington Division of the Metropolitan Counties Branch of the British Medical Association.

Winnie (secretarial help given voluntarily): 'A good deal of voluntary help has been given, one lady coming two mornings weekly to help with the secretarial work whenever she is in town' (LMA reference H71/RF/R/01/001).

Alexander Hargreaves: The philanthropist is a character loosely drawn from the businessman Mr Harford Green, a fundraiser, magistrate and philanthropist who was charged with the indecent assault of a fifteen-year-old girl in 1925.

In an echo of the crimes that were to be committed by Jimmy Savile a century later, Mr Green used his fundraising efforts for St Thomas's Hospital as a cover to gain the trust of those he groomed.

In the trial that followed, the full details of Green's crimes would emerge; the jury heard that once the philanthropist had managed to lure the girls to his home, he claimed that he was able to project their figures onto a screen using a 'wonderful wireless invention'. They were told that, for this new invention to work, they had to undress.

Once naked, he carefully and attentively measured their vital statistics (although he never bothered to make a note of the measurements) and then dismissed them from the premises. One witness, a fifteen-year-old girl, would tell the court that he offered her six guineas to pose naked for him, and eight if she danced as well. According to her testimony, the philanthropist told her that she had a lovely figure.

The jury would find Harford Green guilty of improper assault, although he was to be praised in court for the restraint he had shown in not committing a more grievous crime.

See article entitled 'Wireless Pictures of Girls – Charges Against Hospital Fund Secretary', *Evening Telegraph*, Thursday, 4 February 1926.

Male visitors to Banstead Hospital – on the discovery of a body in the grounds of one of the Surrey psychiatric hospitals in the 1980s, detectives from the Metropolitan Police arrived to investigate and found dozens of lone men lining up to go inside. Officers were told by locals that the men turned up regularly to take female patients out.

ACKNOWLEDGEMENTS

Firstly I would like to thank my wonderful agent, Laetitia Rutherford, for championing me and getting me to dig deeper every time I send a draft her way. I am so grateful for all the help, support and encouragement she's given me over the years, as well as her gentle humour in steering me away from some of my wackier ideas and onto sensible projects instead.

Huge thanks also to the lovely Vicky Eribo for the opportunities she's given me as well as her warmth and support, and to the rest of the team at HarperCollins.

I am obliged to David Chave for being an enthusiastic and helpful sounding board, to Liz Foster, Derek Sims and Hannah Brown for giving feedback on the manuscript, and to my late aunt, Sylvie, for her insight into nursing and hospital procedures in years gone by.

Lastly, thanks to my amazing family for their unwavering love: Irene, Philip, Paul, Pete, Jean, Toria and Alex, and to my three children, Hannah, Daniel and Lexi.

Moving Memoirs

Stories of hope, courage and the power of love…

If you loved this book, then you will love our
Moving Memoirs eNewsletter

Sign up to…

- Be the first to hear about new books

- Get sneak previews from your favourite authors

- Read exclusive interviews

- Be entered into our monthly prize draw to win one
  of our latest releases before it's even hit the shops!

Sign up at

www.moving-memoirs.com